Making Sam's life miserable twenty-four hours a day was not easy.

True, Delilah thought, she'd had a lot of practice being mean; a girl didn't grow up in the Jones household and live to tell about it unless she learned to get tough when she had to.

Yet, since she'd grown up, it hadn't been necessary to be mean with any consistency. She was out of practice.

Being mean to Sam for two days running had practically worn her out. It took fortitude and stamina. And it was even harder since the meaner she became, the nicer he seemed to get.

To be honest, being alone with him, *feeling* his presence and constantly remembering that he was with her on a wager and that she'd only be asking for heartache if she softened one bit, was driving her right out of her mind....

Dear Reader,

Welcome to Silhouette **Special Edition** . . . welcome to romance. Each month Silhouette **Special Edition** publishes six novels with you in mind—stories of love and life, tales that you can identify with—as well as dream about.

This Valentine's Day month has plenty in store for you. THAT SPECIAL WOMAN!, Silhouette **Special Edition**'s new series that salutes women, features a warm, wonderful story about Clare Gilroy and bad-boy hero Reed Tonasket. Don't miss their romance in *Hasty Wedding* by Debbie Macomber.

THAT SPECIAL WOMAN! is a selection each month that pays tribute to women—to us. The heroine is a friend, a wife, a mother—a striver, a nurturer, a pursuer of goals—she's the best in every woman. And it takes a very special man to win that special woman!

Also in store for you this month is the first book in the series FAMILY FOUND by Gina Ferris. This book, *Full of Grace,* brings together Michelle Trent and Tony D'Allessandro in a search for a family lost . . . and now found.

Rounding out this month are books from other favorite writers: Christine Rimmer, Maggi Charles, Pat Warren and Terry Essig (with her first Silhouette Special Edition).

I hope that you enjoy this book and all the stories to come. Happy St. Valentine's Day!

Sincerely,

Tara Gavin
Senior Editor

CHRISTINE RIMMER

WAGERED WOMAN

SPECIAL EDITION®

Published by Silhouette Books New York

America's Publisher of Contemporary Romance

For M.S.R.,
with absolute conviction—and all my love.

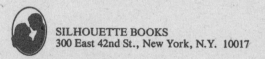

SILHOUETTE BOOKS
300 East 42nd St., New York, N.Y. 10017

WAGERED WOMAN

Copyright © 1993 by Christine Rimmer

All rights reserved. Except for use in any review, the reproduction or utilization of this work in whole or in part in any form by any electronic, mechanical or other means, now known or hereafter invented, including xerography, photocopying and recording, or in any information storage or retrieval system, is forbidden without the permission of the publisher, Silhouette Books, 300 E. 42nd St., New York, N.Y. 10017

ISBN: 0-373-09794-8

First Silhouette Books printing February 1993

All the characters in this book have no existence outside the imagination of the author and have no relation whatsoever to anyone bearing the same name or names. They are not even distantly inspired by any individual known or unknown to the author, and all incidents are pure invention.

®: Trademark used under license and registered in the United States Patent and Trademark Office and in other countries.

Printed in the U.S.A.

CHRISTINE RIMMER

is a third-generation Californian who came to her profession the long way around. Before settling down to write about the magic of romance, she'd been an actress, a sales clerk, a janitor, a model, a phone sales representative, a teacher, a waitress, a playwright and an office manager. Now that she's finally found work that suits her perfectly, she insists she never had a problem keeping a job—she was merely gaining "life experience" for her future as a novelist. Those who know her best withhold comment when she makes such claims; they are grateful that she's at last found steady work. Christine is grateful, too—not only for the joy she finds in writing, but for what awaits her when the day's work is through: a man she loves, who loves her right back, and the privilege of watching their children grow and change day to day.

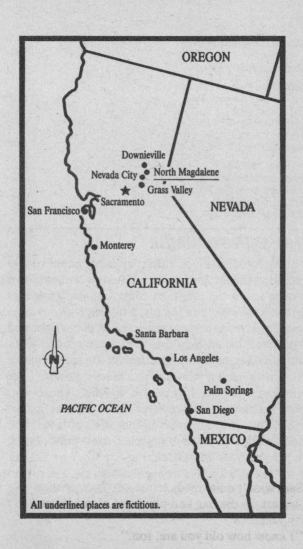

All underlined places are fictitious.

Chapter One

"Sam, whatever's eatin' you, I'd like to help." Oggie Jones let out a tired sigh and shifted the cigar he always kept clamped between his teeth to the other side of his mouth. "But it's creeping up on 3:00 a.m. Either spit it out or call it a night."

Sam Fletcher took a pull off the beer that had been sitting in front of him since closing time, only realizing after he had a mouthful of it that it had grown warm. He scowled, swallowed and pushed the mug away.

"It's about a woman." Sam said the words so low that if Oggie hadn't been standing less than two feet away, he would never have heard them.

Oggie leaned closer. "What woman?"

Sam wasn't quite ready to answer that question yet, so he leaned on the bar and pondered aloud instead, "I'm forty years old."

"I *know* how old you are, son."

"I own a store. I own a house. I own a cabin up at Hidden Paradise Lake—"

"You done all right for yourself, no one's arguing there."

"I should be happy."

"Damn straight."

"And I *am* happy."

"'Course you are."

"Almost."

Oggie wiggled his eyebrows again and chewed his cigar but said nothing. One of the jobs of a bartender was to know when to keep his mouth shut, and Oggie Jones had been tending bar for a long, long time. Oggie sensed that he should let Sam proceed at his own pace.

And Oggie sensed right. If Oggie had rushed him right then, Sam would have clammed up. But Oggie gave him a little time, and Sam put off getting to the point for a few minutes more by staring into the mirror over the bar, studying his beard.

Once a pause long enough to drive a train through had elapsed, Oggie did just the right thing: he gave a meaningful cough.

Sam bestirred himself and picked up where he'd left off. "I'm *almost* happy, Oggie. But not quite..."

Oggie dared to prompt, "So somethin's missing, is that what you're getting at, son?"

"Yeah. There's an...empty place in my life."

Oggie picked up Sam's rejected beer, tossed the last of it down the drain and washed the mug. "So this ain't about *a* woman, it's about *the* woman," he sagely suggested.

Sam leveled his gaze on the old man, impressed at the depth of his perception. "That's right."

Oggie nodded. "You got it all—now you need someone to spend it for you." Oggie let out a rheumy cackle.

Sam granted the old codger a wounded frown. "Oggie, this is no joking matter to me."

"All right, all right. No disrespect intended."

"Fine. None taken."

Oggie leaned toward Sam. "So who's the lucky lady? And what's the problem?"

"The lady *is* the problem."

"She's playin' hard to get?"

"She's playing nothing."

"Well, then what—?"

"There *is* no lady. That's the problem." At last Sam had reached the crux of the matter. "I haven't found her yet."

Oggie, clearly gratified that at last they were getting somewhere, breathed, "Ah-ha." Then he slid his thumbs under the frayed suspenders that held up his pants and inquired, "Not even a prospect?"

Sam stared down at the ring on the bar where his beer mug had been. "No. And not because I haven't been looking. I've been dating. Nice women, too."

"And?"

Sam shook his head at the ring. "There's nothing there. Zero. I want fire, you know? I can't even raise a spark." He sighed. "Maybe there's just no one out there for me."

Oggie Jones straightened up at those words. "Don't say that, Sam Fletcher. There's someone out there for everybody."

"You think so?"

"I know so."

Sam smiled. Oggie knew all the bartender's jokes about women, and he was willing to use them just between him and other men. But he believed a man needed the right woman deep down, which was why Sam had decided to go ahead and consult him about this.

Oggie had been married only once, to Bathsheba Riley, who'd given him three big handsome sons and one spiteful little daughter and then died of a stroke at the young age of thirty-seven. To this day, nearly a quarter of a century later, Oggie would still on occasion wax poetic about "beautiful Bathsheba, the empress of my heart..."

"Okay then, Oggie," Sam said. "I could use your help."

"For what?"

"Finding that woman out there who's right for me."

Oggie beamed. "You got it, son. What do you want to know?"

"Oh, suggestions, I guess. Ways to meet women. And the women here in town who might be right for me. It would be good to find the right woman here at home. Someone who loves this town as much as I do and never wants to leave."

Oggie was cackling again. "This here's North Magdalene, son, in case you ain't noticed. Population 215, er, 219, now that Beatrice Brantley's had those twins, and those two ladies from Oakland moved into the Luntman place over on Pine Street."

"I realize that. But you know how it is. I think I've thought of everyone who could conceivably be right for me. But maybe I've missed someone. It's always a possibility."

"Hmm." Oggie considered this, then said, "By my count, there are seven women in town who might remotely be eligible for a serious relationship with a man your age—I'm discounting anyone married, living with a man, under eighteen or over fifty, as well as those two ladies from Oakland I just mentioned. Rumor is they are in love with each other.''

Sam lifted his head. Hope stirred his blood. ''Seven? You count seven? I could only come up with six myself. And I've discounted all of them.''

Oggie wrinkled up his nose, as if counting once more to make sure. ''Yep,'' he said at last. ''Seven. I count seven.''

''Who?''

''You want me to name them off?''

''Yeah, if you don't mind.''

''Hell. Okay.'' Oggie began, ''Alma Santino?''

''I thought of her. But she's barely twenty. That's way too young for me.''

''Regina Black.''

''Uh-uh. She's nice, but she's so shy. I've tried to strike up conversations with her more than once.'' Sam shook his head. ''It added up to zero. No, Regina is out.''

''Betty Brown.''

''No way. She is one bossy woman.''

''Angie Leslie?''

''Too flighty. You know she's been divorced three times.''

''Now wait a minute here. Jared's been divorced twice. Jared ain't one bit flighty, and you know it.''

''Well, I'm not thinking about getting involved with Jared,'' Sam said of Oggie's eldest son, ''so I'll make no judgments about him. But Angie Leslie is not for me.''

''All right, all right. So Angie's out.''

''Right.''

''Too bad. She's a fine lookin' woman.''

''No argument there, but looks aren't everything. Where were we?''

''Er, Cathy Quail. Hey, didn't you take her out last month?''

"Yeah."

"And?"

"Nice woman, no spark."

"Okay. Chloe Swan."

Sam shook his head. Everyone knew Chloe would wait until the end of forever for Oggie's second son to pay attention to her. "Chloe's always been in love with Patrick," Sam said. "No, Chloe's not for me. That's the sixth one. Did you miscount?"

"Hell, no. I said seven, and I meant seven."

"Then who else?"

Oggie's crafty smile made Sam a little nervous. Sam understood why when Oggie proudly announced, "Why, my Delilah, a course."

Sam felt the little ember of hope that had glowed warm in his chest wink out and turn cold. Oggie's venomous only daughter was the last person he'd want to curl up with on a cold winter's night.

"That's a real humorous suggestion, Oggie," he muttered dryly, then went on with a sigh. "So all the local ladies are out. I guess I knew that, but you can't blame a guy for hoping."

"Wait a minute." Oggie jerked his mangled cigar out of his mouth, looked at it, and stuck it back in. "My Delilah's no worse a prospect than any of the others."

Sam squinted at his friend and realized he'd hit a nerve by rejecting Delilah out of hand. He'd heard Oggie complain more than once that Delilah should be finding herself a man before she was too old to present her dear old dad with a few grandchildren. But never before had Oggie dared to suggest that Sam might be that man. Of course, Sam had never before confessed he was looking for someone special, either.

Sam decided to smooth the old man's ruffled feathers before going on. "Okay, Oggie. Objectively speaking, Delilah's..." He hesitated. He wasn't in the habit of trying to think of nice things to say about Delilah Jones. "She's fine, just fine," he said at last. "But she's not the woman for me, and you know it. So let's move along to other ideas."

Oggie's feathers were not smoothed. "No, let's the hell not," he growled. "Let's think serious about my girl for just a damn minute here. Let's give her a chance."

Sam decided to try pointing out the obvious. "She hates my guts, Oggie."

"Now, son. She don't hate you. She *despises* you. There is a difference."

"Yeah. If she found me dying in a ditch, she'd step over me instead of finishing me off."

That gave Oggie pause, but only for a minute, during which he thoughtfully chewed his cigar. Then he spoke confidentially. "Try to see her side of it. She lost her mom when she was only eleven, and after that she got nothing but headaches from her rowdy brothers and me. She swore to better herself, and she did. She went to college. Now she's part of a noble profession; she's a teacher of young minds. She ain't got a lot in common with any of us anymore. She can't help looking down on us lowlifes even if we are her family—and she thinks of you as just another one of my boys, you know that damn well. But she's got a true heart. If the time came when any one of us needed her, you know she'd be right there."

In spite of his own personal dislike for Delilah Jones, Sam had to admit that Oggie was right. "Yeah, okay, Delilah's loyal and true-hearted to a fault. I know that. But that still doesn't make her right for me. I'm talking about finding someone sweet to come home to. Delilah is about as sweet as a treed bobcat."

"My girl can be sweet." Oggie's slight wince contradicted his words.

Sam had had enough. "Oggie, this is pointless. I don't want Delilah, and she damn sure doesn't want me. Let it be."

Oggie shook his head, looking rueful but determined. "I just plain *can't* let it be, son. The more I think of it, the more sense it makes."

Sam realized he was becoming uncomfortable. He didn't like that gleam in Oggie's eyes. The old man was looking downright zealous, all of a sudden. It was spooky.

Oggie went on, "It's..." He paused, as if grasping for just the right words to explain some unforeseen and marvelous revelation. "By God, Sam, it's like something that's been in front of my nose all the time but too obvious to notice. You're exactly the man my girl needs, and she's just what you need! And you *did* say you wanted fire. My girl's got fire."

Sam groaned aloud. "Damn it, Oggie. Face it. I couldn't get along with her. Never in a million years. She'd as soon sic the sheriff on me as look at me."

Oggie's little raisin eyes were suddenly red with unshed tears. "She's my little girl, after all. And she's the only one of my kids who ain't been married at least once. I'd like to see her happy, settled down with the right man, before I meet her mama in the great beyond."

"I'm not that man, Oggie." Sam was getting worried. He was beginning to realize that confiding in Oggie hadn't been such a great idea after all. But hell, it had just never occurred to him that Oggie could stretch things so far— that he could delude himself into believing there could ever be anything between his spinster schoolmarm daughter and the man she'd always hated with all her mean little heart.

"You're like a fourth son to me," Oggie wheedled.

"Damn it, Oggie..."

"And you've done yourself proud since you showed up in this town with nothing but a bad attitude and the clothes on your back. Lord, Lord, why didn't I think of this before?"

"Oggie—"

"It's perfect. You even got...artistic leanings, what with the jewelry you make and your whittling. That one boyfriend Delilah had way back in college was an artistic type. I think if anyone will ever get a chance with her, he'll have to be artistic."

"I've heard enough of this." Sam stood up.

"I ain't through, son."

"Maybe not. But I am." Sam turned for the double doors.

"I got a proposition for you, boy!"

"'Night, Oggie."

"Get back here."

But Sam only waved a hand and headed for the doors.

Oggie was forced to voice his proposal to Sam's retreating back. "The day you and Delilah tie the knot is the day I deed over The Mercantile to you!"

Sam hesitated when he heard that. The Mercantile was an ancient brick barn of a building adjacent to the bar, which Oggie had bought forty years ago for a song. It was big enough to house Sam's expansion plans for his gold sales store. But it was also promised to Oggie's second son, Patrick, when Oggie died. Or at least, that was the excuse Oggie had given him for not selling it the last time Sam had made an offer.

"You hear me, Sam Fletcher?"

Sam heard, and he couldn't help considering. He wanted The Mercantile—and it was true what Oggie had said about Delilah and him. The spark was there, all right. He had to admit that the thought of Oggie's little witch of a daughter didn't leave him with that nothing, empty feeling that all the other women he'd considered inspired. Thoughts of Delilah Jones invariably made his temperature rise. Too bad the heat was caused by animosity rather than desire; he couldn't stand her, and she hated him right back.

No, he had to face facts. Even with The Mercantile thrown in to sweeten the deal, he and Delilah Jones would never make a go of it. Sam shrugged and pushed through the doors.

"Got that?" Oggie shouted, as Sam went out into the star-thick night. "You been after me to sell that building for how long now? But I ain't never sellin'. You'll be takin' it for free, Sam Fletcher, the day you make a fulfilled woman of my little girl!"

Chapter Two

Delilah Jones stood outside the small, weathered building at the north end of town that housed Fletcher Gold Sales and wondered if she should even bother going in. She certainly didn't want to go in. Sam Fletcher owned it, and to her that was reason enough never to step inside the place.

But she'd agreed to contact all the merchants in town. She just hadn't thought too carefully before volunteering, or she would have realized that there were only six merchants in all of North Magdalene—and two of them were her rascal of a father and that troublemaking wild man who owned Fletcher Gold Sales.

She'd already acquired pledges from Lily's Cafe, Santino's BB&V—Barber, Beauty and Variety—North Magdalene Grocery, Swan's Motel and finally The Hole in the Wall Tavern, which her father owned and ran.

That had been unpleasant, asking her father for a donation. He had cackled and chomped his smelly cigar and wondered aloud, as he always did, if she'd found herself a man yet. The few local yahoos with their bellies already up to the bar at one in the afternoon had chortled right along with him.

Goodness, how Delilah had longed to be outside again where the clean, spring sun was shining and the mountain lilac was in glorious bloom. Instead, determined to fulfill her obligation, she'd stood there in the stale-smelling dimness, waiting grimly for her father to say yes or no to her request for money toward the renovation of the Community Church's collapsing bell tower.

At last he'd cracked open the till and handed over several grungy bills. "There you go, gal. That oughtta help."

"Thank you, Father." She'd stuffed the bills in the donation envelope, dashed off a receipt and whirled for the exit.

But Ogden Elijah Jones just couldn't let it go there. Oh, no. He'd had to call after her. "I'm serious as a heart attack about you givin' me some grandkids, gal. In fact, I have taken matters in my own hands. Expect a man to come knockin' on your door one of these days soon. Be ready. You hear?"

Delilah had kept right on walking. She had not paused in the least, though the rude laughter of the men in the bar followed her out into the light. She'd walked briskly up Main Street, putting her father's absurd threats right out of her mind.

Now, there was only Sam Fletcher left to approach and her obligation to the Bell Tower Committee would be fulfilled. Delilah brushed at her slim skirt and straightened her collar and then pushed open the door to Sam Fletcher's store.

Overhead, as she entered, a little bell chimed.

"Be right out!" The deep voice came from beyond a door at the back.

Delilah said nothing. She was here to beg for money for the church's sake, after all. If she called out, it was just possible Fletcher might recognize her voice and refuse to speak with her. Who could say ahead of time what that wild man might do?

They hadn't shared two words together in the last ten years that she could recall. Maybe, just maybe, they could manage to be civil with each other now if she handled things right. Nervous, she clutched the donation envelope and receipts and her small handbag, and tried to calm herself by looking around.

What she saw elicited a tiny gasp of disbelief.

Beneath the sun that streamed in the spotless many-paned windows, the old wooden floors gave off a smooth, buffed shine. Glass display cases gleamed, filled with a wide variety of gold samples, jewelry and eye-catching souvenirs. Oils and watercolors of wildlife and the disappearing wilderness—the back country of which, in California at least, so little remained—brightened the walls. The rows of shelves stacked with mining gear were scrupulously neat and free of dust.

There were several excellently carved wooden sculptures: a rearing horse, a bald eagle, a delicate foot-high fawn. Delilah had heard somewhere that Sam Fletcher did beautiful carvings in wood. She wondered if these pieces could possibly be ones he had made himself.

How strange, she thought, bewildered. Could this beautiful little shop actually be crude Sam Fletcher's place of business? He'd had it for—how long now? Eight years or thereabouts, as she remembered. Before that, he'd sold his gold samples and the jewelry he made right out of that beat-up van he used to own.

People had told her that the store was a gem. And she knew tourists came from all over to rent panning and dredging equipment from him. But she hadn't paid much attention to what Sam Fletcher was doing with his life, as long as he kept away from her. And never before had she had the slightest reason to see for herself.

Not that it mattered what his store was like. It didn't matter at all. It just…didn't fit with her idea of him, that was all.

As Delilah stood and stared, the little bell over the door tinkled again. A man and a woman, tourists out for a Saturday drive in the gold country from the look of them, came in.

The woman went immediately to the jewelry cases and began exclaiming over the rings. "Walter, you must look at this one. Please, darling, look. Here."

Delilah backed away, not really thinking that she was moving into the shadows, until she stood in a corner near a tall stand filled with long picks and shovels. The door to the back room opened. She jumped a little, knocking the stand with her elbow and causing it to clatter slightly. At the sound, the man called Walter glanced over and saw her.

But then Delilah forgot all about anyone else, because Sam Fletcher came out of the back room, huge and imposing as always, his lion's mane of red-gold hair bright as fire, his full beard combed and gleaming.

Delilah blinked, recalling, for some strange reason, their first confrontation two decades ago, at her private place by the river.

The memory came at her, swift as a diving hawk. She had no chance to shut it out. She saw Sam Fletcher come out of the back room of his store, and suddenly she was fourteen again and going out the front door of her father's house on her way to her special place by the river where she always went to be alone.

It was early summer, late-morning, and the trees had all their leaves. She was wearing her bathing suit under her jeans, and her hair was braided down her back. The sun was warm on her face when she opened the door.

She let herself out of the house, heaved a little sigh, and felt relief. She was escaping that house, really. Since her mother had died, there was rarely any peace and never any order there. Her father and her brothers thrived on trouble and confusion.

The house, as she left it, was quiet for once. They were all sleeping late as usual. The night before had been pretty bad and each of her brothers had done his part to make it that way.

First, her youngest brother, Brendan, who was thirteen years old, had fallen asleep in his room with a lit cigarette between his lips. Luckily, Delilah had smelled something funny and burst in to find him stretched out on the bed, dead to the world, encased in a greasy cloud of smoke.

Terrified that he might already have suffocated, she tore back to the kitchen, filled the dishpan with water, flew to his room again and threw the water over him. He woke spitting and swearing and calling her terrible names.

But finally he got up and helped her drag the ruined mattress outside where they could douse it thoroughly. Then he stalked back toward his room. She'd followed after him, to insist he not smoke anymore in there.

"Don't lecture me about smoking, Delilah, damn you. You're my sister, not my mom. Mom's dead. Get that through your thick head. I'll smoke if I damn well please!'' He'd slammed the door in her face. She'd stood there for a moment, fuming, wanting to pound on the door until he opened it—and then to spit in his mean little face.

But she'd controlled herself. She'd returned to her own room and read for a while, then gone to bed.

She was sound asleep when Patrick, her second brother, came crashing into the house. She woke with a start, and saw that it was almost 2:00 a.m. Patrick kept slamming around out there, so she threw on her robe and went out to see what was the problem.

''What the hell are you sneakin' around about, sis?'' Patrick demanded when he saw her. Then he held out his right hand, which had a gash above the knuckles and was dripping blood all over the kitchen floor. ''Well, while you're up, find me some bandages, will you, and take care of this?''

She'd gotten him patched up and gone back to bed. But she'd no sooner dropped off to sleep than her oldest brother, Jared, had started beating on the front door.

''Damn it, let me in! Let me in, damn you all to hell!''

Delilah waited for one of her other brothers to do something, but neither of them did. Her father hadn't come home from the bar yet. Jared went on pounding, yelling louder and louder. She knew soon enough he'd go ahead and kick the door in—he'd done it before. So she pulled on her robe once more and went out to let him in.

He shoved the door back violently when she unlocked it, swore something crude under his breath about women and barreled past her and back to his old room, sending the door in there crashing shut behind him. Delilah knew what had happened without having to ask; he was drunk and his wife, Sally, had kicked him out again.

And, she thought, as she walked down the trail to her private place, her father was no better than his sons. Right now, at 11:00 a.m., he was still passed out on the couch, snoring away. He'd stayed out after his bar closed toasting the memory of her three-years-dead mother with his friends.

But she had left all that behind, she reassured herself. At least temporarily. She was on her way to her special place, her secret place, where beauty and tranquility reigned. She thought to find peace.

What she found instead was a greasy-haired giant and a huge, ravaging machine.

She stood there, where the trail ended at the willows near the beach, and stared, unable to believe what she was seeing.

Her place was savaged, the river a swirling pool of mud. Someone had decided that her special place would be a good spot to dredge for gold. The dredger, which floated near the rocks on black inner tubes, pumped and pounded, spewing water and gravel a foot into the air and filling the mountain quiet with hideous hungry gulping sounds.

A man was kneeling among the boulders on the bank in a black wet suit, fiddling with the big hose that nosed into the river. His mask and his rubber diving helmet had been tossed aside, and his long hair, dirty and uncombed, but boasting at the same time a burning, crude vitality, gleamed in the early summer sun.

She recognized him then: her brother Jared's new buddy, Sam Fletcher, who'd shown up in town out of nowhere a few months ago, a rowdy troublemaker, who got drunk every night just like Jared did, and lived out of his van.

Something snapped in her. She started yelling—screaming, really. She leapt across the small beach to his black-suited back and attacked him, pounding him with clenched fists, beating him about the head and shoulders, calling him all the awful names she'd always despised her father and brothers for using, ordering him and his horrible machine to get out of her place.

He froze for a moment. And then he reacted, throwing her off with a rippling shrug of his huge shoulders.

He switched off the pumping mechanical monster and then loomed over her as she lay half-stunned on the sand where he'd thrown her down. "What the hell's the matter with you, you stupid brat? Get your butt off my claim."

That did it. She started screaming again. "Claim! Your claim? This is my place, mine! *You* get out of here, you . . . dirty, good-for-nothing tramp!"

The insult stung him. "Why, you little—" For a moment she thought he might actually hurt her. She cowered back. But he seemed to control himself. His eyes narrowed, and he peered at her closely. "You're Jared's little sister, aren't you—Oggie's girl, Delilah Jones?"

She shrank backward some more, wanting only to escape him, but too proud to scramble to her feet and run. "*Miss* Jones, to you," she announced with a bravado that seemed absurd even to her. "Now you get that dredger out of here."

He grunted. "You've got it backward, kid. You're the one who's getting out. Now."

Her rage came back, pure and strong. "No, I'm not, you creep. *You* leave! You've got no right to be here!"

"Go on," he said quietly. "Get lost."

"No, *you* get lost. You get out of here, you bum! Get out right now!" She kept on shouting at him. He must have realized that arguing with her would do him no good. So he didn't say another word.

He lunged at her. She scrambled back, but not fast enough. He caught her by the ankle, dragged her toward him, and slung her over his shoulder like a bag of meal.

Then he started up the trail. He didn't even bother to toss her into his van that waited up by the road, but stomped on bare feet the two miles to her father's house, down Bullfinch Lane to Sweet Spring Way, with her hammering his back and screeching all the way.

He marched right up to the door and pounded on it. All three of her brothers and her father came out, looking as scruffy and disreputable as the black-suited giant who had her slung over his shoulder.

"What the hell, Fletcher?" her father groused. "I was sleepin' real peaceful five minutes ago. I heard you comin'." Delilah screeched again. Her father looked pained. "Delilah, honey. Can't you keep it down?"

So shamed and past caring was she at that moment, that she screamed once more, louder than all the screams that came before. And her father and brothers just stepped back, clearing the way, so that Sam Fletcher could carry her into the house and toss her on the couch.

"Keep her off my claim, Oggie," he said then, and turned and walked back out the door, closing it quietly behind him.

Once he was gone, there was silence. But not for long. Her father and brothers looked at each other. And then they started to laugh.

They laughed and laughed, they thought it was so funny. And she screamed at them to stop. At last, she leapt from the couch and ran to her room and locked herself in for the rest of the day.

Her father came knocking later, to try to make up with her. She pulled herself together and came out and more or less forgave them—her father and her brothers.

But she never forgave Sam Fletcher. He was trouble and she knew it, and as time passed she grew to hate him more and more.

"Can I show you something in that case?" Sam Fletcher, an older, cleaner version of the giant who'd once treated her so intolerably, strode toward the couple bent over the ring display.

"Yes." The woman's voice was eager. "This one. And this one as well, please."

Walter, beside her, coughed politely and tipped his head toward Delilah where she lurked in the shadows. "Anna, there's someone ahead of us, I think."

Anna—and Sam Fletcher—turned to look. Delilah froze, her back pressed against the wall. Sam Fletcher's blue gaze found her, pinning her to the spot.

Delilah, who up to that moment had remained half-lost in a long-ago summer day, wished she could close her eyes and disappear right through the floor. To have him catch her cowering behind a shovel stand like a shoplifter caught in the act was a thousand times worse than having to seek him out in the first place. For a minute that seemed like half a lifetime to Delilah, no one said a word.

Then Fletcher muttered, "Well, I'll be damned."

And the woman at the display case demurred, "Of course, I didn't realize . . ."

Delilah, who knew something had to be done immediately if she hoped to salvage one shred of her self-respect, forced herself to step out from behind the rack of shovels. She squared her shoulders, straightened her cardigan sweater and said with as much nonchalance as she could muster, "No, no. I'm not here as a customer. You two go ahead. I'd just like a word with...you, Sam." Lands above, she'd addressed him directly in a pleasant voice, and actually called him by his Christian name. When in heaven had she ever done *that* before? His mouth dropped open for a moment, and he looked as stunned as she felt. She made herself go on. "I'd like a moment of your time, when you can spare it...."

His frown told her that he didn't trust her for a second, but luckily the two customers politely waiting for him to help them kept him from saying whatever rude things might be in his mind. "Fine," he muttered curtly. "Be with you in a minute, then."

"Great." She actually forced her lips into a brittle pretense of a smile.

After that, he turned his back on her and gave his full attention to his customers. When the couple left twenty minutes later, Anna was wearing a new ring and a nugget necklace and Walter was fully outfitted for recreational gold panning.

"Okay, what the hell's going on?" Sam Fletcher demanded without further preamble, before the little bell over the door had even stopped tinkling behind the two tourists.

Delilah, who'd been pretending to study a painting of a spotted owl on the far wall, suddenly felt as if the small store had grown smaller still—as well as much too warm. She stared at him.

And it came to her in a suffocating rush: this was never going to work. A person did not approach the man she most loathed in all the world to ask him for a donation— even for the sake of her church's collapsing bell tower. Nellie Anderson or Linda Lou Beardsly would have to handle this one, and that was that.

She whirled, in a hurry to get out of there and not caring in the least if he knew it, and made for the door. "Never mind," she said tightly as she rushed past where he stood behind the register counter. "This was a bad idea, that's all. Someone else will be contacting you."

The scoundrel laughed, a low, rolling kind of chuckle, and he stepped out from behind that counter and right into her path. She had to jerk herself back from plowing into him. And then, worst of all, in order to scowl at him, she had to look up. Way up. The rat was well over a foot taller than she was.

"Contact me about what?"

She held on to her temper. She was a grown woman now, not an anguished fourteen-year-old. She made herself answer his question. "Making a donation. For the church bell tower. It's been condemned and has to be rebuilt." The words came out through clenched teeth.

His ice blue gaze froze her to the spot. "That's the only reason you came? For the church tower? You haven't been . . . talking to your father?"

"What do you mean? Yes, I spoke with my father. He gave two hundred dollars."

"Two hundred dollars." He looked at her sideways. "For the bell tower?"

"Yes. That's what I said."

"He didn't mention . . . anything else?"

"What *are* you talking about, Sam Fletcher?" she demanded. The temper she was holding onto was doing its best to get away from her. If he kept pushing, she might just let it run free.

"Nothing. Never mind." He smiled then, she could see it, his thin slash of a mouth curling beneath all that mustache and beard. "Just a little coincidence, that's all."

"*What?*"

"Nothing."

They stared at each other, she fuming, he grinning. And then she told him in carefully measured tones, "All right, then. That's all. Will you please step aside?"

His grin faded, as if he remembered they'd always been enemies, and he strove to reestablish the status quo. "Don't you want what you came for?"

She longed to tell him that the church could do without his money just fine. But that wasn't true. So she swallowed her pride and said tightly, "I . . . certainly. If you'd like to make a contribution, that would be fine."

"All right, then," he said, and stepped away. He went behind the counter and pulled out one of those big commercial checkbooks, and wrote out a donation for five hundred dollars.

She scribbled him a receipt. "Thank you," she said, though the words came out a little strained.

"Anything for a good cause," he told her, accepting her forced pleasantry with more grace than she had shown in giving it.

She turned and got out of there, sure that he watched her go, but determined not to let him know that she felt his gaze on her back, cold as twin icicles, sending dangerous shudders up and down her spine.

And she was right. Sam did watch her go.

Worse than that, once the door closed behind her, he actually pushed aside the Help Wanted sign in the window and observed her progress as she skedaddled down the street. And as he watched, he remembered the offer her father had made him less than forty-eight hours before.

The day you and Delilah tie the knot is the day I deed over The Mercantile to you! The shouted proposition echoed in Sam's mind.

Not that it mattered what the old scoundrel proposed. The old man could offer him everything he owned, and it wouldn't be enough to make him go after a woman who had never had a single agreeable word to say to him in all the time he'd known her.

Still, Sam shook his head in mild perplexity as he realized he hadn't really looked at Oggie's daughter in years. Somehow, in that time, the damned little witch had gone and turned into a good-looking woman.

By God, when he'd stepped out from behind the counter and she'd almost run into him, he'd looked down and seen that she had grown a pair of breasts—and a luscious-looking pair, as well. How long ago had that happened?

And her hips, he observed, sweet heaven if they didn't roll smooth and easy beneath her pencil-thin skirt as she trotted off away from him, fast as those nicely shaped legs would carry her.

Strange. He'd known the woman for two decades, and in his mind he'd always seen her as the scrawny little brat of fourteen who'd jumped on him kicking and biting and calling him a good-for-nothing bum. He shrugged. Oh, well, even if she did seem to be better looking than before, it didn't *mean* anything. He'd noticed she'd grown up now, that was all. It was no big deal. And it *was* only a coincidence that she'd appeared in his store so soon after her father had come up with the outrageous idea that Sam was just the man for her.

He wasn't the man for her. And she certainly was not the woman for him. He and Delilah Jones couldn't stand each other. It had always been that way, and there was no reason on earth that what had always been should change.

However, he kept on watching her, staring out the window feeling downright dazed, until her tempting little backside had disappeared from view.

Chapter Three

For Sam, the rest of the weekend went by with a minimum of excitement, like most weekends in North Magdalene. The only commotion worthy of even passing mention occurred Saturday night at The Hole in the Wall when Owen Beardsly accused Rocky Collins of moving the eight ball during a pool match. Rocky took immediate offense and dived at Owen right across the pool table. Oggie broke it up straightaway by firing a warning shot into the ceiling with the .38 special he kept behind the bar.

Sam heard the story secondhand on Sunday. He'd decided to keep clear of The Hole in the Wall for awhile. He wasn't in the mood to have Oggie Jones start in on him about Delilah. Sam didn't want to be badgered about Delilah, especially not after having gotten such a close look at her Saturday afternoon.

And that was another thing Sam decided, after considering it way more than he should have. He wasn't going to spend any of his time thinking about Delilah Jones and how good-looking she'd turned out to be all of a sudden. Only a man with a self-destructive streak as big as the San Andreas fault would let himself imagine what might happen in a bedroom alone with her.

And Sam was not self-destructive. Not anymore. The years when he'd been his own worst enemy were over. He went to the store Monday morning firm in his resolve not to think of Delilah Jones.

At nine sharp, Julio Santino's third son, Marty, came in. Marty asked about the Help Wanted sign in the window. Sam, who'd been handling things on his own since he'd had to let Roger McCleb go two weeks before, explained that it was full-time work.

Marty, fresh out of high school last June, said that was just what he was looking for. There was no place for him in the family business, Santino's BB&V. His sister helped his mother with the variety store and the beauty shop, and his father could easily handle the barbering alone. In fact, his two older brothers had long since left town for lack of work.

"There aren't a lot of heads in North Magdalene, Mr. Fletcher," Marty explained glumly. The boy eyed Sam's hair and beard with a rueful expression. "And there's a heck of a lot of longhairs—no offense meant, sir."

Sam, who'd put up with more snide remarks about his grooming over the years than he cared to think about, simply shrugged and got back to business. "You can start right now."

"Gee, great, Mr. Fletcher!"

They shook on it, and Sam began showing Marty his duties. By noon, Marty was handling things just fine. At three-thirty, Sam decided to go across the street and pick up his mail at the post office.

North Magdalene wasn't big enough to support its own door-to-door carrier. The mail was dropped off at the post office, and the postmistress sorted it into private boxes. For most people in town the process of picking up the mail was a daily ritual.

"No problem, Mr. Fletcher," Marty said brightly when Sam told him of his plans. Sam left the store feeling the next thing to jaunty. He'd come close to giving up on finding good help, and now it looked as if good help had been right next door at Santino's all along.

Once inside the post office, he waved at Melanie Swan, the postmistress, in the counter room beyond an interior door and went to the wall of private boxes in the long main room, which was left open seven days a week for the convenience of the box-holders. He just had his own box opened and was reaching in to get the rolled pile of flyers, cards and bills when he heard the door open and felt the slight, chilly breeze from outside.

He glanced toward the door.

And there was Delilah Jones.

She paused in the doorway when she saw him, and the afternoon sun from behind her made a gold rim around her thick black hair. She wore a gathered skirt today, its swirling colors rich and deep, with a dark red sweater on top. Most likely, he thought, she'd just come from the school that must have let out a few minutes before. He thought, with her inky hair and the strongly colored full skirt, that she looked like a gypsy, slightly wild, a little dangerous. When she spotted him, she froze for a moment.

Then she seemed to shake herself. She nodded, tightly. He nodded back. She swept into the narrow room and went to her own box, beyond his. She passed close to him. He got a whiff of her perfume, woodsy and faintly musky, too. A damned alluring scent. He snatched the envelopes and brochures from the mailbox, slammed the little door without bothering to spin the combination dial, and got the hell out of there.

The rest of the day, he kept catching his mind picturing black hair and dark, turbulent eyes. That was when he decided he was letting his mind get out of hand. And he was going to have to stop it. He just plain wasn't going to think about her anymore. He wasn't even going to think her *name* anymore, and that was all there was to it.

Later, after he'd sent Marty home and was locking up the store, he realized what was wrong with him. He'd been spending too much time without pleasant feminine companionship, and that was causing him to imagine the most ridiculous things about a woman who was as far from what he was looking for as it was possible for a woman to be.

He needed a date, that was all. If he had a pleasurable evening with a nice woman to look forward to, his overactive imagination would settle itself right down.

That evening, when he got home, he called Sarah Landers, a medical technician who lived in Grass Valley and whom he had dated twice before. He asked her to dinner Saturday night. She accepted, sounding pleased that he'd called.

When he hung up, he tried not to remember that the last time he took Sarah out, he'd more or less decided she just wasn't the woman for him. After all, he really did like Sarah. She was everything he'd been looking for in a woman: sweet and gentle, with a soft touch and a quiet voice.

Not like some women he could mention, whom he *wouldn't* mention, whom he'd promised himself he wouldn't even let himself *think* of. . . .

* * *

It happened again on Thursday.

Sam was rearranging the main window display while Marty cleaned the shelves by the side wall. With no warning, *she* drove up in her little hatchback car.

Forgetting every solemn vow he'd made to himself about how he would ignore her, Sam pressed his nose against the edge of the window so he could watch her pull up in front of Santino's next door. She and a passenger, little Emma Riggins, got out of the car. They went together into Santino's store.

"Looks like Emma's won the book."

At the sound of Marty's voice, Sam jumped as if he'd been caught doing something reprehensible. He glanced over to where Marty dusted the shelves, near a side window with an angled view of the street.

"What do you mean, the book?"

"Last Thursday of the month," Marty explained, busily dusting away as he spoke. "Kid with the most book reports turned in gets a book of their choice from my mom's store. Miss Jones buys it herself. She's been doing that forever. She did it when she taught me, and that was almost seven years ago now."

"I didn't know she did that," Sam remarked.

"No offense, but everybody knows that, Mr. Fletcher."

The bell over the door rang, and Sam was spared having to decide whether or not to reply to Marty's comment. Marty rushed to help the customer, and Sam returned to his window display.

Not long after, Oggie's daughter and Emma Riggins emerged from Santino's. Emma clutched a brown bag against her chest. The woman and the child got back in the car and drove away.

"Er, Mr. Fletcher?"

Sam sprang back from the window. Somehow Marty had stepped right up beside him and was looking out the window, too.

"Haven't you got a customer?" Sam challenged.

"He just left, Mr. Fletcher." Marty was grinning all-too-knowingly for an employee, Sam thought.

"Then get back to the shelves."

"Right away, sir." Marty flew to the shelves, and resumed cleaning them with great enthusiasm.

For a few minutes, the young man and the mature one worked without speaking. Then Sam said, "All right, Marty. What's on your mind?"

"Well, sir, no offense, sir..."

"Spit it out, Marty."

"If you got your eye on Miss Jones, sir, you better visit my dad's barbershop before you go asking her out. She's a teacher, sir. She likes a clean-cut look."

Sam looked at Marty for a moment, recalling with a rueful sigh his last short-lived employee, Roger McCleb. Roger never would have noticed if Sam had been staring out the window at Oggie Jones's daughter. Roger had had his hands full trying to remember how to make change. Maybe, Sam found himself thinking, there were a few drawbacks to hiring a go-getter like Marty; Marty saw too damn much.

"Mr. Fletcher—did I say something wrong, sir?" Marty inquired nervously, when Sam had been glowering at him for a while.

"Just finish the shelves, Marty."

"Er, you betcha, Mr. Fletcher."

Saturday evening, Sam drove to Grass Valley for his date with Sarah Landers. They shared a meal, and took in a movie. It was a pleasant evening.

And Sam knew halfway through dinner that calling her again had been pointless.

She invited him in when he took her home, smiling at him sweetly, the light of anticipation shining in her soft hazel eyes. He declined the invitation, knowing for certain this time that he would see her no more. She kept her sweet smile, but he watched the light fade from her eyes.

After he left her, he drove the twisting highway for home, feeling a depressing mixture of sadness and relief—sadness that he was alone, relief that he'd finally faced the fact that Sarah was not the right woman for him.

At the edge of town, he thought for a moment of stopping in at The Hole in the Wall. Maybe Jared would be there, in from the logging camp in the woods where he lived most of the time after his second messy divorce. Though Jared no longer touched liquor, he sometimes hung out in the bar for companionship when he was in town. If Jared were there, Sam would buy him a soda and they could talk about old times . . .

But Sam vetoed that idea before he let himself act on it. Oggie would be there, and Oggie, next to *she-who-could-not-be-named,* was the last person he could afford to get near right now. Oggie would be after him about *her*. And he didn't want to talk about *her*.

He turned off Main Street and drove home. Once there, he went to the workroom over the garage where he kept his woodworking tools. He labored for a while on a hunk of white pine he'd found, one in which he had recognized the vague shape of an owl waiting in the wood to be set free. He boasted, or roughed out, the basic shape of the bird, finding peace in the concentration, comfort in the feel of his own hands on the wood. Then, his spirit somewhat soothed, he showered and watched some late-night television, eventually falling asleep on the couch.

He dreamed of his first claim, that spot at the bend of the river that Oggie's vindictive little daughter had called hers. He dreamed he was working that four-inch dredge he'd spent his last five hundred dollars to buy, down below the surface of the water with the hose, vacuuming the crevices for placer deposits trapped there. Something stuck in the hose. He surfaced, and as he fiddled with the machine, he felt someone watching him.

He looked up. And *she* was standing there.

He stirred in his sleep, moaning a little, because he was trying, valiantly, even while unconscious, not to think her name. But then it came to him, rolling off the tongue, sweet and tempting as the smell of her: Delilah Jones.

No. Wait a minute. Not Delilah. Lilah. Yeah. Lilah, that's what he would call her if he ever said her name again. Lilah. He muttered it aloud in his sleep, though of course no one heard.

Lilah...smiling at him. She held out her hand. In her palm gleamed the biggest, purest nugget he'd ever seen in his life.

She said, "The gold's over here, Sam. Come on and get it." And she tucked that big nugget down her shirt, right in the sweet valley between her full breasts....

Sam sat bolt-upright, kicking the coffee table with the leg that was hanging off the side of the couch. He stared blankly at the television he'd left on, watching a giant reptilian bird tear the head off of a man in swim trunks as a pretty woman in a bikini cowered screaming nearby.

Then he groaned, raked his hair back with both hands and switched off the television. Soon enough he staggered groggily to his bedroom and fell across the bed, asleep before his head hit the pillow. The next morning, he told himself that he had no memory at all of his dreams the night before.

Around eleven, he dropped in at Lily's Cafe for a late Sunday breakfast.

And there *she* was.

In a booth at the back with Nellie Anderson and Linda Lou Beardsly, in for a snack after church. Sam almost turned around and got out of there. But he couldn't spend his life running from the sight of her.

He slid onto a counter stool, resolutely turning his back to her, and ordered his usual. But he could see her in the mirror that took up the whole wall behind the counter, and he knew she saw him, too.

Nellie and Linda Lou noticed him as well, though they sat side by side facing the other way. More than once, each of those old biddies turned and shot him a sour glance. He didn't let it bother him. He'd had run-ins with both of them, way back when, as he had with most all of the town's really upstanding types.

Once, after a particulary wild night out with Jared, he'd awakened to find himself in Nellie's flower bed. Nellie herself, out in her robe and slippers to pick up her paper, discovered him right after he realized he was awake. She'd started screaming. He'd thrown up on her slippers. It had not been his most shining hour.

But that had been years ago. Still, he was sure Nellie and Linda Lou continued to think of him as the rowdy young fool he had once been. And he just bet they were having a hell of a time reconciling the young wild man of whom they'd so thoroughly disapproved with the local merchant who'd just given five hundred bucks to help prop up the church bell tower.

But Sam didn't really give a damn what Nellie Anderson and Linda Lou Beardsly thought. He was too busy trying to pay no attention to *her*.

It shouldn't have been so difficult to ignore her. She hardly moved or made a sound, sitting there in the corner in a blue wool dress while the two battle-axes she called friends, Linda Lou and Nellie, jabbered away about the bell tower fund and the declining attendance at church. It should have been a piece of cake, to keep his eyes on his omelet and forget about her.

And maybe, if she'd never moved a muscle, he might have done all right. But suddenly, when she'd been sitting very still for a long time with her hands in her lap beneath the table, she raised her right arm.

For no reason he could fathom, Sam had a crystal clear mental image of her smiling at him, holding out something golden and gleaming. He almost choked on his coffee, and it sloshed in the saucer when he put the cup down. He looked again, furtively, and saw there was nothing at all in her hand. She had only lifted it to smooth her black hair.

His appetite, he realized then, had fled. He paid for his untouched ham omelet and left.

Good God, was there no escaping her? He couldn't go on like this.

He saw her twice in the following week. Both times, mercifully, were at a distance. It was what happened on Saturday that finished him off.

Saturday afternoon, Sam left Marty in charge of the store and drove to Grass Valley to stock up on staples.

He went to the big supermarket on Brunswick Road. He was actually feeling about as contented as he'd ever felt the past two weeks, strolling the wide aisles picking up his flour and his bacon, far away from the never-ending temptations of Oggie Jones's one and only baby girl. Or so he thought.

Until he came around the floral display to the produce section—and there she was, leaning on the handle of a big basket just like his, and chatting with the produce clerk. Sam froze in the aisle and listened as she asked for fresh mushrooms and the clerk pointed to them. She smiled and thanked him. It was a downright gorgeous smile.

Had she always smiled like that? Sam wondered. And if she had, why not for him?

Because she can't stand the sight of me, he reminded himself grimly. *And I've never been able to tolerate her, either. She's a prissy little twit half the time, and mean as a riled rattler the rest, not what I'm looking for at all....*

But he stood there, transfixed, as she wheeled her cart away from him, her beautiful hips swaying provocatively in trim jeans, and rolled down a plastic bag to begin choosing her fresh mushrooms. She selected them with great care, never looking up, and Sam found himself wishing he was one of them, a pale, fresh mushroom in her slender hand.

After the third or fourth irritated shopper murmured a pointed "excuse me" at him, Sam realized he had to get moving again.

Like a thief in the night, he pulled his cart backward, around the floral display and out of her sight. He simply could not make himself stroll past her, have her look up and glare at him, or worse, stare right through him, as if he didn't exist.

He headed for a check-out lane and paid for what he'd already picked out. Then he loaded the bags in his new Bronco and returned to North Magdalene. He took the food home, put it away, and then joined Marty at the store.

He and Marty worked smoothly together until nearly closing time, when he left Marty alone again to pick up the mail. As he entered the long room, he did not let his mind even consider the thought that *she* might be lurking there among the mailboxes, ready to drive him insane with her fierce, frozen glances, with her perfume that mingled a woodland morning with musk.

But everything was fine. There was no sign of her. He spun the dial. The little door swung open, and he took his mail in his hands. He left the long room quickly, not wanting to tempt fate. He made it outside, where the sun was nearing the western hills and all was as it should be. He crossed the street to his store again.

And then he saw her. Getting out of her car up by Lily's Cafe. She shut the car door and began strolling right toward him.

He saw her stride break when she recognized him. She gave him that tight little nod, like she had in the post office a week before—that nod that, he supposed, was a concession to the fact that they'd spoken more or less civilly Saturday-before-last, when he'd donated five hundred dollars to her bell tower fund.

But the nod was all he got. After that, she kept right on coming, her face blank, like it always was, not acknowledging him further, as if, in reality, he was no longer there at all. He wanted to rush forward to meet her. He wanted to grab her by the arms and shake her, until she looked in his eyes at last, until her mouth went soft and yielding and she held it up to his. . . .

He heard a low growling sound and knew it came from him. And then he ducked into the next doorway, into Santino's store. He went straight to the back, to the little room where Julio Santino presided, with the Naugahyde couch and scarred side table stacked with tattered magazines by one wall, and the barber's chair in the middle of the floor.

"Well, shut my mouth and call me a rug," Julio Santino exclaimed at the sight of him. "I never thought I'd see the day."

Sam sat in the chair. "Just the mustache and beard," he said flatly. "Don't touch the hair."

"Well, it's a start," remarked Julio.

"Shut up and cut."

Chapter Four

That wild man Sam Fletcher was sitting on her front porch when Delilah drove up. It took her a moment to realize it was him. For some inexplicable reason, he'd shaved off his mustache and full beard. He'd also tied back his shoulder-length hair into a ponytail. From the front at least, he almost looked respectable.

But not quite. There was still that troublemaking gleam in his eye and the arrogant way he carried his big, powerful body. Even crouched on her front step, his shoulders hunched over a stick of wood as he worked at it with a knife, he looked alert and ready to pounce at a moment's notice.

Delilah shot him a ''get lost'' look from behind the wheel. It had absolutely no effect. He didn't budge, but just went on slicing away at the little stick of wood.

For a moment, reluctant to get out of the car and deal with him, Delilah didn't move. What in heaven's name could he be doing here? she wondered. He'd never come to her house. Yet here he was, sitting on her step like he belonged there, causing her stomach to knot in a distressing way.

And that really bothered her—to feel anxious about Sam Fletcher. Seething, furious, indifferent, disgusted, enraged—all those emotions came to mind when she thought of the man. But anxious? Never. Until recently.

Oh yes, there was definitely something going on with him lately. Since the day she'd solicited a donation for the bell tower fund from him, it had seemed like the man dogged her every move.

He watched her in the mirror while she tried to enjoy her Sunday brunch at Lily's Cafe. He stared at her in the post office as if she had her skirt on backward. His icy gaze chilled her when she passed him in the street, and she could swear he peered at her out of the windows of his store every time she passed by.

It just didn't make sense. For over a decade, they'd lived in a perfectly good state of truce. They'd put the battles they'd fought during the years she'd lived with her father behind them. They'd learned to ignore each other; each had developed the habit of pretending the other wasn't there. And it had worked out just fine.

Now, all of a sudden, the rotten rogue was changing the game plan on her. And Delilah didn't like it. Not one little bit. It made her nervous, very nervous. And, worse than that, it made her *think* about him. Which was crazy. She had better things to do with her time than to think about Sam Fletcher.

Well, she thought grimly as she emerged from her car, whatever the incorrigible wretch was doing here, she was going to give him a large piece of her mind for his trouble. She would take this opportunity to tell him in no uncertain terms that she wanted him to stop giving her the eye every time she walked by him. She wanted him to start ignoring her again, and that was that.

Also, he had no business being on her porch, which was the first thing she said to him once she'd marched around the nose of her little car and planted herself at the base of her own front steps.

"Sam Fletcher, you have no business being on my porch."

He shot her something that resembled a grin—a sort of flattening out of his lips. Then he stood up and pocketed his whittling knife. "Good to see you, too, Lilah."

She glared at him, shielding her eyes with her arm because, to the west behind the house, the sun was dropping low. "What do you want?"

He held out the bit of willow that he'd been slicing away at. "For you."

Dropping her shielding arm, Delilah looked down at his outstretched hand where a wooden raccoon sat, balanced on its hind legs, paws up. The little figure was primitive, but utterly charming. She stared at it for a moment, realizing with alarm that she itched to finger the grooves where his knife had shaped it. Then she pointedly looked away.

With a shrug of his muscular shoulders, he stuck the lovely thing in a pocket. Delilah felt a stab of regret for that small object of rough beauty, lost to her because she mistrusted its creator.

"What do you want?" she demanded again, more forcefully than before.

He looked over her shoulder, into the windows of her car. "You've got groceries. I'll bring them on in."

"No, you won't."

Ignoring her words, he took the few steps down to where she stood. She didn't budge.

He feinted around her. She mirrored his step. She wasn't exactly blocking his way; Sam Fletcher was six-five and broad as an oak. She could no more block his way than a gnat could stall a buffalo. But she *was* standing, quite purposefully, in his path.

"Come on, Lilah," he said.

"I don't need your help."

He looked minimally annoyed. "I didn't say you needed it. I just said you're getting it, that's all."

"What for?"

"Why not?"

"You're up to something. I want to know why you're here."

He looked at her for a moment, sighed as if he were the one whose patience was being tried, and then casually took her by the shoulders and moved her out of his way. He'd reached her car before she even had time to sputter her outrage that he'd dared to lay hands on her.

"You have absolutely no right—"

"I want to talk to you." He tossed out the words casually, overriding her budding fury with nonchalance, as he pulled open the hatch at the back of the car and hauled three grocery bags into his powerful arms.

"Stop that," she snapped. "I told you, I didn't want—"

"Settle down, Lilah," he said, sounding weary. "Let's get this stuff inside, and then we can talk."

He mounted her steps again and went to the front door, where he waited quite patiently for her to let him in.

"Oh, all right," she muttered, when a few seconds of vituperative glaring did her no good at all. She had some frozen things in the cooler, and the groceries had been waiting in the car for a while now; she'd had errands to run in town before coming home after her trip to Grass Valley to get them. It would probably be best to get the perishables put away as soon as possible—even if that meant putting up with Sam Fletcher for a few grueling minutes more.

Grabbing up a bag herself, she climbed the steps, slid around Sam Fletcher's imposing bulk, and unlocked the door. "This way," she instructed. He followed her in.

They set the bags on the kitchen counter. Then he went back for the cooler, which he said he could handle himself. She quickly set about putting the milk and meat in the refrigerator and when he returned she took the frozen vegetables out of the cooler and put them away.

Once that was done, she faced the clean-shaven giant. "Now, what do you want?"

He glanced around at the bags on the counter, almost as if, now the moment had come, he shrank from it. "There's more here to put away."

"It will wait. Talk. Now."

He looked at her, an unnerving look that seemed to drink in the whole of her, though his eyes never moved from staring into hers. "It's Saturday night," he said finally.

"So?"

"Do you have a date?"

She gaped at him. What in the world difference could it make to Sam Fletcher if she had a date or not? "As a matter of fact, no. Though it's none of your business."

"You aren't... seeing anyone, then?"

"What are you getting at?" This was becoming stranger by the second. These were the kinds of questions a man only asked a woman when he was considering...

Heavens, she couldn't even bear to finish the thought. It wasn't possible. Not wild Sam Fletcher who detested her just as much as she loathed him. He couldn't be thinking of asking her for a . . .

Delilah shook her head. No. She wouldn't think it. It was too appalling. There had to be some other perfectly reasonable explanation for the way he'd been behaving lately.

"Sam." She was so taken aback by her own thoughts that she actually forgot to be hostile for a moment. "Sam, what is going on?" The pleading note in her voice shocked both of them. They stared at each other.

He was the first to look away, smoothing his already tightly pulled-back hair with his hand. "Look. I'm thirsty. Could I have—"

Without letting him finish, she whirled, popped open the fridge, and yanked out a can of cola. She shoved it at him. "Here."

He looked down at the can, as if he couldn't figure out how it had gotten in his hand. "Mind if I . . . sit down?" Good heavens, he was being so *polite*. There was something the matter with him, no doubt about it now.

She peered at him more closely. He didn't look well. His face was pale, and his breathing seemed rapid. Maybe he was sick, maybe that was what was wrong with him. Maybe he'd been sick for a couple of weeks now, and that was why he'd been behaving so strangely. Yes, that must be it.

Though it made no sense. If a man was sick, why would he show up at the house of a woman he hated just to tell her he was ill? Unless he hoped she'd catch what he had.

"Lilah?"

And why was he calling her Lilah all of a sudden? "What?"

He looked longingly at the table in the window nook a few feet away. She remembered he'd asked for a seat. "Oh. Of course. Go ahead."

He dropped to a chair and popped open the cola. She waited, her heart doing erratic things in her chest, as he took a long drink.

He set the can down. "That's better. Thank you."

"It's okay. Now, tell me—"

"I am. I will... Lilah, I—"

Suddenly, she didn't want to hear. "You know, you're absolutely right."

He blinked. "I am? About what?"

"These groceries. I really should put them away."

She sprang to life, peeling herself off the refrigerator where she'd been drooping in dread and flying around the roomy kitchen as if getting the bags unloaded meant life or death.

"Lilah?"

She grabbed a bag full of produce and whirled to yank open the refrigerator door. Then she knelt, the bag beside her, and began frantically piling lettuce and celery, radishes and zucchini, into the crisper drawer.

"Lilah?"

"Won't be a minute..."

"Lilah?"

Slowly, she looked up. He'd left the chair and now loomed above her, looking down. His eyes, always so cold in her every memory of him, shone now with a strange blue fire.

She shot to her feet and confronted him. "You stop. You just stop. I won't, I will not, do you hear?" She backed away, stepping over the half-unloaded bag.

Gently, he closed the refrigerator door. "Lilah."

She shook her head. "It's no. No ahead of time. So don't bother to ask."

He smiled then, a smile that charmed and beguiled her. Stars above, with all that hair gone, his face was downright...handsome.

"Ask what?" he said tenderly and took a step toward her.

Out the window over the sink, the day was going. The sun gleamed on the rim of Sweetbriar Summit, which rose on the other side of Main Street, past the river and the woods. Shadows claimed the edges of the bright room. Oh, she had to get rid of him, she knew it. Before dark, before he could say what he'd come to say.

"I want you to leave. Please," she told him on a mere whisper of sound.

He only shook his head. "Not until I ask you..."

"No. Don't do it. Please."

"I have to."

"Oh, heavens, Sam, don't..."

But it was too late. He said, *"How about a date, Delilah?"*

She turned away and looked out the window, as the sun slid behind the mountain. For a moment the room lay in soft, tempting shadow. She could feel his hopeful, tender gaze.

And then Delilah turned, edged around him swiftly, and went to the wall by the living room arch. She flipped on the light. "No. Never. Forget it. No way."

His gaze was hard now, his big body tense. When he spoke he almost sounded like the rotten scoundrel she'd always known. "Why the hell not? It's only a date."

"Because."

"That's no answer."

She looked past him out the window over the sink again, at the near-darkness where the trees were only dim shapes now and the rim of Sweetbriar Summit shimmered with the very end of day.

"Why not?" he demanded again. "Give me one good reason." He took a step toward her. She slid around him once more and went back to the sink.

"A reason, Delilah."

She said, rather mindlessly, "You want a reason."

"That's what I said."

"Fine. I'll give you a reason." She crossed her arms under her breasts. "I don't go out with jailbirds, for one."

"What the hell do you mean, jailbirds? I'm no jailbird."

She shook her head, feeling self-righteous. "Don't stand there and lie to me. Sheriff Pangborn is always tossing you in the jail, for being drunk and disorderly, for getting in fights."

"Lilah." He spoke with infinite patience. "I haven't spent the night in jail in fifteen years—and even then, the sheriff was more giving me a place to sleep it off than anything else. Charges were never filed. Not once."

"Sheriff Pangborn's a forgiving soul. Too forgiving, as far as a lot of people in town are concerned."

"That was fifteen years ago, I'm no jailbird now. Let's talk about now, that's fair, don't you think? Why can't you go out with me now?"

"Well…" She glowered a little and bit the inside of her lip. "There are a hundred reasons."

"Fine. Start with one."

"All right—you drink too much."

"I *used* to drink too much. Past tense again, Lilah. We're talking about now."

"Drunk or sober, you're always hanging around my father's bar."

"My friends are there, and I drop in once or twice a week. But that's tops. Lately, I haven't even been stopping in that often."

"You love to gamble. You're a gambling man."

"Lilah. I like a game of poker with the guys every now and then as much as the next man. But that hardly adds up to a dangerous habit."

"Of course you'd say that."

"Because it's the truth."

"Well, it doesn't matter anyway. My answer is still no."

"You still haven't given me one solid reason."

"I . . . I have the best reason in the world for not dating you. I don't need any others."

"All right, what? What is the reason?"

"Because we've *always* hated each other!"

He looked completely unconcerned. "No reason that can't change."

"It can't. It can't change. It's how it's always been."

"Past tense, Lilah. Give right now a chance."

Delilah uncrossed her arms and recrossed them again. She felt more than uncomfortable now. She felt . . . like her whole world was fraying at the edges. He sounded so reasonable. She was weakening, and she knew it.

She was actually starting to wonder why she shouldn't say yes to him—a man exactly like her father and brothers, a man she'd always been careful to avoid like the plague. Oh, what was wrong with her? She must be getting desperate, though she'd always believed she was perfectly happy with her single life.

She'd had one love affair, in college. It had not amounted to much in the end. In fact, the physical part of it had been awkward and groping, and had left her se-

cure in her conviction that she could get along just fine
without whatever it was that everyone else got so excited
about.

But, heavens to Betsy! If she was as completely im-
mune to passion as she'd always thought, why was it that
right this minute, she was actually pondering what it
might be like to kiss Sam Fletcher on the lips?

Could it be, she wondered, even though she wished she
hadn't, that she'd always loathed Sam Fletcher as a defense, because deep down she was *attracted* to him?

Delilah recoiled from such an impossible idea. Frantically, she sought a fresh defense against this forbidden
new fascination with a man who would never in a thousand years be the right man for her.

And then it came to her: her father, two weeks ago,
tossing off that ludicrous taunt that he'd picked out a man
for her. It was crazy to think that he might have really
done such a thing. However, if Oggie *had* done it, who
better to choose than Sam Fletcher, fellow troublemaker,
son of his heart if not of his blood?

And, come to think of it, Sam had begun acting
strangely on that very day....

Delilah, who'd felt her bones starting to melt, now
stiffened her spine. She glared at the handsome giant
across the room from her. "My father put you up to this,
didn't he? I know him. He wants to see me married. He
doesn't care to whom. He's probably offered to *pay* you
if you can put a ring on my finger. Do you actually think
I'd have anything to do with a man who was paid by my
father to take me out—let alone, if that man was *you*...."

Though Delilah didn't know it, this particular indict-
ment gave Sam a moment's pause. After all, Oggie *had*
offered him The Mercantile if he married her.

But then, Sam shrugged. Two weeks ago, there wasn't enough money in the world to bribe him to go after Delilah Jones. And today, there wasn't enough to hold him back.

He answered her accusation with heavy irony. "Why, thank you, Delilah. Your high opinion of me never ceases to amaze me. But you're wrong. I'm not here for money. I'm here for *you.*"

Delilah eyed him warily. He sounded grim, but sincere. She found, against all wisdom, that she actually believed him, though to believe he'd only come here because he wanted *her* seemed impossible. Incredible. Downright dangerous.

And yet—Heaven help her—captivating, too.

She stared at him, feeling suddenly bewildered by her own forbidden thoughts.

He smiled, knowing as men have always known, what her dazed look meant. She was softening, giving ground.

"Lilah." His voice was a caress. His gaze spoke of things she knew she shouldn't let herself imagine. He took a step toward her.

"No..." She stepped back and came up short against the sink.

"Lilah..."

"Stay away. I mean it."

He took another step.

She had to stop him. Frantic, she fumbled behind her in the dish rack, and felt the handle of a heavy frying pan. She grabbed it and held it up. "Get back."

He smiled. "God, Lilah. You are something."

His eyes were sea blue mirrors in which she saw herself. Oh, foolish, foolish, she thought vaguely. Never before, in all their years of battles and armed truces, had she let herself be alone with him. Alone in her kitchen after dark.

She should never have let him in. She should have grabbed her groceries from him on the front porch, and refused to let him cross her threshold into her personal space. At the least, she should never have allowed him to tell her why he came. She should have ordered him out the minute he set her groceries on the counter.

Yes, order him out. That was the thing to do. She was going to order him out. Now . . .

But he took the final step. And she said nothing. Her weapon, the frying pan, grew too heavy to hold high. She let it sink to her side.

He whispered her name again, and she felt the warmth of him, radiating out, enveloping her. His big hand, rough and tender, was on her cheek, stroking, guiding her chin up so her mouth would be ready.

Oh, my gracious, he was going to kiss her. His mouth was going to cover hers, and she was going to know the taste of her enemy on her lips. And she wanted it, *wanted* it, couldn't wait for it. She felt her head droop back on the stem of her neck. His mouth descended. . . .

And the forgotten frying pan in her nerveless hand clattered to the floor.

The jarring sound saved her. With a choked cry, she shoved at his chest. He grabbed her arms. She struggled, briefly, and then she just glared at him, into those seductive blue mirrors that now looked hard, and hungry as well.

Slowly, so she would know he did it by his own will, he released her and stepped back. There was a long silence, which she broke at last by retrieving the frying pan and setting it on the counter beside the remaining grocery bags.

Then he tried that voice on her again—that soft, tempting voice that soothed her and beguiled her into forgetting who he was.

"Lilah..."

"No."

"Lilah."

"I want you to go. Now."

He shook his head, his expression bemused. "I know what you want, Lilah. I saw it in your eyes. Felt it, in the way your body—"

She put up a hand. "No more."

"Aw, Lilah. Why run from it? You can't get away anyway. Believe me. I know." They looked at each other, and she wondered if her own face mirrored the barely restrained longing she saw in his. "Come out with me. Tonight," he said. "We'll drive down to Nevada City. I know this nice, quiet little restaurant there, where we could—"

She couldn't let him continue, it sounded too lovely. "No. Please leave. Now."

"Lilah..."

She looked him level in the eye and spoke with some force. "Get out of my house."

"Come on. It's only dinner."

"No. I mean it, Sam Fletcher. No dates, no nothing— ever—between you and me." He went on looking at her tenderly, and her frustration at his unwillingness to leave loosened her tongue. "I've spent thirty-four years proving that being a Jones doesn't necessarily mean I'm a person who likes to brawl over things that make no difference, and shoot out the lights rather than walk across the room to reach the switch. Do you actually imagine that I'm going to let myself become involved with a man who's more of a Jones than the Joneses?"

"You want me."

"There has to be more than that for me."

"Give it a chance. We can find more."

"No way. Find yourself some other woman."

His eyes glittered at her, the way moonlight reflects on a night pond, in gleaming ribbons. Then he reached in his pocket and took out the willow raccoon she'd refused on the front step. He set it on the table.

"I made it for you. Sitting there, nervous as hell, waiting."

"I don't want it."

He was already on his way to the door. "Fine. Throw it away."

She gave a little gasp at the thought. She didn't want it; to take it would somehow speak of intimacies between them. But beauty like that was rare, however unrefined. She could never toss it away.

She heard the front door close. He was gone. She listened as his booted feet retreated down the porch steps. Then she looked again at the figure on the table. The tiny animal gazed back at her, too appealing to bear, through its roughly etched raccoon mask.

Quickly, Delilah turned away from the tiny creature and finished putting her groceries away. After that, she made herself a simple dinner and sat down to eat.

The raccoon, which she hadn't touched since *he* set it down, watched her every bite. When she could tolerate its fetching glance no longer, she grabbed it up, rushed into the living room and, balanced on a stool, stuck the thing on top of a high bookcase, all the way against the wall, where she wouldn't be able to see it from anywhere in the room unless she stood on a chair. Then she returned to her solitary dinner and enjoyed it very much.

* * *

The phone rang at eight, while Delilah was getting a head start on the papers she had to have graded by Monday. It was Nellie Anderson.

Nellie hardly gave Delilah time to say hello before she was off and chattering. "I just spoke with Loulah Bends, and, of course, I had to call right away and let you know."

"What is it, Nellie?"

"Loulah says that Janie Fashland says that Billie Rae Naylor claims she drove by your house before dark and saw that crazy Sam Fletcher sitting on your porch, bold as brass."

"Oh?" Delilah set her papers aside. She'd been expecting Nellie's call—or one just like it from Linda Lou Beardsly. Not a lot went on in North Magdalene that everyone didn't find out about sooner or later. As a child, Delilah had been hurt more than once when the gossip turned on some insane thing that her father or her brothers had done. But when she decided, after college, that she missed her hometown and wanted to return here to live, she also decided how she would handle rumormongering when it came her way. She would listen quietly while it played itself out, and not contribute to it in the least.

"Well..." Nellie had temporarily run out of steam. Delilah's noncommittal *Oh?* had given her pause—just as it always did. But then she got herself going again. "I thought you should know that he was hanging around there earlier."

"Yes. I know."

Nellie's breath caught, a little eager gasp. "You saw him then?"

"Yes. He was here when I drove up."

"And?"

"He helped me with my groceries."

"And?"

She bent the truth just a smidgen, by not telling all. "He left."

"But what was he *doing* there in the first place?"

Delilah considered. She hated to lie. But Nellie would be burning up the phone lines, calling everyone in town with the news, if she admitted Sam Fletcher had asked her for a date.

"Well?" Nellie prompted.

Delilah removed her reading glasses and rubbed the ache at the bridge of her nose. "Nellie, I'm just not at liberty to say. It was a private matter, and now it's settled. And that's all there is to it."

Nellie said nothing for a moment, her disappointment palpable. Then, "Delilah, honey. You know you can trust me."

"Of course I do. But it's all over now."

"*What's* all over?"

"Nellie." Delilah's voice was kind and firm. "It's over. Let it be."

Nellie sighed. "Oh, all right. But if you need a listening ear..."

"Thanks. I'll remember that."

They talked for a few more minutes, but Delilah knew her friend was eager to hang up and burn the wires a little with the small amount of information she'd been able to glean from their conversation. Delilah didn't hold this against Nellie. That would be a little like blaming the wind for blowing.

After Nellie said goodbye, it was a few minutes before Delilah put her reading glasses back on and resumed correcting the stack of papers she'd set aside. She did feel a bit uncomfortable, knowing that tongues would be wagging for a day or so, hypothesizing what might have gone on between her and Sam Fletcher.

But then she told herself the talk would die down soon enough. She kept a very clean profile in North Magdalene. She led a sober, quiet life. She'd been born into a family whose antics gave all the local gossips one thrill after another. And she'd made sure, as soon as she could choose her own way, that she lived the kind of life that put scandalmongers right to sleep.

Yes, give it a day or two, and the gossip would die out. She was sure of this because she intended to give them nothing more to go on. And because she knew that Sam Fletcher would never say a word.

Delilah put her glasses back on and reached for her papers and her red felt pen. She returned to her work, not letting herself think about Sam Fletcher anymore. Or about how she could be so certain that the man she'd always despised had too much integrity to tell a soul what had passed between them in her kitchen earlier that evening.

She worked diligently for half an hour. Then the phone rang again. She almost let it ring. And then, with a sigh, she answered.

"How about *next* Saturday, then?" Sam Fletcher asked in her ear.

"Never," she quietly replied. "Goodbye." She hung up, but not before soft laughter, deep and beguiling, tormented her from the other end of the line.

After that, he called nightly. She learned to have the phone back in its cradle before he'd even finished saying hello.

And that wasn't all. Every morning, a new and charming wooden figure would greet her from an outside windowsill—an owl, a squirrel, a dove. She resolutely ignored them.

Moreover, she discovered that she could no longer walk on Main Street without seeing him. He popped out of his store and lounged against the wall by the door the moment she set foot in town.

He never tried to speak to her, either. And somehow that made it worse. He just stayed there by his store, not even looking at her, managing maddeningly to respect her privacy at the same time that his very presence telegraphed his unspoken message:

He was not giving up.

So she ended up scurrying for the post office every day, promising herself that she would keep her eyes completely averted as she passed Sam Fletcher's store. She was doing just that on Tuesday, making a dash for the post office door, when a loud diesel honk caught her up short.

She whirled around. It was her brother, Brendan, up behind the wheel of the like-new Long Nose Peterbilt he and his wife Amy had put themselves in hock to buy. Brendan signaled that he'd pull over down the street.

Delilah, still hoping to get her mail and get away before Sam Fletcher appeared, almost shook her head. But then she reconsidered.

Truth was, in recent years, she didn't see much of her brothers. She avoided them because they'd driven her insane during the years she was growing up. But now, in the few seconds before Brendan drove by, she felt a little guilty. Maybe she wasn't really being fair. Almost two decades had passed since they'd all lived at home. Maybe Brendan—and Patrick and Jared as well—had changed.

Unbidden, she recalled a seductive voice suggesting, *Past tense, Lilah. Give right now a chance....*

"Oh, shut up," she muttered under her breath, as if the voice in her head had been real.

Then she nodded at Brendan and waved. After all, she'd never even seen the Peterbilt, Brendan's pride and joy, up close. It seemed only right that she stop and take a look. That seductive remembered voice had nothing to do with her decision—nothing at all....

Just then, Brendan's truck rolled by, its spotless chrome gleaming. Delilah caught a glimpse of her own face in the deep maroon gloss of the flawless paintwork. Her expression was a beleaguered one.

And why shouldn't she look beleaguered? Sam Fletcher was driving her crazy, after all. Every single thought she had seemed to lead right back to him.

Down the street, Brendan had found a space long enough for the big truck. Delilah hurried to meet him. Brendan jumped down to greet her, explaining how he was off on a run from Sacramento to Phoenix before dawn the next morning.

They talked for a few minutes, exchanging pleasantries. Delilah found herself charmed by Brendan's eagerness—as well as heartened by his obvious happiness. Could this be the sullen baby brother who took up smoking at the age of eleven and displayed an astonishing command of imaginative profanity whenever she asked him to pick up his room?

He and Amy expected their first child in a little over a month. He'd given up smoking, he told Delilah, when he learned about the baby. He spoke with a grateful kind of pride, and said softly that he fell more in love with his wife with each passing day.

And Brendan's adoration for Amy shone on more than his face. The big truck was a rolling personification of his unabashed love. On either side of the matching trailer,

Brendan had talked a talented friend into painting portraits of Amy—very vivid portraits, five times life-sized, from which Amy's wide doelike eyes regarded the world with shy allure and her long blonde hair flowed away behind, as if blown by the wind. Beyond that, both the gleaming front grill and the sleeper declared the truck to be the Sweet Amy in fanciful, flowing script.

Brendan insisted Delilah climb into the sleeper to see what a home-away-from-home it was. He gave her a hand up. Inside, there was actually a small section of flooring to stand on as well as a double bed—and a microwave. The colors were a soothing silver-gray. Quite comfortable, Delilah decided, for a man who lived so much of his life on the road.

Brendan, still outside on the sidewalk, explained that once the baby was a few months old, Amy would be riding with him at least part of the time again. He mentioned how difficult it was for her now, with him gone so much and the baby almost due. Then he insisted on shutting the sleeper door, so Delilah could get a feel for how comfy and private it was.

After a moment, Delilah pushed open the door to step down—and found Sam Fletcher grinning up at her. "Let me help you, Lilah...."

Nonplussed, Delilah gaped at him. His red-gold hair, pulled back as always lately, gleamed in the sun. He wore a pale blue ski sweater that hugged the massive contours of his shoulders and emphasized his trim waist. The sweater matched his eyes, which looked at her with humor and understanding and carefully restrained desire.

Something hot and forbidden bloomed in her stomach. He grinned wider, as if he knew just what she felt. She had to resist the ridiculous urge to shrink back into the sleeper and slam the door, to cower there, hiding from her own taboo reactions as much as anything else, until he finally went away—which, of course, he wouldn't do.

Seeking a more viable escape, she looked beyond him. She spotted Brendan a few feet away. Brendan shrugged— as if there was nothing *he* could do about it if Sam Fletcher had a sudden urge to pop up out of nowhere and assist his sister to the ground.

But Brendan's shrug didn't fool Delilah. She recognized the wayward gleam in his eye. He hadn't changed completely, after all. He might have cleaned up his act for sweet Amy's sake, but he still had enough hell-raiser in him to want to see what would happen when his sis was offered a helping hand by the man she most despised in all the world.

Nothing, Delilah thought. *Absolutely nothing is going to happen, baby brother. So there.*

She composed her face into cordial lines and said sweetly, "Why, thank you, Sam. How kind of you."

She must have sounded convincing, because she saw out of the corner of her eye that Brendan's jaw dropped. Quite pleased with herself, she held out a hand. Sam's huge paw engulfed it. Tempting heat, like that in her stomach, shivered up her arm. With an effort of will, she kept her expression tranquil.

She stepped down, figuring she could handle it since the only contact between them was their clasped hands. But Sam Fletcher knew how to exploit a situation. Just as she stepped free of the sleeper, he released her hand and caught her about the waist. The heat of his touch seemed to spin and close around her as he swung her to the ground.

She came up against his broad chest. He looked down at her, pale eyes alight. "There you go."

Somehow, she smiled. "Yes." She delicately placed her palms on his chest, felt the deep thudding of his heart for an instant, and gave a light shove. "Thanks again."

His hands fell away. She resisted the mad urge to sway back into his arms, to feel her breasts brush against his chest one more time.

He said softly, "I'll talk to you tonight."

She murmured so only he could hear, "Get smart. Give up."

"Never."

"Hey!" Brendan interjected. "What gives between you two?"

Delilah turned her back on Sam. "Nothing," she told her brother calmly. "Nothing at all."

That night when Sam called, Delilah hung up even more swiftly than usual.

The next morning, a wooden rabbit looked at her hopefully from beyond the window over the kitchen sink. She closed the curtains on it.

In town that afternoon, as usual, Sam lurked by the door to his store. She ignored him.

He called that night. She hung up.

Thursday, a doe, poised in the moment of scenting possible threat, stood on one of the sills of the windows around the kitchen table.

The doe astonished her. She stood looking out the window at it for a long time. What skill he must have, to shave the wood away from those delicate legs without cutting too deep and destroying the whole.

That night, when he called, she stayed on the line too long, long enough to hear him ask, rather sadly, when she was going to stop being so stubborn. Then she made herself hang up.

Friday, a bear cub waited in the next window over from the doe. It was plump and appealing, rolled over on its back batting the air with its paws. She couldn't help it. She smiled when she saw it.

But then, strangely enough, he failed to materialize by the door to his store when she went to get her mail that afternoon—which was just fine with Delilah; a relief, as a matter of fact.

Then, Friday night . . . nothing. He failed to call. Delilah felt great about that. It was just what she'd hoped for, that he'd leave her alone.

Saturday morning, the same wooden animals greeted her when she peeked through the drawn curtains. But no new ones had joined them.

That was just terrific, as far as she was concerned.

That afternoon, after her weekly trip to Grass Valley for groceries, she walked over to Main Street as usual to pick up her mail. She ducked into the post office swiftly, sure that his absence yesterday and the lack of a new wooden creature in the window this morning had been only a fluke to make her let down her guard. She just knew that when she emerged, *he* would be standing there, by the door to his store.

No such thing happened. He wasn't there when she came out.

Saturday evening, after dark had come, she sat in her living room easy chair and read a mystery novel. Tonight, there were no papers to correct. Easter week lay before her, and she looked forward to the break.

Beside her, the phone sat silent. And she was really and truly relieved. She was finally beginning to believe that Sam Fletcher had at last given up. And that was good. That was just what she wanted. She was grateful to have her privacy and peace of mind restored. She was. She really was.

In fact, now that she thought about it, it all made sense. More than likely, he'd called someone else for a date yesterday. He was probably out with that someone tonight. Taking her to that nice restaurant in Nevada City he'd mentioned, and having a wonderful time.

And that was great; that was just great. If some other woman wanted to go out with Sam Fletcher, that was okay with her.

Just then, Delilah realized she'd let her book drop to her lap and she was staring blindly at the far wall. She made a disgruntled little sound, took off her reading glasses and put the book aside. She got up and turned on the television and tried to concentrate on it, though she found her mind still insisted on wandering where it shouldn't go—to thoughts of Sam Fletcher and where he might be tonight....

Chapter Five

Sam hadn't gone out with another woman. He'd gone instead where he knew he shouldn't: to The Hole in the Wall.

Oggie greeted him with a muttered, "It's about damned time," and a cold mug of Sam's favorite brew. "Drink up," he suggested, before Sam even had time to slide onto a stool. "You look like you need it."

Sam grunted, sat down, and lifted the mug.

Oggie leaned on the bar. "Go ahead, son. Tell me all about it."

"What?"

"Whatever's got you lookin' discouraged as a woodpecker in a petrified forest."

"I'm fine, Oggie. Just fine."

Oggie gave Sam a disbelieving wiggle of his eyebrows and then remarked, "Well, one thing I gotta tell you—you shoulda shaved fifteen years ago. Great balls of fire, if I was a woman, I could go for you myself!''

Sam saluted the old rapscallion with his beer before draining the last of it. Oggie leaned closer and pitched his voice low and confidential. ''By the way, how you doin' with my little girl?''

Sam set his mug down. ''I don't know what you're talking about, Oggie.'' He pushed the mug toward the other man. ''How about a refill?''

Oggie poured out another draft and slid it to Sam. ''C'mon. Don't tell me you ain't been givin' my offer some thought. Julio Santino tells me his boy Marty says—''

''Marty's a real self-starter. If he's got a flaw, it's too much imagination.''

''Marty's a good, honest kid,'' Oggie argued.

''I didn't say he wasn't honest.''

''Good. So let me tell you what Julio says—''

''If it's true, I already know it, and if it's a lie, I don't want to hear it.''

''Sheesh.'' Oggie shook his head. ''You're as testy as Brendan tonight.''

Sam looked around. ''Brendan's here?''

Oggie tipped his head toward the heavy green curtain at one end of the room. Beyond it was the poker table. ''He and Amy had words, from what I could pull out of him. He showed up here a half hour ago, ordered a double whiskey and bought a pack of smokes. Now, if he's lucky, he won't go and lose his shirt to those two slick out-of-towners in there before he gets up the courage to go home. Which is where he oughtta be right now, if anybody asked me. He's a rotten rascal for fightin' with that sweet girl.''

''It takes two to make a fight, you know, Oggie,'' Sam pointed out reasonably.

"It don't matter. That little girl is carrying my grand-baby... And don't go thinkin' I don't know what you're doing, son. I'm old but not that old. I know when a subject's been changed on me."

"What are you talking about, Oggie?"

Oggie grunted. "Good enough. Keep your own council about you and Delilah. For tonight. Just don't you forget this is North Magdalene, son. Secrets around these parts got all the stayin' power of a frozen daiquiri in hell."

Sam knew the wisest thing to do right now would be to set his mug down and leave. He felt edgy and antsy, the way he used to feel in the old days just before doing something crazy. In this kind of mood, there was no telling what he might do. Sheriff Pangborn might end up extending the hospitality of the local jail to him once again—thus proving Delilah's accusations of last week correct.

But hell. Another Saturday night staring at four walls when he knew what he wanted, and what he wanted kept saying no, was enough to make a man do foolish things.

Like show up at The Hole in the Wall when he'd sworn to himself he was going to keep away.

"Sam? Sam, you in there?" Oggie cackled gleefully.

"Lay off, Oggie."

"Well, pardon me for breathin'," Oggie groused, looking much less hurt than he was trying to sound. In fact, if anything, Oggie Jones was looking downright delighted.

"Hey, Oggie. 'Nother round down here," someone called from the end of the bar.

"Keep your pants up. I'm comin'." Oggie moved down the bar.

Sam, relieved to have the interrogation at least temporarily suspended, turned and sat, facing out, sipping his beer and staring at the room.

At the pool table nearby, Chloe Swan, who ran Swan's Motel, was playing eight-ball with some guy Sam had never seen before—and beating the pants off him, too. But the guy didn't seem to mind. He looked gone on her, grinning in frank appreciation of her ability every time she made a shot. And she was nice to him. She joked and she was friendly. Probably the poor guy didn't have the faintest idea that he didn't have a chance. No one really had a chance with Chloe. She was Patrick Jones's to the core, even though the whole town had started to doubt that Patrick would ever get smart and claim her.

Sam shook his head. Who could figure the things that went on between women and men? Not him, that was for sure. Take Delilah—which he'd love to do, but which wasn't damn likely, the way things were stacking up. Sam had been absolutely positive, after what he'd seen in her eyes last Saturday, that with a combination of persistence and patience on his part, she'd drop right into his arms.

But it was not happening. She left his carvings, the gifts of hand and heart, outside in the cold and damp. And she hung up every time he called. Persistence and patience, with Delilah Jones, at least, were getting Sam exactly nowhere. He'd given up on them yesterday.

He was still foolish enough to hope that just maybe she was sitting home tonight, longing for his call. But if she was, he knew it was for only one reason—so she could hang up on him again.

He was just going to have to get real about this, Sam admitted. He was going to have to forget all about the hard-hearted little witch and start looking around again.

He rubbed at his jaw. Maybe he'd grow his beard back. Hell, yes. Then he'd go out looking for a woman who could appreciate him just the way he was.

At the pool table, Chloe sank the eight ball. The stranger applauded. Chloe laughed and began racking the balls for another game.

Oggie approached once more. Sam, who in recent years always limited himself to two a night, signaled for a third beer, and soon after that, another. Five minutes later, he was signaling again.

"That's your fifth," Oggie pointed out.

"Don't worry. I'll make this one last awhile."

Oggie, looking doubtful, filled the mug once more. When he set it down, Sam picked it up and carried it to the end of the room and through the split in the green curtain to the poker table beyond.

In the smoky recess on the other side of the curtain, eight men were playing: the two strangers Oggie had mentioned and six locals, including Brendan Jones. Brendan, a cigarette hanging from one side of his mouth and an empty drink at his elbow, looked like a man who'd lost his best friend.

Brendan's mental state didn't seem to have hurt his card playing, though. The stack of bills in front of him was triple the size of any other stack on the table.

In fact, the game itself appeared to have gotten pretty serious. Some real money was changing hands.

One of the strangers, a rangy character with a black mustache, made a tight comment about Brendan's playing style just as Sam slid through the curtain.

Brendan's smile was humorless. "I may not have your style. But I do have a lot of your money, my friend."

"That'll change," the stranger said.

Brendan gave a mirthless laugh. "Ante up."

Owen Beardsly, across the table from where Sam had entered, looked up. "Sam. You want in? This table's too rich for my blood."

Sam considered. "What's the game?"

"Texas Hold'em."

Sam rubbed his chin. Texas Hold'em was a chancy game to get involved in. Two cards were dealt to each player, with five cards in the center, face down. The betting commenced as the dealer flipped the center cards, two first, then one at a time. Each player built a five-card hand from the two he held and the five cards in the center. The problem was that a player saw too much. It was easy to assume the hand the other guy was building. And too often, it was easy to assume wrong.

But Sam had purposely brought along a wad of cash. He'd been thinking a good game might be just what he needed on a lonely night like this, that maybe a few hands of cards would settle down the reckless feeling that was eating at his nerves.

"Bump limit?" Sam asked.

"Nope."

"Betting limit?"

"Fifty."

"Hell, why not?" Sam said. He took the chair Owen Beardsly vacated and laid his money down.

The game resumed.

Sam more or less held his own, winning a hand now and then only to lose several times soon after that. He was down a few hundred by eleven o'clock. But he didn't really care. Keeping his mind on the cards was working. The edgy feeling that could get him in trouble stayed in control.

The real game was between the black-mustached stranger, who called himself Parnell, and Brendan. Tension grew higher between them as the hours ticked by. Brendan, apparently suffering over whatever had happened with his wife, took his frustration out on the thin stranger.

Whenever Brendan won a hand—which was often—he'd haul in the pot with a big, smug grin on his face—a grin directed at Parnell. Parnell would remark that, where he came from, only fools gloated while they were still sitting at the table.

And Brendan would chuckle. "I'd rather be a fool than a loser, that's for sure."

There would be a charged moment of silence, where every man wondered if Parnell would go flying across the table to grab Brendan by the throat. But then the next dealer would mutter "Ante up," and there would be another round of play.

As the hours went by, though, Brendan's playing became reckless. He started losing. The pile of bills in front of him shrank. He then became morose, sipping steadily at his double whiskeys, his handsome face growing more sullen with each hand. Parnell, cold-eyed and quiet, seemed to radiate a wintry satisfaction as his own stack of winnings grew.

Sam, who'd finally started to win himself, considered advising Brendan to go home. But he knew if he did that he would have found the trouble he'd been trying to stay out of. You didn't give a Jones advice when he'd had a fight with his wife and was losing at poker—unless you wanted your face rearranged.

Maybe, Sam thought, Brendan's luck would turn again. But it didn't. Brendan Jones continued to lose.

At a little past one, Parnell suggested in a toneless voice that they play a hand with no betting limit. Brendan, grown even more reckless with frustration, agreed. And

Rocky Collins, who'd always had more nerve than sense, said that was just fine with him. Three men opted to sit out the hand, including the other out-of-towner, Bernie Flack.

Tim Brown, to Sam's left, dealt. When all the cards were out, Tim flipped over the first two center cards: deuce of diamonds, Ace of diamonds.

Parnell, first to bet, shoved two hundred dollars into the center of the table. Brendan, whose pile was dangerously low, saw it and raised a hundred. Rocky Collins, Sam and Parnell all stayed in. Tim Brown dropped, and then turned over the next card: five of hearts.

Parnell shoved another two hundred into the center of the table. Brendan pushed out two hundred to match it, and raised a hundred once more.

Rocky sighed and shook his head. "I'm out." Glances were exchanged around the table. Who could tell what in the hell Rocky Collins had in his head for brains? He'd stay in for no reason anyone could see—and drop out the same way.

Now, as the game continued, there were only three players left: Sam, Parnell and Brendan. Sam and Parnell shoved out their money to stay in.

The next card was a Queen of diamonds. Parnell, who must have got what he was hoping for with that, shoved out five hundred dollars. Brendan was forced to do a little counting, but he had it and covered the bet. Sam, whose hand was also looking good, stayed in, but played it safe and didn't raise. He stole a glance at Brendan, who now had nothing but bare table in front of him. What the hell was Oggie's youngest son planning to use for money on the final round?

Tim flipped the last card: the black lady, Queen of spades.

Parnell calmly pushed another five hundred dollars into the center.

Brendan looked at the pile of money for a long while. Then he turned to face Parnell and stated the obvious in a flat voice. "I don't have it on me."

Parnell replied, "Then you're out."

Brendan stared at the other man, his black eyes burning. And then he took the ring of keys that always hung at his waist and threw them on the table.

Rocky Collins shook his head and muttered something disbelieving under his breath.

Brendan said, "That's to my truck. She's a beauty, and she's worth eighty grand. I've got over fifteen thousand in her. Will you take that as a guarantee—say, for a thousand?"

Parnell turned to Sam. "What do you think?"

Sam thought Brendan Jones was acting like an idiot. But he didn't say that. He considered his own hand and came to a decision. Better let him do it, he thought. Give him a good scare, then make sure everything worked out okay.

"I've seen the truck," Sam said. "I'll allow it as collateral on a thousand."

Parnell shrugged. "All right, then. If it's okay with you, it's okay with me."

Brendan spoke right up. "Agreed then. That's your five hundred—and a five hundred raise."

Sam looked at his two cards, and thought about making a little mischief himself. But no. He was getting soft and sentimental in his old age. If he raised, who knew what the hell Brendan would throw in next. He'd give Brendan a break, because right now Brendan was very close to the edge of a cliff as far as Sam could see. Sam shrugged, and he pushed a thousand into the center of the table.

Parnell kicked in his own five hundred to call. Then he laid his cards on the table: a three and jack of diamonds. With the cards in the center, his best hand was an Ace-high flush.

Brendan smiled. He laid his cards down: a pair of deuces. with the other deuce and the two queens on the table, he beat Parnell. "Full house," he said.

Sam almost felt guilty laying down his hand, but he did it. He laid down his two queens. "Four of a kind," he said gently and glanced at the huge stack of bills with the keys to the Sweet Amy right there on top. "I guess that's all mine."

After that, it was all over but the goodbyes.

Parnell, none too happy, but not as incensed as he might have been had Brendan cleaned him out, gathered up his remaining winnings and left. One by one, the others stood and went out through the green curtain, too. In minutes, only Brendan and Sam remained, looking at each other over the pile of booty in the center.

Now the other men were gone, Brendan had the grace to look sheepish. "Amy will have my hide on a stretcher," he muttered grimly.

Sam grunted. "Then why'd you do it?"

Brendan shrugged. "That crazy Jones blood, I guess. Amy accused me tonight of not loving her. And after that, nothin' meant anything anyway. And I did think I could take that sucker. Hell, I *did* take him. It was you I couldn't beat." Brendan fell silent for a moment, staring at the keys in the center of the table. Then he went on, "Truth to tell, I haven't got the faintest idea where I'm going to come up with your thousand, Sam. I just made the monthly payment, so I'm a little short. I was playing tonight on just about all I got left. Will you give me a day or two to work it out?''

Sam looked at the other man, thinking. He'd planned to simply give the fool back the keys and be satisfied with the tall stack of bills. But he'd just had an idea.

In his mind, he saw Delilah, the way she'd looked that night in her kitchen, just before she dropped that damn frying pan and shoved him away. Her mouth had been turned up to his, soft as a full-blown rose, her body had been pliant to his touch. She'd been ready, he was sure, to fall into his arms. She did want him, he knew it. All he needed was some time alone with her, some time to make that flicker of desire he'd seen in her eyes burst into a hungry flame.

Brendan was standing up, casting a rueful glance at the keys he'd just lost. ''I guess no answer is answer enough. You'll be wanting to keep the keys, and I don't blame you. Just think about giving an old friend a few days before you do anything with her, okay?'' Brendan waited. Sam still didn't speak. Then Brendan shrugged. ''Well, I suppose I better head on home. I got the feelin' I'm gonna be doing some serious crawlin' before the night is through. I've not only got to soothe Amy down for the harsh words we shared, but now I've got to tell her I've lost our livelihood as well.'' He laughed mirthlessly. ''Hell, maybe this solves all our problems, now I think about it. Amy was on me because I've got a run out of Marysville at six Sunday night. She was upset because I'm never home. But now, unless I find me a thousand bucks under a rock somewhere, it looks like I'll be home a lot.''

''Maybe not,'' Sam said.

"What do you mean?"

"Sit back down a minute, Brendan. Maybe we can both get what we want out of this deal."

Chapter Six

Delilah, sound asleep, stirred and tried to block out the knocking that kept intruding on her dreams. But then it came again, urgent and demanding. She turned over and wrapped her pillow over her head.

"Go away," she mumbled at the mattress.

But talking to the bed did no good. The knocking continued—along with some idiot calling her name.

Finally, she surrendered to wakefulness. She sat up and listened.

More pounding. On the front door. "Delilah. Hey, sis!"

Delilah grabbed the little bedside clock and glared at it. 2:30. One of her insane brothers was pounding on her door at 2:30 a.m.

"All right, all right," she muttered. Then she called out, "Put a lid on it! I'm coming!"

She grabbed her robe and shoved her arms into it, belting it as she strode through the short hall and the living room to reach the front door. She flung it back.

Brendan stood there, looking horrible. Delilah gaped at him for a moment, worry replacing vexation. Had something terrible happened? Had their father breathed his last? Were Amy and the baby okay?

But then she noticed that he was smiling that smarmy smile that all three of her brothers used to bestow on her whenever they wanted something out of her. A warning buzzer went off in Delilah's head. She closed the door most of the way, and peered around it suspiciously.

"Brendan." She made his name an accusation.

"Sis." The smarmy smile widened.

"What do you want?"

"Well..."

"Is there an emergency?"

"Well..."

"Is there?"

"Well, sort of."

"*Sort of* does not cut it at 2:30 in the morning, Brendan Jones."

"Look, I'm sorry to bother you—"

"Don't be sorry. Just don't." She tried to close the door on him. He stuck his foot in it.

Grudgingly, she pulled it open once more. "All right. What do you want?"

"I have to talk to you."

"Now? Can't it wait till morning?"

"No, it can't wait. Look, I really am sorry, but I don't have much of a choice. I can't go home to Amy until—"

Delilah looked beyond his shoulder at the darkness, which smelled of coming rain, at the black sky where the clouds were gathering, and at her neighbors' houses across the road. She was a respectable citizen, not the type to conduct urgent conversations through a crack in her front door. She reached out, grabbed Brendan by the collar, and yanked him into her living room.

"Hey, back off, " he complained, swatting her hand away.

They stood facing each other by the door. She could smell him now—he reeked of cigarettes and whiskey.

"You can't go home to Amy until what?" Delilah demanded.

Brendan rubbed his eyes. "Can you spare a cup of coffee? It's been a hell of a night."

"All right. Come on." She led him into the kitchen, told him to sit at the table, and then quickly set about spooning grounds into the filter basket and setting the maker up to brew. When the coffee had dripped, she plunked a full mug in front of him and allowed him a few fortifying sips.

Then she said, "Talk."

He looked at the table, at his own fingers wrapped around the handle of the mug. "Amy and I had a big fight tonight." Brendan winced, at the painful memory no doubt. Then he tossed back more coffee, until he'd emptied the mug. After that, he got up and poured himself a refill.

"Brendan," Delilah said, her patience hanging by a thread.

"I'm getting to it. I am." Brendan returned to the chair and sat down again. "Okay, now. Where was I?"

"You and Amy had a fight ..."

"Right. And I slammed out of the house and went over to Dad's bar."

"How surprising."

He gave her a look that only brothers give sisters. "Delilah, if you're going to make sarcastic comments, I could start getting crude. You remember how I used to swear. I still know how."

"Sorry. Go on."

He looked at her for a moment more, as if to press home his threat. Then he acquiesced to continue. "I went over to The Hole in the Wall, and I got into a poker game—"

"Very bright," she remarked. He glared. She mouthed another "Sorry."

He went on, "And for quite awhile I was rakin' it in. And then . . ."

"You started to lose."

He gave her a quelling look. "Who's telling this?"

She sighed. "Keep talking."

"I'd had a few hundred on me, and I'd built it up to near four thousand at one point."

"That's a high stakes game," Delilah couldn't help but point out in obvious disapproval. "Father is always swearing that the games that go on at The Hole in the Wall are just friendly little—"

"Delilah. If you want to start preaching the evils of gambling, will you do it in church tomorrow, and let me get on with this?"

"Well, I'm only saying that this just goes to prove what Nellie and Linda Lou and I have always claimed. Gambling is a dangerous pastime—not to mention the fact that it's illegal in California."

"*Organized* gambling is illegal in California, Delilah. Not a friendly game of cards with the guys."

"*Friendly?* You call losing thousands of dollars on a Saturday night *friendly?*" Brendan just looked at her. "All right. I'm sorry. You're right. I've interrupted."

"Thank you." Brendan dragged in a big breath. "Anyway, I started to lose, and I kept on losing. And before you know it, I had this hand I *knew* I could win with—and not a red cent for the final bet. So I threw in the keys to the Sweet Amy."

"Oh my heavens," Delilah muttered, knowing exactly what her brother would say next.

"And I lost."

In the grim silence that followed, Delilah stared at her brother, unable to comprehend how he could have done such a harebrained thing.

Brendan looked up. "Okay. It was about the stupidest thing I've ever done in my life."

"No comment." Delilah stuck her hands in the pockets of her robe. "Now what's this got to do with me?"

Brendan swallowed. "Well, see. There *is* some good news here."

"Oh, really. What's that?"

"*You* can make everything all right."

"Me?"

He nodded, looking earnest.

"How?" The faint warning buzzer inside Delilah's mind that had started when she saw his smile at the front door was reaching full volume now.

"If you do me one little teeny favor," Brendan said, "I get the truck back and I can go home to Amy down only five hundred or so—not good, but not the end of the world, if you know what I mean."

"What is the favor?"

Brendan swallowed again. "Well, see. It's who won the truck that makes this all possible...."

"Who won the truck..." Delilah repeated the words blankly. Then she asked, with some force, "Well, who was it?"

Brendan raked back his black hair with both hands. "Well..."

"Who?" she asked again, and then suddenly she knew. She uttered the rotten scoundrel's name. "Fletcher." Delilah closed her eyes and groaned. Then she forced herself to look again at her brother. "Sam Fletcher."

"Now, sis—"

Very quietly, she asked. "What does he want?"

"It's really hardly anything."

"What?"

"I mean, compared with the Sweet Amy..."

"*What?*"

"Just..."

"Yes?"

"... a date with you."

For a moment, Delilah stared at him, as his words sunk in. And then she hit the roof.

"*You wagered your own sister in a poker game!?*"

Wincing, Brendan put out his hands in a fruitless plea for reason. "Settle down, sis. How're we supposed to work this out when you get like this? I already explained. I didn't bet *you*. I bet my rig—or at least, I put down my rig as guarantee on a thousand. But I haven't got the thousand, so Sam would be completely within his right to take the Sweet Amy. But he said he'd be willing to take you instead."

Delilah felt like the top of her head was going to pop off when he said that. She managed to keep from shouting, barely, as she asked, "Do you realize what you're telling me? That my person will do as a substitute for a truck and trailer?"

"Sis, you got that look you used to get back in the old days when me and the other boys would pull a harmless little joke on you. It worries me, it truly does. I thought we were beyond all that now.''

Delilah felt like she might explode. "You are not listening to me, Brendan Jones. I asked if you comprehend what you've done? You've . . . you've offered me up like a sacrifice to the man I most despise in all the world so that you can keep your truck.''

Now Brendan was the one to look offended. "That isn't so. And you know it. Sam never asked for you. Just a date with you. You know...dinner, drinks and a show? Lord, sis. This isn't your *virtue* we're talking about. It's a few hours of your time . . . to save me and Amy and the baby from ruin.'' He looked at her with a kind of defensive self-righteousness that set her teeth on edge. "And besides that, you two seemed downright friendly in town last week. You were smiling at him and saying 'why, thank you, Sam,' when he helped you down from the sleeper. It seems to me it couldn't be *that* horrible for you to spend an evening with the guy. . . .''

Delilah longed to box her brother's ears. "Oh, what do you know, Brendan Jones? What do you know about anything?''

Brendan had sense enough not to answer that one. He was quiet for a moment, having said all he imagined he could get away with right then. Then he resumed, looking doleful, "Okay, sis. This is a free country. I can't make you do it.'' Now his voice dripped resigned nobility. "And I suppose it *is* way out of line. To ask you to do such a disgusting thing just so Amy and the baby will have food on the table and a roof over their heads.''

"You are pushing it, Brendan.''

"I'm only stating the facts.''

"Fine.'' She recrossed her arms. Her brother went on looking at her as if she held the lives of his wife and unborn child in her hands. Finally, she couldn't stand it anymore.

"Stay here." She headed for her bedroom where she could change into jeans and a sweater. "I'll deal with you as soon as I get through with *him!*"

In less than ten minutes, Delilah pulled up in front of the new house Sam Fletcher had recently built.

The house stood, framed by cedars and birches, on four acres near the end of Bullfinch Lane. Though there were few homes nearby as of yet, there would be soon enough. Bullfinch Lane was a neatly paved road now, and little resembled the dirt trail down which Sam, barefoot in a wetsuit, had carried the kicking and screaming teenaged Delilah twenty years before.

As she sat in her car after turning the engine off, bolstering her courage to do what must be done, Delilah noted that the porch light was on. The rest of the house appeared unlit. But *his* room could be at the back, after all. And he could be asleep. Though, the way she'd always heard it, the devil never slept.

Maybe he wasn't there. Maybe she should come back in the morning.

Delilah banished the cowardly thought the moment it took form. If she had to wait all night, she wasn't going away until she'd told the rotten rascal just what she thought of him. She'd yell at him so long and so loud that he'd give her the keys to the Sweet Amy just to get her to stop.

With that idea firmly in mind, Delilah bolted from her car and gave the door a slam. Then she hesitated for a moment, as she breathed in the moisture on the cold air. The crescent moon had already gone down. The sky was a mass of turbulent shadows as the clouds that obscured the stars churned, black and heavy with rain. A spring storm was on the way.

That's the truth, Delilah thought grimly, a doozy of a storm. And it's hitting Sam Fletcher's house right about now....

She marched up the front steps. Once at the entrance, she began alternately pounding on the front door and leaning on the bell, discovering great satisfaction in making such a ruckus—especially considering that he lived far enough out that no one else in town was likely to hear her at this hour of the night. Or rather morning...

"Sam Fletcher!" she shouted. Ah, what gratification to holler out his name with all the loathing she was feeling for the rogue right then.

Normally, she liked to think of herself as a very calm person, a self-controlled person, a no-nonsense person, level-headed and reasonable above all. The passion and tumult of her painful childhood and adolescence had passed, she always told herself, and she had grown into a mature, rational woman, who never went in for rash displays.

But tonight was an exception. Sam Fletcher had finally pushed her one step beyond rationality. She was a one-woman storm, to match the one in the sky.

She bellowed, "I know you're in there! You come out this instant! I want to talk to you!"

She pounded on the doorbell in several sharp bursts, and then hit the door some more with a tightly clenched fist.

"Sam Fletcher, I warn you! I'm not leaving this spot until you come out here and—"

The door was pulled back, suddenly, cutting her off in mid-tirade and nearly causing her to go sprawling into the small foyer beyond. Delilah gasped, and pulled herself up.

And then she fell back a little, her mouth dropping open in surprise.

It was her nemesis, all right, standing there with that knowing grin spread over his too-handsome face. He was soaking wet. And wearing only a towel.

"Why, Lilah," he murmured cordially. "How nice of you to drop by. I was just cleaning up and getting ready for bed."

She blinked, and licked her lips and struggled desperately to match his composure, though her heart pounded like jungle drums in her ears and her face felt aflame from within. He had...why, he had silky reddish hair on his chest, and his little nipples were hard, from the chilly night air. In fact, his golden skin, beneath which the hard muscles rippled and bulged, had goose bumps all over it. He stood with one powerful arm fisted on a hip. The reddish hair on that arm was matted with moisture, as was the hair on his chest. The hair on his head looked darker, all wet like it was. It was loose, too, falling on his shoulders in snaky water-weighted curls. He looked—primitive and magnificent, like a viking or some feral barbarian from a lost, untamed age.

Her insides, as they had on the street the other day, bloomed with heat once again. And she saw herself stepping forward, her lips parting, pressing herself up against him, running her hungry hands over his huge shoulders as she licked him dry with her tongue.

He chuckled. "I'm glad to see you too, sweetheart," he said softly, as if in response to a greeting she had never—she was sure—uttered. "Why don't you come in?"

She stepped forward in a kind of daze, and was beyond the threshold before she really let herself decide if such a move was wise. He gently pushed the door shut behind her. And there she was, alone with him in his house. . . .

He was standing behind her after shutting the door. She turned, too quickly, like a small frightened animal cornered by a large beast. She retreated a step, though that brought her backside in contact with the wall.

She realized she was staring. And from the look in his eyes, she knew there must be way too much of the sensual longing she didn't want to feel written clearly on her flaming face.

She forced herself to croak, "I want to talk to you."

"Okay. Talk."

She sucked in a breath. In the closed space, so near him, she was having great difficulty deciding what to say next. He smelled of soap and water and man, a delicious, arousing scent, one that messed up her thought processes, short-circuited her synapses.

She had to get control of herself, she knew it. Otherwise this encounter was going to end up a rout. Silently, she castigated herself for a fool. She'd indulged in a stormy scene by pounding on his door and yelling as she had. And stormy scenes were something she never allowed herself since she'd matured. And now she was paying the price. She'd been caught off guard, with her adrenaline flowing, when he'd pulled back the door—off guard and vulnerable in the worst and most dangerous way.

She decided a little retrenchment was in order. She drew herself up.

"Go put something on first," she instructed in the same tone she used when one of her students dared to misbehave. She poked her head around the corner and saw a living room. "I'll wait in here." She flew out of the foyer and into the larger space.

He chuckled behind her. "Yes, ma'am," he said softly, and then left her alone.

She ignored him as he padded up a switchback staircase. Then, while she waited for him to return decently covered, she pretended to study the angled ceilings and the full bookcases and the gray leather furniture accented with bright-colored pillows and throws.

But even looking around worked against her. As she had in his store three weeks ago, she couldn't help but notice how different this was than what she would have imagined—if she'd ever felt like imagining where Sam Fletcher made his home. The room was attractive and inviting. The books, both hardbound and paperback, looked as if he might even have read a lot of them, and the prints and paintings on the walls were ones she herself might have chosen.

Oh, it was all just too...disorienting. She'd rushed over here without stopping to consider, caught him in the altogether, and now she was wandering around waiting for him to cover himself, thinking that she liked his house better than her own.

"Do you like that table?"

Her head shot up, and she spotted him, barefoot but otherwise decent, dressed in faded jeans and that blue sweater he'd been wearing the other day. His long hair, still wet, lay in coils on his shoulders. A key ring—the keys to the Sweet Amy, Delilah had no doubt—dangled from one hand. He came down the stairs toward her.

Delilah, positive the keys constituted an outright taunt, decided to ignore them for the moment. She'd already put herself in enough trouble by reacting without stopping to think.

Keeping her expression composed, she looked down again at the huge table to which he'd referred. It was of some pale wood, perhaps white pine. It was very beautiful in its simplicity.

She said, "Yes, I like it."

He smiled, and then went on, as if she'd come here at 3:00 a.m. for the express purpose of learning more about him and his woodworking skills, "I saw it in my mind, just what I wanted. And since I couldn't find it anywhere, I made it. I don't go in much for furniture making. I mostly sculpt in wood. But you already know that."

She thought of the figures, so perfect and fine, abandoned by her on her various windowsills, and she felt a sharp stab of something like shame, to have left such beauty outside in the elements to fend for itself.

Oh, she thought desperately, it had been a mistake to come here. She should have let Brendan go on home, and confronted this beguiling, continually surprising knave someplace tomorrow, in the bright, safe light of day.

He dropped to one of the gray leather couches, and casually tossed the ring of keys on a table beside him. The sound of them dropping made her stiffen. He saw that, and the ghost of a grin lifted a corner of his mouth.

"Sit down," he suggested.

She swallowed and gathered herself. "No. Thank you. I'll stand."

"Suit yourself."

They looked at each other. And, in this graceful room where the paintings intrigued her and the man on the couch watched her with an interested air, this whole melodramatic mess seemed suddenly silly and pointless. A man who'd read Shakespeare and seemed to enjoy John Le Carre for light entertainment, who fashioned incredible sculptures out of wood in his spare time, surely couldn't be serious about forcing her to go out with him by stealing her baby brother's Long Nose Peterbilt.

And that, she decided with some relief, was how she would approach this. As a silly, pointless misunderstanding that two mature adults could easily clear up.

She said, "I really appreciate this."

He frowned, momentarily, and then his brow smoothed out. "You do?" he asked casually.

She smiled, a smile she hoped appeared midway between embarrassed and grateful. "Yes. And I'm sorry things got so out of hand. But I see now that you've made the wisest decision."

"I have?"

"Yes. And, as I said, I'm grateful."

"You are?" He watched her with great interest.

Boldly, she approached. She reached for the keys...

Before she could grab them, his hand shot out and closed on hers.

The familiar hot shivers quivered up her arm. She forced herself to ignore them, to keep on smiling, though her instinct was to jerk away as if she'd been burned.

She said, faking bewilderment, "But you *have* changed your mind, haven't you? Otherwise, why would you bring me the keys?"

Slowly, he released her. "No, I haven't changed my mind. Brendan told you the terms. They stand. And you know damn well why I brought the keys to you. So you can give them to your brother once you've agreed to hold up your end of the deal." He was grinning again. "Nice try, Lilah. But you didn't really believe it would work, did you?"

Delilah glared at him, dropping her pose of civility since it had done so little good. She said, "I despise you, Sam Fletcher."

He answered, "Why doesn't that surprise me?"

"You're a low-down, mean, rotten scoundrel, and I was right about you all these years."

"Why, thank you, sweetheart."

"I am not your sweetheart."

"Allow a poor fool his fantasies."

"You have left me no choice."

"That was the idea."

"And I *hate* you for that."

"So you say now."

"And a night out with me isn't going to do you one bit of good."

"It's not?"

"No. It is not. But if that's the price for Brendan's rig…" Oh, it almost choked her to say it, but she did. "I'll pay it. You'll have your pointless date. Next Saturday, all right? You can pick me up at seven. And you will have me home by eleven, and that will be that."

"Oh, will it?"

"Most definitely. Now, give me those keys." She reached again, he caught her arm. This time, she didn't even try to pretend his touch didn't affect her. She yanked away and jumped back. "What now?" she fairly shouted. "I said I'd do what you want."

"You're a hardheaded woman, Delilah Jones."

"What is that supposed to mean?"

"I think you've made a real point here."

"What? What point?"

Casually, he picked up the key ring and spun it on a finger. The keys tinkled with nerve-shattering cheerfulness. "Next Saturday night. Seven to eleven. That's what? Four hours? How can even the most persistent of men get through to a woman like you in four hours? It's my guess that if it could have been done, it would have been done already."

"What in heaven's name are you babbling about?" she challenged tightly. She clenched her fists and ground her teeth—because what she longed to do was fly at him and claw his glittering eyes out.

"I mean," he said pleasantly, "if I only get one chance at you, I'd be wise to make it a damn good one."

She didn't like this, not one bit. Something unbearable was coming, and she didn't want to know what it was. She said, "A date. That's what you told Brendan. Those were your terms, dinner, drinks and a show—"

He spun the keys again. "I said a date. That's all. Brendan assumed what kind of date it would be."

"A date's a date. Saturday night, seven to eleven is a perfectly reasonable—"

"From your point of view, yes. But from my point of view, it's a bust."

"What do you mean, a bust?"

"I lose what I won fair and square—either a thousand cash or fifteen thousand equity in a great little piece of equipment. And what I get is you, for exactly four hours, glaring at me across a table and telling me you hate my guts."

Delilah clenched her fists so hard, her nails bit into her palms. She had to keep her temper, she just *had* to.

She pointed out, through lips pale with her effort to keep from screaming out loud, "It's not your truck, anyway, not really. It's Brendan's. And you took it from him by gambling—which you swore to me a week ago was something you never did any more. You came to my house and you told me you'd changed, and I...well, I started to believe that maybe you had. But you have not changed one bit, Sam Fletcher, and now I know that with certainty. And no matter what you do, I will never in my life spend a willing hour in your company. Do you understand?"

"Completely," he replied. "I understand completely."

"Good."

He rubbed his chin thoughtfully, as his gaze moved over her, caressing and bold. "And since I *do* understand, these are my terms—"

"We've already named the terms. And I agreed to them, I—"

He waved the keys. She fell silent. "These are the terms. I want a week."

"A *week?*" she croaked.

He went on as if she hadn't made a sound. "This week, to be exact. It's Easter Vacation for you, so you're free. Marty can handle things at my store. We're going away together, you and I. Go home and pack for a camping trip. There's a cabin where we're going, but expect low temperatures, it's still the tail end of winter there. We're leaving at dawn."

"You are insane...."

"You'll be my *date* for a week, Sunday to Sunday. You'll give me seven days, and Brendan can go home to Amy with the keys to his rig in his pocket where they belong."

Chapter Seven

Delilah stared at the rotten rat who sat on the gray couch, grinning and holding the keys to the Sweet Amy in his big hand. Oh, how she longed to call him a name so foul it would burn her own ears to utter it.

A week. He wanted a week, for those keys.

And she might as well face it. Her own temper had gotten her into this mess. She should have left well enough alone. If she'd only kept her mouth shut and sweetly agreed to his original terms, she'd be looking forward to a grim Saturday night—and no more.

Instead, she was doomed to spend a week at his side— or let Brendan stew in his own pot. Letting Brendan stew would have been quite easy. But unfortunately, a pregnant woman and an unborn child would be stewing right along with him. Delilah just didn't think she could stand by and let that happen, not when it was in her power to stop it.

Stars above. Now she knew all over again why she always kept herself out of her brothers' lives. Getting involved with them meant trouble. Pure and simple. And being grown up wouldn't change them, they would always be that way: The Jones Gang, wild, crazy and nothing but trouble for any woman foolish enough to get close to them, be she wife, mother, girlfriend, or sister....

Fletcher hefted the keys again, so they clinked together on the ring. "Well?"

She looked at him sideways. *Think fast,* she told herself. There just had to be a way to get out of this mess. Camping. He said they were going camping. Lots of people hated camping. Maybe he would believe she hated it, too.

"I can't go camping with you," she said. "I hate camping. Ugh. There's nothing worse, as far as I'm concerned."

"Oh, no?" He didn't look convinced.

She elaborated. "No, absolutely nothing. Who in the world would consciously choose to sit around a smelly open fire, swatting at biting insects, eating things out of cans? And don't forget about hygiene."

"What about it?"

"That's just it. When you camp, there isn't any. 'Facilities' consist of disappearing behind a boulder with a wad of paper towels. And there's never, ever a place to take a real bath." She shook her head emphatically. "No way. Give me indoor plumbing, and somewhere to plug in my hot rollers."

Sam chuckled. "Nice try, Lilah. But I'm not buying."

She tried to look guileless. "What do you mean?"

"I mean, even if you hate camping, you seem to do it three or four times every summer."

"I never—"

"Yes, you do. You go camping with your church group. And you're usually the one in charge, as far as I can remember. At least, it's always your name and phone number that are plastered all over the flyer." He granted her a superior smirk. "You know what flyer I mean, don't you? The one Owen Beardsly always brings in and asks if he can put up in the front window of my store?"

Delilah resisted the urge to slap his smug face. The blasted flyer, she thought heatedly. How was she supposed to remember that—let alone imagine that a heathen like him would ever bother to read anything with the church logo on it?

He went on looking at her, still smug, still waiting.

She considered telling him she suddenly felt ill—too ill to go *anywhere* for at least a week. But then she knew what he'd do: send her home to recover *without* Brendan's keys.

He asked, "Well?" again.

The sinking feeling in her stomach told her that this dreaded trip was inevitable. But before she gave in and agreed to his terms, she intended to make one thing crystal clear.

She stared him straight in the eye. "All I have to do is go, right? I don't have to like it. And I don't have to...be intimate with you."

He went on looking smug, the misbegotten cad. "Why, Lilah? What are you implying?"

"I'm not *implying* anything, I'm saying it straight out."

"What?"

Oh heavens, she loathed him. She forced herself to speak even more plainly. "I'm not going to...go to bed with you."

He shrugged. "That's fine with me. You can threaten me with a frying pan any time I dare to come within two feet of you."

He was still smiling. She knew just what he thought. That all he needed was time, and she'd be sure to change her mind about intimacy with him. And the hideous truth was, she wasn't absolutely positive that he was wrong.

Well, there was no point in dwelling on how long she'd be able to keep her forbidden desires at bay. She would manage, one way or another. Maybe, if she was lucky, she could stall for a little while before the grueling ordeal began....

She said flatly. "All right. You win."

He nodded. "Be ready to leave in three hours."

Trying for breezy indifference, she suggested, "I'd like to leave Monday morning instead of today, if that's all right. I do need some rest, and I'll need time to find someone to, um, water my plants."

"Your plants will survive. I'll pick you up in three hours."

"But I—"

He shook his head. "Three hours. Don't argue."

She almost told him again exactly what she thought of him, but then resigned herself to the fact that he already knew.

"The keys," she said.

He tossed them to her. She caught them neatly, and then got out of there.

At her house, she found Brendan in the kitchen making another pot of coffee.

He turned from the counter where the coffee was dripping when he heard her come in. "Well?"

He looked so downtrodden, his black hair a tangled thatch, his eyes red and tired, that she almost felt sorry for him, though she tried to remind herself that her sympathy was the last thing he deserved.

"How'd it go?" he asked.

She remembered how she'd planned to tell Brendan exactly what she thought of him once she was through with Sam Fletcher. But now it was settled, yammering at her brother seemed pointless; a waste of good energy. She said, "It's all taken care of," and held out the keys.

Brendan took them. Then he just stood there for a moment, looking at her, his brows drawn together, as if he were trying to decide what exactly to say. At last, he shrugged. "Thanks, sis. I owe you one."

Delilah nodded. "It's okay."

It wasn't, of course. But she supposed she had to admit that things could have been worse. Brendan could have lost the truck to someone who wasn't willing to give up his winnings for the privilege of hauling Delilah off to the wilds for a week.

And she had to remember that even a week wouldn't last forever. In seven days, the debt would be paid. She could go back to her life. Everything would be as it had always been once again.

Or would it? After a week alone with Sam Fletcher, would anything ever be the same?

Delilah sank into a chair. She remembered Sam Fletcher's broad chest, the reddish hair there, the beads of water that had clung to his skin, the clean, moist scent of him, the blue mirrors of his eyes . . .

"Sis? You okay?"

Delilah blinked. "What? Yes, fine. Just tired, that's all."

Brendan looked chagrined. "Well, I...suppose I oughtta head on home now, get it all worked out with Amy and everything...if you're sure you're okay."

Delilah stood up. "Yes. I'm fine. You go on." She went to the coffee pot and poured herself a cup. "And give Amy my best."

"You bet," Brendan promised. His voice came from behind her, near the door to the living room. " 'Night, then."

Delilah glanced over her shoulder at him, waved, and then turned back to the counter to sip from the coffee.

"Sis?"

Delilah looked around again. Brendan was still standing there. "What?"

"You're a hell of a sister, you know?"

"Yes." She sighed. "I'm wonderful."

"In a pinch, you always come through."

She turned around to face him. "Brendan. I said it's okay. You can spare the testimonial."

"But I..." Brendan raked his hair back.

"What?"

"I...well, I'm sorry, damn it. For being a horse's ass. I don't deserve a sister like you, any more than I deserve a wife like Amy...."

Delilah didn't know what to say. He was right, of course, he didn't deserve her or Amy, but that had never seemed to bother him before. Now, however, he seemed honestly moved by what she had sacrificed for him. His frank apology struck a chord in her. She didn't know how to react.

"Brendan, I...It's all right. Really..." Delilah's voice trailed off as she stared doubtfully at her brother, who looked sweet suddenly, so flustered and unsure.

Then, out of nowhere, he muttered something ear-burning and strode the few steps to where she stood. He took the coffee from her, set it on the counter, yanked her up against him and hugged her so hard it knocked the breath out of her.

"Brendan!" Startled, she shoved at his shoulders.

He held on. "Thanks. Just thanks," he whispered fiercely in her ear. With that, he released her just the way he'd grabbed her, in an instant. She fell back against the counter, nearly knocking over her full coffee cup. She grabbed it and steadied it.

And when she looked up he was gone.

Delilah stared after him for a moment before she returned to the table and sat down again. He *was* different than the mean little boy he'd been, even if trouble still followed him around. She realized she was glad now that she hadn't had the energy to tell him he was exactly the horse's behind he'd called himself, let alone inform him that his *dinner, drinks and a show* had become a week-long ordeal in the woods.

And where? In what woods? Delilah realized with increasing exhaustion that she hadn't the faintest idea. But she'd be finding out soon enough, since she was leaving right away.

She sat down, but only long enough to drink the coffee. And then she plodded to her room to start packing.

In a way, it was soothing to her frazzled nerves to prepare for the trip. She concentrated on packing and tried not to think that at dawn she would be off for a week in the wilds with her worst enemy for a companion. As Sam Fletcher had already deduced, she had all the necessary gear.

She set out long underwear, sturdy pants, bulky sweaters and flannel shirts, a down vest and jacket, hiking boots, heavy socks and a good sleeping bag. She also took along her little vanity pack which contained the bare necessities for grooming and hygiene.

It was while she was fumbling in the back of a bathroom drawer for that special small bottle of shampoo which just fit in the pack, that her groping fingers found the little foil pouches she'd stuck there two years ago.

Delilah pulled out one of the condoms and looked at it. She'd bought them after she'd taken that required course for teachers in sex education. She supposed they were still usable...

Delilah looked up from the small pouch to her own face in the mirror. What, really, was she thinking?

Nothing but the truth, she thought grimly. Because the attraction she felt for Sam Fletcher was powerful. It was just possible, given the long days together, and the longer nights...

No. She shook her head. It was not going to happen. She wasn't going to surrender to this...pull he exerted. And there was absolutely no need to be prepared.

She tossed the condom back where it had come from and firmly shut the drawer.

Then she went to the service porch off the kitchen, where she stored a pack full of basic, sturdy cooking equipment—things like tin plates, flatware, a cup, a saucepan and a frying pan.

She smiled for the first time in hours when she found the frying pan. He'd suggested she have it ready in case he got near her. She would—though unfortunately it was only aluminum and wouldn't be near as threatening as her nice cast iron one had been.

She also kept plenty of high-energy snacks and freeze-dried food on hand for camping trips. She filled another pack with these items, since she had no idea what kind of cooking setup they'd have or how much he would bring. Basically, she assumed he would be taking care of the food problem. But she didn't intend to starve if she was wrong.

After that, she straightened her house.

She considered, for about half a second, calling Nellie and asking her to look after the plants. But dealing with Nellie and her passion for other people's business was more than Delilah felt she could handle right then. It was going to be rough enough when she returned next Sunday. By then, she had no doubt, the whole town would be buzzing. She and Sam Fletcher were going to be grist for the gossip mill, she was certain.

Delilah almost felt like crying when she realized that. Her spotless reputation as the only Jones in North Magdalene who led a civilized life was not long for this world. Everyone would be saying that she was just as wild as the rest of them after all.

Well, Delilah told herself firmly, she'd lived through it when she was little, and she could live through it again. And besides, there was no point in borrowing anguish anyway. She had a whole week with the wild man to get through before she worried about the gauntlet of whispering and rumors that would come next.

Pushing concern about what hadn't happened yet to the back of her mind, Delilah set a tray of water under each of the plants to keep them going until her return.

After that she was ready—a full hour before Sam Fletcher was due to pick her up.

She tried lying down, thinking a little rest would probably do her good. But her eyes stayed wide open and her body wouldn't relax. So she got up and wandered around her little house, checking the back door and the window locks.

The sky lit up beyond Sweetbriar Summit as she lifted the curtain over the sink. The rabbit beyond the glass stood out for a moment in sharp relief. Its wide eyes seemed to look at her, startled, full of reproach and dumb entreaty. Then the sky went dark, thunder rolled, and Delilah was looking at her own tired reflection and the first rain drops blown against the glass.

For a frozen moment, she remained there, poised with the kitchen curtain raised, staring at her own shadowed face. Then the sky lit up again, the rabbit flashed and disappeared as the thunder crashed once more.

Delilah Jones, who despised foul language as much as she loathed gambling and mind-altering chemicals, swore roundly. Then she whirled from the window and stomped outside in the rain to gather up the wooden figures one by one.

She would have left them, she reassured herself, she really would, if only the rain hadn't come. But they were simply too fine to leave to be destroyed by the storm. In spite of who had made them, they were beautiful and deserved to be treasured.

But not by Delilah, of course. Oh, no. She would never keep them. She would insist that he take them back, that was all, once the wagered week was over. And if he wouldn't, why she'd return them to him the same way he'd brought them, by stealth. She'd wait for a time when he wasn't at home, and she'd drop them off, and that would be the end of it.

Back inside, she set them on the kitchen table. They appeared undamaged, as far as she could tell, and seemed to have been coated with a thin layer of shellac or varnish which had protected them quite well. But they were wet from the rain.

She found a clean cotton cloth and wiped each one carefully. Sweet heavens, they were marvelous to touch, the wood smooth as tumbled stone, only warmer, more alive. She palmed the plump stomach of the bear cub, and stroked the long legs of the doe. And then she thought of the little raccoon, stuck up there in the shadows of her tallest bookcase.

She found a stool and brought the raccoon down and set it on the table with the others and thought that it was as beautiful in its unfinished roughness as the others were in their smooth and varnished splendor.

She sat down at the table, still holding the little raccoon. She smiled at it.

And then, beneath the pinging of the rain in the gutters, she heard the sound of a vehicle pulling up out in front.

Good gracious, it was Sam! A frantic glance at her watch told her she'd been mooning over the wooden animals he'd carved for the best part of an hour.

Swiftly, she pushed the figures toward the far side of the table, near the windows. That way he couldn't possibly see them from the front door—which was as far as he was going to get this time. She'd learned enough after what had happened last time never to let him into her house again.

But then, as soon as she pushed the animals out of sight, she felt foolish. Why shouldn't he know she'd brought them in, after all? Leaving them outside had been childish anyway. And she wasn't going to keep them. She could make that perfectly clear.

She heard his boots on her step, followed by his knock at the door. She went to answer.

He smiled when she opened the door, and for a crazy moment, she almost felt like they were partners—long-time companions heading off on some grand adventure.

Behind him, in the east, the orange glow of the rising sun bled through a space in the heavy cover of clouds, creating the most miraculous of effects, a quarter of a rainbow arch, glimpsed for the briefest of seconds, and then gone as the clouds rolled and reformed once more.

His hair, pulled back tidily now, was dewed with water, and he smelled of the rain, as did the whole brightening, glorious, cold world.

He said, "Where's your gear? Let's get loaded up." And he stepped forward, gaining entrance as she'd sworn he wouldn't, because she was too busy thinking forbidden thoughts to remember her intention to keep him on the porch.

"I..." She stepped back, and then decided that ordering him out would be ridiculous. They should get her things together and they'd be out of there soon enough. "I have two packs out on the service porch—cooking utensils and some food."

"We probably won't need the utensils. The cabin has all that, or at least it's supposed to. But I haven't been there in a year, and someone could have helped themselves. You never know these days. How about if we go ahead and take your cooking gear, just in case?"

"Sounds fine."

"Okay. Now what kind of food?"

"Some canned meat and snacks and some freeze-dried entrées and fruits and vegetables, too."

"Great. We can take that for backup, just in case. What else?"

She gestured toward the hall that led to her room. "My clothes and sleeping bag."

"Fine. You get your clothes." He headed for the kitchen, beyond which lay the service porch.

She remembered about the carvings at the same moment that he saw them. He paused, his huge frame filling the kitchen doorway. Then he turned and looked at her, one sandy eyebrow raised.

She just stared back for a moment, since her voice had somehow become hung up in her throat. Then she managed to mutter defensively, "Well, it was raining. So I brought them in."

"I see." He went on looking at her, his expression different than ever before. It was a rather soft expression, actually. A rather vulnerable one. . . .

Delilah swallowed. "I'll get my things."

"Good idea."

Neither of them moved.

"Well . . ." she said.

"Right." He turned and headed for the service porch.

She shook herself and went to her bedroom where her sleeping bag and clothes pack waited.

When she slid into the passenger seat of the shiny Bronco 4×4, he handed her a notepad and a pencil. She shot him a questioning look.

"We'll drive down to Grass Valley first, to shop for food," he explained. "We can plan the menus on the way, so we'll know just what to buy."

"Where *are* we going, anyway?"

"Hidden Paradise Lake."

"Where's that?"

"You'll see." He started up the engine and turned on the wipers and lights.

She shot him a grim look as he pulled out of her driveway and onto her street. "Gee whiz." Her voice dripped sarcasm. "Here we go, on our way to who knows where. Maybe we'll get lost, and *never* find our way back."

"Don't worry." Sam reassured her, "I called Marty Santino and had him meet me at the store so I could show him how to handle the receipts while I'm gone. I also drew him a map. He knows where to send the search party if we don't return Sunday."

"Terrific," Delilah said, thinking exactly the opposite. Marty still lived at home, with Julio and Maria and their only daughter, Alma. In her mind's eye, she could see all the bleary-eyed Santinos, awakened by the departure of Marty in the middle of the night, waiting up for him to come home and tell them all about how Sam Fletcher was running off with Delilah Jones for a week. Delilah stared out at the pouring rain and beat the pencil on her knee for a moment. "Did you . . . tell Marty that I was going with you?"

"No."

She stilled the pencil from its nervous tattoo. "Oh." She felt a sweet wash of relief.

Sam swung the Bronco onto Pine Street, and then from there onto Main. In a few hundred yards, Main became the highway. In the rearview mirror, North Magdalene, gleaming in the rain, disappeared around a turn.

They drove for a few moments in weighted silence, and then Sam swore softly. "Damn it, Lilah. Someone in town *will* put two and two together, you know. If not Marty, then Brendan. Or your father. Or your pal, Nellie Anderson—"

"Look. Let's drop it, okay?"

He gave her a narrow look. "Did you tell *anyone* you were leaving?"

She shook her head. "I'm a single, self-sufficient adult. I can go where I please, and I'm accountable to no one— during my vacations from school, anyway."

Sam muttered a few more choice expletives.

"Will you please stop swearing?"

"Nellie and Linda Lou are a couple of nosy bit...er, cows, as far as I'm concerned," he said. "But they do care about you. Did it ever occur to you that they'll worry when you don't show up at church this morning?"

It hadn't, Delilah realized. She'd been too busy dreading the way their tongues would wag when they heard where she'd been. "That is my business."

"Fine." He shook his head in an I-give-up sort of way, and gave all his attention to the twisting road.

Delilah raised the pencil. Suddenly planning the menu seemed very attractive. "Does this cabin have a stove and refrigerator?"

"Yes."

"Okay, then, we can have real meals. We can get some steaks, and some hamburger, a few vegetables, salad stuff. Not to mention eggs, bread, milk—all the staples." She cast a glance at Sam. He was glaring at the road. "Sam?"

He waved a hand. "Fine. Whatever you say."

She lowered the note pad to her lap. "Sam. What do you want from me?"

He shot her a look that sent a bolt of heat right down to her core, but all he said was, "Honesty. And a little plain sense."

"What is that supposed to mean?"

"You are a schoolteacher. A highly respected and admired member of your community. If you disappear into thin air for a week, there will be hell to pay."

Delilah felt her temper rising. She grimly reminded herself that it had gotten her nothing but trouble the last time she let it loose. She said, through clenched teeth, "You are absolutely right. So why don't you turn this vehicle around and take me back home?"

He slowly shook his head, never taking his eyes from the twisting, rain-slicked road. "I paid well for this week. By God, I'll have what I paid for. And you agreed to it—including whatever inconvenience it might cause you."

"Inconvenience?" She breathed the word in restrained fury. "You force me to go away with you against my will, and you think all it will be is *inconvenient* for me?"

"Nobody forced anybody. It was your choice."

She gripped the pencil in a tight fist and stared at the streaming windshield. "I am not even going to dignify that remark with a reply."

"Glad to hear it."

There was a seething silence. Delilah reminded herself that they had a week to get through. She was going to have to watch herself, or she'd murder him before the day was out.

After a few minutes, when her adrenaline had settled down and she thought she could look at him without leaping across the stick shift and scratching his eyes out, she said, "Now. What else do we need?"

"Gasoline. There's a generator to run."

"Gasoline. Fine. What else?"

"*You* need to decide who you're going to call."

"Call? What do you mean, call?"

He spoke with steady patience. "When we get to Grass Valley, you are going to call *someone* and explain that you've gone camping for a week and will return sometime next Sunday."

"I loathe and despise you, Sam Fletcher."

"Tell me something new. Who will you call?"

She slapped her knee with the note pad. The sound was sharp and final in the enclosed space. "All right. I'll call someone. Will that satisfy you?"

He shrugged. "It's a start."

When they reached the big supermarket on Brunswick Road, Sam went inside while Delilah trudged to the phone kiosks by the newspaper racks.

She had no trouble finding a phone that was not in use. Delilah picked up the headset and sighed.

Whom to call?

She knew she should probably contact Nellie or Linda Lou, but she just couldn't bring herself to do it. Right now, on her way to who knew where with Sam Fletcher, she didn't think she could bear to hear another woman gasping in shock and then palpitating to get off the line so she could spread the news.

She decided to call Brendan, since he knew the basic background of the situation anyway. Delilah found his number through information and grimly punched the buttons.

A soft, feminine voice answered. "Hello?"

"Amy. It's Delilah."

"Oh. Hi." Amy panted a little, as very pregnant women often did. "Gee, Delilah. Brendan told me. About everything that happened. I can't thank you enough."

"It's okay. How's the baby?"

"Fine. The baby's fine."

"May I talk to Brendan?"

There was a silence. "Well, sure," Amy said at last. "Give me a minute. I'll have to wake him up."

"Wait. Amy?"

"Yes?"

"Does he have to be on the road again soon?"

"Yes, tonight."

"Well, then, maybe you'd better let him sleep. I can just as well tell you."

"What?" Worry crept into the soft voice. "Are you okay? Is everything—?"

"Fine. Nothing's wrong. Um, Brendan told you everything, right?"

"Yes, he did."

"That I'd agreed to go on a date with Sam Fletcher, to get back the Sweet Amy."

"Yes, and that was wonderful of you, Delilah. I can't tell you—"

"It's okay. Really. But I'm calling because I . . . didn't explain, about the date."

"You didn't?"

"No. You see, it wasn't just for an evening."

"It wasn't?"

"It was for a week. This week, to be exact."

Amy gasped, and then began panting harder than before. "Maybe you *should* talk to Brendan. You just hang on. I'll get him—"

"No. No, Amy. Listen. Don't wake him. Just, please, listen. Okay?"

"But a week? A week *where?*"

"I don't know. Camping. At someplace called Hidden Paradise Lake."

"Never heard of it."

"Neither have I. But Marty Santino knows where it is, if for some reason somebody has to know. I just . . . realized I should let someone know, just in case. That's all."

"But, Delilah . . ."

"Really, Amy. I know what I'm doing. I'll be fine."

"You're sure?"

"Positive."

"Delilah?"

"Yes? What is it?"

"That Sam Fletcher must really be gone on you, huh? I mean, it's awfully *romantic,* don't you think? Him givin' up the Sweet Amy for a week alone with you?"

"Amy."

"Okay, okay. I know you two are famous around here for how much you hate each other. And I should mind my own business. I know. But maybe you ought to give a guy like that a chance...."

Delilah wanted to scream. Just what she needed. Advice from a hopelessly romantic pregnant twenty-two-year-old—one who'd married a Jones, to boot.

"Amy," Delilah said in her best no-nonsense tone. "I am going camping with Sam Fletcher. I'll be back next Sunday. Marty Santino knows where we are. I would appreciate it if you wouldn't spread it all over town. That's all I called to say."

"Okay." Amy's voice was softer than ever. She sounded hurt.

Delilah felt like a bully. "Look, um, you take care of that baby—and that brother of mine."

"I will." A pause. "I promise. And you take care...of yourself."

"It's a deal."

"Bye."

Delilah hung up.

"Good. That's handled," Sam Fletcher said from behind her.

She whirled from the phone kiosk to confront him. "I thought you said you'd go on into the store."

"Well, on second thought, I decided to make sure you went through with it."

"What did you do with yourself before you had my life to control?"

"Ah, Delilah. Relax. Take things easy. We have a whole week to go."

"Don't I know it."

"Come on." He gestured out at the parking lot, beyond the overhang which protected them. "Cheer up. Before you know it, it'll be a gorgeous day."

She looked where he pointed and saw he was right. The rain had eased up quite a bit. The clouds were thinning. It was just possible that in an hour or two, they'd be enjoying a sunny spring day. Yet Delilah felt far from sunny. She gestured toward the glass doors. "Let's just get the food."

He gave a mock bow. "After you."

Chapter Eight

Within an hour, they were back on the road. A half hour after that, as Sam had predicted, the storm had passed. The sky was a flawless blue overhead, the road was a winding ribbon lined with tall conifers, and they were climbing ever higher into a sea of cedar and pine.

Eventually they left the highway, switching back onto a road that was paved at first, and then became a bed of moist pine needles splotched with patches of melting snow. They crossed a wooden bridge over a creek swift with spring runoff, and then the road became so rutted and rough that they had to proceed much more slowly. After a while, Sam switched to four-wheel drive.

They came to more than one crossroads, and Sam always seemed to know which raw, half-frozen route to take. Once or twice, Delilah spied small lakes or ponds through the tall trees, like huge puddles of sapphire, reflecting the smooth perfection of the sky. She also saw the occasional cabin nestled among the tall cedars.

Then the land opened up. The far mountains became rolling carpets of fir, spiked now and then with rugged rock faces, still heavily bearded with snow. Nearer, moraine from an aeons-ago glacier dotted the low hills.

For some time they drove up and down the moraine-dotted hills, where melting snow lay in the cracks and crevasses between the giant stones. Then once more they left the open country behind and entered the tall, silent trees where the snow lay on the banks of the rutted road, growing thicker with each mile that passed.

They went on, into the dark tunnel of the trees, through which, now and then, the sun would find its way in bright, stunning shafts, cutting the shadows like a heaven-sent spotlight and picking up jewel-like gleams in the white drifts of the snow.

At last, up ahead Delilah saw a patch of blue. It glimmered through the trees, then disappeared, then winked at her again. Finally they trundled around a curve, and the trees opened up to a clearing where most of the snow had melted away. The clearing ended at her teasing patch of blue: a small lake.

The lake glittered in the sun and reflected back the blue bowl of the pristine sky, as well as the mountain that rose on the other side, high and craggy, a moonscape of granite rock and glistening, wind-crested snow.

Sam pulled the Bronco to a stop and turned off the engine. Delilah, seduced by the beauty of the scene, only sat and stared. Heaven help her, faced with splendor like this, she could almost forget that the man beside her had held her brother's livelihood hostage to get her here.

Delilah glanced at Sam. He smiled at her. She smiled back. Right at that moment, it was simply impossible for her to do otherwise.

He gestured at a spot out her passenger window, and she saw a log cabin, at the edge of the trees. "That's where we'll be staying."

She found she couldn't hide her excitement. "How did you find this? Whose is it?"

"Ten acres, back into the trees, including the cabin and up to the lakefront, are mine. The rest is national forest."

"Ten acres?" She was awestruck. Land like this was rare now in overpopulated California. "But how did you ever convince anyone to sell a place like this?"

"I didn't," he said flatly. "It was my father's."

Delilah blinked. His *father's...*

The idea that Sam Fletcher had once had a father struck her as terribly strange. But then, everyone did have a father, after all. So she supposed Sam would be likely to have had one as well.

She'd just never thought of his having parents or a family. He'd shown up in town alone twenty years ago, and no evidence of a family had surfaced since. Until now.

She said, puzzled, "Your father? But Sam, I didn't even know you had a father..."

"I don't," he replied in that same flat tone. "He's dead."

"But—"

"Let's go inside," he said, suddenly brisk. "We have work to do getting settled in." He leaned on his door and got down from the Bronco before she could demand to hear more about this father she'd never known he had.

And then, when she thought about it, she decided she would only be asking for trouble to hear too much about Sam Fletcher anyway. Hearing his life history would be getting to know him better. And getting to know Sam Fletcher better was exactly what she'd sworn *not* to do.

In fact, she determined, the wisest course over this entire week would probably be to keep conversation to a minimum whenever possible. The less they talked, the smaller the chance she'd be drawn into the intimacy she'd sworn to resist. Also, every time they talked, things seemed to get out of hand. He either stirred her temper or her senses—two equally dangerous occurrences.

Yes, she thought, pleased with herself. As much as possible, she would keep her mouth shut. She'd be reasonable and helpful in getting things done. She'd be...polite. She'd do her best not to cross him. And just maybe she'd get through this week without killing him— or dropping right into his waiting arms.

That decided, she got out and joined him at the back of the Bronco, where he handed her a box of groceries. Then he took the other two boxes of food and led the way to the cabin. There, he balanced the stacked boxes in his arms against the door frame as he fitted a key into the padlock on the rough wooden door. The lock fell open.

He pushed the door inward and led the way into a single room with natural log walls and an unfinished plank floor on which their steps echoed when they walked.

He crossed the room and set the boxes down on a section of counter next to a stained sink. Delilah followed suit, pausing to glance out a rather large, many-paned window above the sink which granted a stunning view of the butte across the lake.

"Nice, huh?" Sam said. The window framed the craggy peak like a picture. "I put that window in myself two years ago. It was pretty dark in here without it."

Delilah, recalling her resolve to keep unnecessary conversation to a minimum, only nodded. Then Sam began inspecting the place. Delilah took the few moments while Sam was poking in cupboards and peering into cabinets to take stock of her surroundings.

The accommodations were far from deluxe, but the cabin appeared sound and dry. Settling in here would be a great improvement over sleeping outside on the half-frozen ground.

She noted most of the basic amenities including a simple pine table with two straight chairs and a fireplace of natural stone before which a pair of battered easy chairs huddled. The walls were lined with rough-hewn shelves and cabinets. There was even a scarred dresser into which they could unpack their clothes.

Also, in one corner, there was an old-fashioned iron bedstead. Its tired-looking mattress was levered up against the wall.

Delilah sighed. One bed. That was it. She glanced resignedly at the braided rug rolled up by the hearth, and realized where she'd be laying down her sleeping bag that night.

There was no sign of a bathroom. "Facilities," as she had predicted, would consist of a roll of tissue and one of those big trees out there to duck behind.

Sam, who'd been looking around himself, announced, "The good news is it looks like the rat bait I put out last time did the trick. The bad news is the dust is pretty thick, and we'll need to do some washing up. But I can't get the water pump going until I start the generator. So maybe I ought to do that right away."

Delilah agreed with him.

"Don't bring anything else in until I get this taken care of. Otherwise you'll only be stirring up dust."

"Okay."

He turned and left her standing alone in the cabin, gazing at the wood stove and the ancient refrigerator. The refrigerator actually had one of those old-fashioned coils on top of it.

In a few minutes she heard a motor start up several hundred yards away. She glanced out the tiny window on the west wall and saw an electric cable leading into the trees. She thought it clever of him to put the generator away from the cabin, where the sound would be less noticeable.

A bare lightbulb dangled from the middle of the ceiling. Delilah pulled the chain on it. The bulb shone brightly. Too brightly, she decided, and switched it off. The light from the big south-facing window would do until the shadows came.

The ancient refrigerator, whose door was held open by a towel for airing, began to hum. She removed the towel so the door would close.

Then she realized that there was only one spigot in the sink fixture, which meant no hot water. She decided to get the fire started. After checking to see that the tap was open, so there would be no pressure backup when the water began to flow, she found kindling, an old newspaper and a couple of logs in the basket by the stove. She started the fire.

As if on cue, the water in the sink began to run. It was the color of the hair on Sam's chest at first: rusty brown. But in a few minutes, it ran crystal clear. She found a big pot and put some on to heat.

After that, she looked in the cabinets for the cleaning supplies, and she started to work. In a few minutes, Sam joined her.

They worked without pausing for an hour, getting things in shape, dusting and wiping down counters and sweeping up the floor. They pulled the mattress flat on the springs and clouds of thick dust flew up, so they coaxed the thing out to the small front step and beat it awhile with the broom.

All this time, they hardly spoke, except to give verbal clues to facilitate the job at hand. Besides the fact that not speaking fell right in with her plans, Delilah found it very soothing to work so smoothly and purposefully.

She remembered, as she hadn't in years, the hardrock mine her mother's brother, Uncle Cleve, had owned, way up in the hills above North Magdalene. When Delilah was little, they all used to pack up and go camping up there, where the cabin was cruder than this one, and everyone had to pitch in to make things livable.

She remembered the starry summer nights, when they'd build a campfire outside, and make *S'mores*, sweet sandwiches of graham crackers, roasted marshmallows and chocolate bars. She remembered her mother, Bathsheba, tall and graceful in her frayed jeans and plaid shirt, her thick dark hair in a bouncing braid down her back, dancing a polka in her father's arms around the open fire as uncle Cleve beat out a tune on his old guitar.

Funny, in that memory, all her brothers were smiling, clapping their hands and cheering the reeling couple on....

"Lilah?"

She realized, with some chagrin, that she'd been wiping the same clean shelf for several minutes now. She stopped, and looked at Sam. "What?"

He stared at her strangely for a minute, as if he wondered what she'd been woolgathering about, but he didn't ask. Instead, he said with frank admiration, "You're a hard worker."

She was pleased at his praise, in spite of herself. "I like to do my share."

"We work the same."

Now what in the world was that supposed to mean? "So?"

"So that's good."

She peered at him warily for a moment, considering asking him just what was so good about it. But she was afraid she already knew the answer, which would have something to do with how two people who could work so smoothly together would probably do other things smoothly together as well. She didn't need to hear anything like that!

He chuckled, as if he could read her thoughts on her face. Then he pointed out, "Things are in pretty good shape now. I'll get the rest of the stuff from the truck."

She tossed her cleaning cloth in the bucket and followed him out. Together, they brought in everything else and put it away.

Delilah was careful to set her bedroll in the corner by the fireplace. But Sam, without a word, went over and picked it up and carried it to the bed. She opened her mouth to order him to put it back. But then he carried his own bag to the corner where hers had been and pointedly dropped it there. She decided not to argue. She could be foolish when it came to Sam Fletcher, but not foolish enough to complain about getting the only bed in the place.

By then, it was well past lunchtime. They made sandwiches and poured cups of milk, and took them out by the lake where they sat on a fallen log and watched the shadows grow longer on the north-facing butte across the water. Delilah found it very pleasant, actually, just sitting there by the lake, filling her growling stomach, feeling no urge to say a word.

It wasn't till the simple meal was through that she began to wonder if she was finding all this a little *too* pleasant. Once or twice, Sam had glanced her way and smiled and she had smiled back without thinking, as if she were here with him of her own free will, as if she were *enjoying* herself.

When they'd taken the empty cups back inside and straightened up the counter, Sam decided to replenish their supply of usable wood. Delilah, who had sense enough not to hang around and watch him flex his muscles, decided on a nice, long walk. She headed off into the woods without saying a word to him.

She followed a trail around the lake to the foot of the big butte. She walked slowly, enjoying the stillness of the woods, which was broken only by the occasional cry of an unseen bird or the scrabblings of small animals off the trail in the trees. She found herself relaxing a little, and was grateful for the time alone, away from Sam and the forbidden temptations he represented.

When she returned, it was nearing evening. She found wood stacked high against the side of the cabin, and Sam inside at the sink.

It was warm in the cabin; he had both the stove and the fireplace going. The bare bulb glared from above, its light necessary now. She hung her heavy jacket on a peg by the door, and looked at Sam's massive back, his narrow waist and tight buttocks. Suddenly, the tension inside her that had eased during her walk began building once again.

"Nice walk?" he asked over his shoulder. His voice was very casual. Too casual, in fact. "Well?" He set down the carrot he was slicing and turned to face her.

"Yes," she said carefully. "I had a nice walk."

"You didn't tell me you were leaving."

"I ... didn't stop to think," she said, though what she longed to tell him was it was none of his business where she went or how she got there.

He lifted an eyebrow at her. "It's stupid to head off alone into country you don't know without telling anyone where you've gone."

"I'm aware of that," she said, feeling her temperature rise a notch, and reminding herself grimly that he was right; it *was* stupid. Delilah knew very well that in unknown territory, going off alone could be foolish. But if she'd told him she was leaving, he might have argued with her. And she'd already decided she must avoid arguing with him at all costs.

"Then why did you do it?"

"I just wanted to get away for a while, that's all. I didn't think."

"Well, you'd better *start* thinking."

"All right!" She realized she'd raised her voice. She reminded herself to keep calm. Things would be getting out of hand. She took a deep breath, and said levelly, "It won't happen again."

"Good." He turned back to the sink, seemingly satisfied with her word that she would not go off alone another time. Then he asked with a backward glance, "Where did you go?"

"Does it matter?"

He glanced at her once more, and she realized she'd been too curt. Oh, this was like walking a tightrope—as

the handsome cad across the room no doubt knew very
well.

She made another stab at being civil. "Well, if you really want to know, I walked to the base of that mountain
around the lake."

"That's a pretty trail," he said, his tone as innocuous
as the statement.

"Yes, it was lovely." Much better, she thought. He's
innocuous, I'm insipid. We'll get through this week alive
yet.

"But next time, take the handgun." He'd brought along
a revolver for routine protection in the woods.

She looked at his broad back for a moment as he continued scrubbing and slicing the carrots, knowing she
should agree. But when she opened her mouth, agreement didn't come out.

"Why?"

He shot her a look. "Come on, Delilah. You know
why." He went on to explain anyway, in a gratingly patient tone. "If you get in trouble, you can fire a couple of
shots. I'll hear them and come for you—as long as I know
where to look. Also, if you come face to face with a
mountain lion or a bear, believe me, you'll feel a lot better with a gun in your hand."

He was right, of course. She knew she should simply
agree to take the gun and let the subject drop, but somehow her mouth just didn't want to take orders from her
brain. She said, "I'll be fine without a gun."

He said, "You won't *go* without a gun."

"Oh, really. And just how do you intend to stop me?"

"That's an interesting question. I'll have to give it some
serious thought." He cast her a grin, and she realized he
was winning this silly argument simply by refusing to take
it seriously.

She reminded herself once more that her intention was to avoid strife, not stir it up. She said, exerting great effort not to sound surly, "All right. To be on the safe side, I'll take the gun next time."

"Good."

There was a silence. Delilah actually dared to hope that she'd managed to pull herself back from the brink of a full-blown confrontation.

Cautiously, she crossed the room to stand by the table, not too close to him, but near enough that she could see his ponytail was wet; he must have washed in the sink, after chopping the wood.

She felt her skin pinkening, thinking of that, of him stripping down and soaping himself standing in front of the big window in the fading light of day. Of him hanging his head over the sink, and ladling water over his thick red-gold hair...

He glanced at her. Something as hot and intense as the fire in the stove arced between them. She thought of the way his big body had looked when he answered the door the night before, of the water drops left from his shower, which she'd wanted to lick off with her tongue.

They were staring at each other. She saw the hunger on his face and the question in his eyes. She knew her own eyes were answering....

Swiftly, she looked away. She stared blankly at the scarred surface of the old table, waiting until her heart found its normal rhythm again and her breath came more evenly into her chest.

When her yearnings were under control and she sensed he'd gone back to cutting the vegetables, she turned to him again.

"So," she asked, absurdly bright, "What's for dinner?"

"Steak, carrots and salad." His voice sounded as falsely cheerful as her own. "Want to help?"

"You bet."

They cooked. They ate. They cleared the table and washed the dishes. When the meal was done, it was dark outside, though the hour was far from late.

Sam suggested, "Come out with me. I'll show you the stars from Hidden Paradise Lake."

Delilah decided that wouldn't be wise. "No, thanks."

"Lilah—"

"I said no."

He looked at her for a moment, and she thought she saw a hint of real frustration in his blue eyes. But then he shrugged. He went to his gear and took out a soft cloth. He unrolled the cloth on the table, and she saw a basic set of woodworking tools tucked into the pouch inside. He then produced some stones of different shapes, a leather strop, and a can of oil and set about the involved process of sharpening the tools.

Delilah watched the whole procedure until it became clear what he was doing. She was curious about his wood carving, and wanted to ask questions. But questions meant conversation and conversation wasn't a good idea.

Suddenly feeling at a loss, Delilah cast about for something to occupy herself. She knew she ought to be exhausted. She'd had perhaps four hours' sleep the night before, cleaned a cabin and hiked around Hidden Paradise Lake that day. But she didn't feel tired. Not the least bit. In fact, her whole body seemed to thrum with unspent energy.

Oh, she just had to do something with herself, instead of standing in the shadows watching Sam Fletcher sharpen his chisels and picks—or whatever the blasted things were called.

Delilah thought of the books she'd brought. She went to her pack and took them out and lined them up on the dresser by the bed. Then she chose one—the one she'd been trying read last night, as a matter of fact—found her glasses and sat in one of the easy chairs to read.

Even with the soft hum of the generator outside, and the occasional far away cry of a nocturnal creature, the night was very quiet. She could hear every stroke Sam made of metal on stone.

She forced herself to look at the page in front of her, but it didn't help. She kept forgetting what she'd just read, so she'd read the same paragraph over and still the book seemed to make no sense at all.

After an interval that seemed to last forever, Sam put the tools and the stones away, took his jacket off the hook and went outside. Since he said nothing, Delilah assumed he was answering the call of nature.

But the minutes dragged by, and he didn't return.

She should have been grateful, she knew, for a few minutes alone. The fire crackled cheerfully in the grate; it was cozy and warm. She had a full stomach and a good book—even if she still hadn't the faintest idea what the thing was about. Now that her nemesis had taken a hike, she should be able to relax and enjoy the moment.

But where could he have gone? It couldn't have taken this long for him to see to his needs, could it?

She thought of hungry mountain lions, suddenly. Of big brown bears awakened and grouchy after their long winter's nap. She remembered that she hadn't seen him take the handgun when he left. He was out there unarmed, against the dangers of the night....

"Oh, this is ridiculous," she muttered aloud. It was so quiet out there, she would have heard any yowling or roaring that went on within a half mile of the cabin. She was letting her imagination get away with her, and that was going to stop now.

He knew how to handle himself in the woods. There was no reason to worry. And she *wouldn't* worry, that was all. She would read her book and enjoy her solitude.

Five minutes later, he was still gone.

She found she just couldn't sit there another moment. She set her book and glasses aside and went to the big window over the sink. She peered out, pressing her face near the glass so she could see beyond the reflected glare from the bulb hanging overhead.

Out in the night, the moon, a thickening crescent, hung over the rugged spires of the mountain across the lake. The sky was cloudless, thick with stars. A dark shape, hunched against the cold, was sitting on the fallen log beside the lake.

It was Sam.

He didn't look like there was anything wrong, she decided. Maybe, as she had, he'd just wanted a little time alone. The forbidden thought came that she might join him—and was as quickly banished. That was probably just what he hoped for, that she'd grow lonely, and come to find him. She was giving him nothing of what he hoped for.

Delilah turned from the window. Even though she loathed and despised Sam Fletcher, she felt better knowing where he was and that he was okay.

She found her vanity pack and cleaned her face and brushed her teeth. Then she went outside herself—staying well away from the lake, of course.

When she came back in, she pulled the curtains over the big window so that, should Sam turn around from his contemplation of the lake, he wouldn't see her undressed. Quickly, she shimmied out of her clothes and put

on her long underwear, which would do well for paja-
mas. Then she rolled out her sleeping bag and climbed in.

She'd just snuggled down when the door opened.

"Lilah?"

She decided not to answer, to let him think she was
asleep. It was easier that way; it saved another exchange
that could only invite one kind of trouble or another.

She heard nothing for a moment, though she sensed
him listening. She tried to make her breathing even. At
last, she could almost feel his shrug.

He began quietly moving about. She heard the water
run briefly as he brushed his teeth. And then he rolled out
his bag on the rug. Then his boots dropped, and she knew
he must be taking off his clothes. After that, he pulled the
chain on the light, and the room, lit only by the fire now,
grew dim. She heard him crawl into the bag.

There was a silence. Far away outside in the darkness,
a coyote howled at the almost-half-moon. Sam shifted in
his hard bed. Delilah curled into a ball with her back to
the room and resolutely waited for sleep. She was actually beginning to think it might find her, when Sam spoke.

"Lilah?"

She said nothing.

"I know you're awake."

She tried to keep breathing evenly. How could he know
for sure whether she slept or not, if she simply refused to
answer? She waited, trying not to go rigid and give herself away, dreading the moment he'd climb out of his
sleeping bag and approach her to see for himself if she
slept.

But he didn't get up. She heard him shift again, and
thought that perhaps he was now sitting up, maybe staring into the fire, contemplating . . . what?

"This afternoon," he said at last, "you asked about my father..."

It was a mistake. Pretend I didn't, she thought, but of course didn't say.

He went on, "And I cut you off." He shifted again, and the fire popped. "I'm sorry about that. Since then, I've given it some thought. And I've decided to tell you whatever you want to know about my father, and about my life before I came to North Magdalene."

Delilah debated the feasibility of sitting bolt upright and ordering him to keep his life story to himself. But she'd already pretended she was asleep, and even if he knew she wasn't, admitting her deception now would only put her at a disadvantage.

"Lilah?"

She almost said *What?* and let him know she was awake.

But then he chuckled—the rat. And that did it. She pressed her eyes closed and determined not to listen.

"You are the most stubborn woman I have ever known." He actually had the nerve to say it fondly. Then he fell silent.

Delilah fumed and waited and wondered what he was doing, over there by the fire where she couldn't turn to see without admitting she was awake.

Just when she thought he was going to show a little mercy and keep his past to himself, he began, "My father. Whew." He paused, thinking. "My father was...a man with a mission. His mission was to save the world from the sin and degradation he was absolutely positive lurked around every corner."

He fell silent. Delilah waited, forgetting to breathe for a moment.

Then he went on, "He was a preacher, a nondenominational preacher." Delilah stifled a gasp. Could he actually be telling the truth? Mad, bad Sam Fletcher had been a minister's son? Sam continued. "By the time I was five, we'd settled down in a little farm town just north of Fresno, and my father had his own church—the Valley Bible Church."

He paused again, a long pause. And suddenly, Delilah understood that he was just trying to get a rise out of her. He expected her to pipe up and stop him before he revealed too much.

Well, she wouldn't, that was all. He should have thought twice before he started telling things he really didn't want to tell. She would say not a word and move not a muscle and he could just go ahead and lay out all the secrets of his heart—and then wonder if she'd heard him at all.

The silence stretched out. Then she heard the poker shoving the logs around in the fireplace and realized he must be stirring the fire. After that came the sound of the poker clinking on the hearth as he propped it back in place.

Sam remained quiet. She pictured him, staring into the flames he'd just stirred. Then he said, "This is your last chance, Lilah. Say something, or hear it all." He sounded tired—and even a little bit sad.

Delilah realized she couldn't do it—lie here unmoving and listen to the man she'd always loathed tell her all about the little boy he'd been, the hurts he'd known, the setbacks he'd suffered. It wouldn't be wise. She could hear too much, *feel* too much. And that would put her in worse jeopardy than she was already in.

"Lilah?"

"I hate you, Sam Fletcher."

He laughed.

"You are lower than low," she muttered through clenched teeth.

"That's my Lilah."

Delilah let out a furious groan. Then she sat up, wrapped her arms around her blanketed knees and glared at him as hard as she could.

"I am not, nor will I ever be, your Lilah. Is that understood?"

He only grinned. He was sitting up, too, his bare torso gleaming in the light from the fire. His lower body was covered by the sleeping bag. He watched her. His smile was tender, his eyes promised delights she'd never known.

"I asked you a question," she demanded, when he went on grinning and didn't say a word.

He still didn't answer her question, but he did point out in a gentle whisper, "So you weren't asleep."

Something inside her snapped. "You are a—"

He wiggled a finger at her. "Lilah. You are about to say something you'll regret. Think twice, now."

She brought herself back from the brink, and then explained tightly, "I don't want you to tell me about your father. I don't want you to tell me anything about where you've been or what you've done. I know all I'll ever need to know about you, so get that through your thick head."

"That's not true, Lilah. You'll end up needing to know more, much more, before this is through."

"You are wrong. I don't need or want to know a thing more than I do now—not that my needs and wants have ever mattered in the least to you."

His eyes changed, lost their teasing look. Now his gaze penetrated, burned. "You want *me*. That matters. It matters a hell of a lot. I'm only trying to get you to admit what you want."

"Oh, are you?"

"Yes."

"Well," she fumed, "here's a hot bulletin for you—I don't want to want you. I don't need to want you. And even if I *do* want you, I won't be doing a thing about it. Ever. So learn to live with it."

He smiled again. "Give yourself time."

"Time won't matter."

"We'll see about that."

"Sam Fletcher—"

Before she could go on, he stood up. His big body emerged from the sleeping bag with a power and grace that shut her mouth and took her breath. She stared at him long enough to register the heartstopping fact that he was utterly naked and achingly magnificent.

Then she gasped and looked away, her face burning, her body flaming with responses she hated herself for feeling. She heard him toss a log on the fire and prod it into place with the poker.

After a few moments he said in a teasing voice, "You can look now."

She dared a glance; he was back in the sleeping bag, covered to the waist and looking smug as a cat who'd cornered a plump mouse.

She said, "I will make one last effort to appeal to any tiny kernel of decency that just might be waiting, undiscovered, somewhere deep down inside you."

"Please do."

"Take me home in the morning."

"No way."

"This will be a totally wasted week for you. Realize that. I will never ever give you what you're after."

"Ah, Lilah. Do you really even know what I'm after?"

"I have a general idea."

"Say it, then."

"Why not? Attention. Affection. Companionship. Sex."

"Not a bad estimation."

"The point is, you are not getting any of those things from me. Ever."

"So you keep telling me."

"I am never going to be your woman. I have learned my lesson the long, hard way, about what a woman gets with a man like you. With a man like you, I'd have just what my mother had, what each of my brothers' long-suffering wives and girlfriends have had—endless nights waiting up to learn what trouble you've got yourself into now."

"You're not being fair, Lilah."

"Fair? Fair! What does any of this have to do with being fair? You used totally *unfair* means to get me here. And I told you from the first that I didn't like it, that I'd *never* like it. But I have tried to be civil about it, thinking that if you would just leave me alone while I'm here, maybe we can get through this with a minimum of conflict. But you will not leave me alone."

"Lilah." His voice was like rough velvet. "I didn't bring you here to leave you alone."

"I have finally come to fully accept that fact. And that is why I am through even attempting to be civil. You do not deserve civility. I despise you and I loathe being here alone with you and I'm through telling myself the best way to get through this week is to avoid confrontation with you. I intend to make you miserable, as miserable as you're making me. Do you understand?"

He looked at her for a moment, his eyes hooded.

"Do you understand?" she demanded again.

"Perfectly," he said at last.

Chapter Nine

Delilah went about making Sam miserable with a vengeance.

For the next two days, Monday and Tuesday, she never said a single pleasant word. Most of the time, she didn't talk at all. She did her share of the work, and when there was no work to do, she would read or walk off by herself.

She was meticulous, also, in never giving him a single reason to engage her by questioning her actions. She always informed him in clipped tones of exactly where she was going. And she'd always take the handgun just in case, so he couldn't even argue with her that she wouldn't be safe out there alone.

Sam, alert to every possible angle for getting through to her, did the best he could over the issue of the gun. The first time she went off alone on Monday, he challenged her about her ability with it, though he suspected that, growing up with the Jones Gang, she'd probably learned at least the basics of how to shoot.

Still, he'd indulged in a brief fantasy of showing her how to use the gun, of explaining how to load it and handle it, and then of stepping behind her, feeling her supple back and soft bottom caressing the length of him as he wrapped his arms around her and steadied her hand.

She quickly demolished his little fantasy. "Do you doubt my competence with this weapon," she buzzed like an angry hornet, "is that it?"

"Sweetheart . . ."

"Don't call me sweetheart, you manipulative snake."

"Sweetheart," he said again, slowly and very clearly. She held her tongue, but her eyes spit fire. "I'm just suggesting that a .357 is only as useful as the person who's carrying it. And I wouldn't be responsible if I simply gave it to you without making sure you know what to do with it."

"Fine." She left him there in the cabin where they'd been arguing and went outside. He heard her at the west wall, fooling with the garbage and recycling bins, which he kept strapped shut with bungee cords to discourage the raccoons. She got the lid off of one. He heard the sound of empty cans rattling against each other, then silence as she apparently found what she was looking for. Her boots crunched on pine needles, headed in the direction of the lake.

He glanced out the south window. She was bending over the fallen log they'd shared their lunch on the day before, setting out three empty beverage cans in a row. Her round little bottom was a captivating sight to see. He watched, smiling in spite of himself, as she stalked back toward him. She disappeared for a moment around the side of the house, and then poked her head in the door.

"Bring the gun, and the cartridges."

He brought the revolver down from its high shelf, grabbed the box of cartridges and did as he was told.

Outside, she took the gun from him, broke it open, shoved the cartridges in and slapped it closed. In one seamless motion, she whirled on the cans and fired off three shots. All three cans went flying.

She turned to Sam. "Satisfied?"

He could do nothing but nod. She was magnificent. Too bad she was also so damn mean. She replaced the cartridges she'd fired, handed him the rest, and demanded the holster he'd left inside.

"You know where it is."

She went and got it and stalked off for her walk with the gun strapped around her waist.

Their every encounter was like that, Sam came to realize quickly enough: pure hell. She wore a sour expression at all times; her attitude varied between impatient and downright nasty.

Sam tried to bear with her, to wait her out. He set up a vise on the table in the cabin, and created his own miniature wood carving shop, which he dismantled for meals. Monday, he began carving a coyote sitting on its haunches, howling at the moon.

As she continued to torment him, he found himself immeasurably grateful for his hobby. When he was working with wood, he could almost forget Delilah's spitefulness. Whenever the slightest opportunity arose, she made sure he suffered endless indignities for daring to want her and then having the absolute gall to go after what he wanted.

She would alternate long spells of silent seething with periods when she would argue about anything. Sam would hardly have believed, until those two days of her crusade to make his life miserable, how many subjects in the world there were to be argued about. Things he would swear made no difference at all, she could make an issue of.

And she didn't seem to care which side of an argument she took—as long as it was the opposite side from the one he was on.

Monday at dinner, he mentioned that he'd seen Chloe Swan out with a stranger Saturday night, and she snapped that that was preposterous, everyone knew Chloe Swan would never look at any man but Patrick, even if Patrick refused for the rest of his life to give her so much as the time of day.

"Well, Lilah, I'm just telling you what I saw."

"You're either lying or mistaken, Sam Fletcher—either way, you're wrong."

"I'm not lying, Lilah. And I know what I saw."

"You know nothing."

"Fine, Lilah. Have it your way."

"You admit you know nothing?"

"I admit this is a ridiculous argument, and I can't wait to find out what you'll accuse me of next."

"Take me home," she suggested. "The ridiculous arguments will stop."

"Not on your life."

She gave him a look meant to freeze his blood in his veins and fell seethingly silent once more.

After they'd cleaned up the meal, he picked up the latest issue of the *North Magdalene News,* which he'd brought along on the trip. He made himself comfortable in one of the chairs before the fire. She sat at the table with that same mystery novel she'd been reading the day before.

He read the front page of the paper and then turned to the Over a Hundred Years Ago section on page three.

There, he discovered a piece by Mark Twain. He began reading it with relish, found it as full of humorous irony as he'd expected, and was soon chuckling aloud.

"What is so funny?" she demanded, as if there were something inherently distasteful about people who indulged in a good laugh now and then.

"Mark Twain."

"What about Mark Twain?" She took off her reading glasses in order to be able to glare at him more effectively.

He read her a little of the article, wherein the author had visited a San Francisco prison and been appalled to find a sweet-looking sixteen-year-old girl doing time there—until he heard her talking to the other inmates and learned she'd done worse than murder in her day.

When he'd finished Delilah demanded, "What's so funny about that?"

He glanced at her, then turned back to the paper. It was obvious she was on the warpath again, and he decided the best response was no response at all. "Never mind."

"I asked what is so funny about a sixteen-year-old girl who's been used and abused all her life by men?"

Sam lowered the paper and, against his own better judgment, decided to hold his own. "I think the point was that the girl had done a little using and abusing of her own."

"She was sixteen. She was only a child."

"She may have been sixteen. But she was far from being a child."

"And whose fault was that, do you think?"

"All right, Delilah. It was all the fault of men. Horrible, wicked men."

"Don't you patronize me."

"I'm not patronizing you. I'm being ironic, just like Twain."

"Ironic." She gave him a sour frown. "What do *you* know about irony?"

He considered the question. "What do I know about irony? Hmm." He stood up. Her eyes widened; she sat bolt upright in her chair. He couldn't help enjoying her obvious apprehensiveness just a little. He pressed on, though he was careful to keep his voice light. "I know plenty about irony, since I've been spending so much time with you." He took the few steps to her side and stood looking down into her flushed face. "And I find a sense of irony very comforting. Especially since you've gotten so far out of hand with this project of yours to drive me right up the wall."

She glared defiantly up at him. "You deserve to be driven up the wall."

"So you've explained to me."

"And I'm not out of hand."

"Oh, no?"

"Absolutely not. Every rotten thing I do to you, I do on purpose."

"How reassuring." He loomed a little nearer, suppressing a smile as he watched her breasts rise and fall in growing agitation.

She was trying her damnedest to pretend that his nearness didn't bother her in the least. Her mouth quivered; she pressed it into a grim line to make the quivering stop.

"Ah, Lilah," he murmured.

"Don't you 'ah, Lilah,' me."

He longed to reach out and touch her. But he knew better. Instead, he dropped to a crouch by her chair. She gasped at the suddenness of the move, and then contained herself.

"What are you up to?" Sitting as far back in the chair as it was possible to sit, she peered down at him.

He faked an ardent sincerity. "I'm *begging* you, Lilah . . ."

"For what?" she asked, then realized the question could only bring her trouble. "On second thought, don't tell me."

He chuckled. "Too late. You already asked."

"Get up off the floor. I mean it. I'm warning you . . ."

"Give me a chance, sweetheart—"

"I told you not to call me that."

"Give *us* a chance."

"Not on your life. Now get up from there."

"You're a hard-hearted woman, Delilah Jones."

"Right. So take me home tomorrow."

"Uh-uh. We had a deal."

"A rotten deal. One you forced on me."

"A deal's a deal."

"Fine. Have it your way."

"I plan to."

"Just don't ever delude yourself that you'll get anything from me but the misery you deserve."

"Oh, no?"

"No."

He moved then, so swiftly she had no hint of what he intended. He grabbed her hand. She gasped, her whole body tensed. And then she sighed.

Sam relished that sigh. He turned her hand, swiftly, and placed a kiss in the heart of her palm. He barely accomplished his goal, before she tried to jerk away.

He didn't let her. Instead, he rose to his full height, and pulled her along with him.

She came up against his chest. He wrapped his arms around her and held her there. He looked down at her stunned face and saw the hunger there, a hunger he recognized, since it was a mirror of his own.

He smelled the woodsy, sweet scent of her, saw the softening of her lips that meant they waited for his kiss. Her breasts were pressed against him, ripe and ready for his caress. He cupped her face, holding her still.

And then she managed to whisper, "Please don't..."

He almost hated her for that. Because if she'd said anything else, if she hadn't looked so crushed and vulnerable, he would have gone ahead and kissed her, and who could say where things might have gone from there?

Instead, with a muttered curse, he dropped his arms and stepped back. His whole body protested at the loss of her softness. He silently called himself ten kinds of fool. Then he turned and grabbed his coat and got the hell out of there.

When he returned a half hour later, she was already in bed with her face to the wall.

After that, things grew worse. She must have decided that arguing with him wasn't a good idea, because she refused to be drawn into any disagreements with him from then on. She seethed and glared and spoke only when spoken to.

Sam spent every spare minute on his carving. He worked on the coyote till afternoon. Then he put it aside for a while and glued three pieces of poplar together, thinking that Wednesday he would begin the fine, strong head of a mountain lion, its sharp teeth bared in a warning snarl.

But by Tuesday night at bedtime, Sam had begun to wonder what the point of this was. If he was going to spend all his time carving away at hunks of wood to keep from fighting with Delilah, he might as well go on home where he could carve in his own shop—and not have to look up from his work and find her glaring at him as if she longed to shoot him dead with his own gun.

That night, as the two previous nights, she got ready for bed early and then lay down with her face to the wall, leaving him to stare at the fire. It was then, as he leaned his head back in the old armchair and watched the flame shadows dance in the beams of the ceiling that he finally admitted to himself that this hadn't been such a hot idea after all. He'd told himself Saturday night, before he won Brendan's truck and got the brainstorm to take Delilah instead, that she was never going to give him a break. And he'd been right.

It was driving him crazy having to be around her night and day, and keep hands off. He just couldn't take it anymore. Her never ending meanness had broken him down—and his own frustrated desire had done the rest. He was ready to give up.

"Lilah?" he said quietly, thinking that if she would only turn, and say one reasonably pleasant word—a plain *What?* would do, as long as it was lacking in animosity— he would tell her she'd been right all along, this wasn't working. They were going back to North Magdalene at dawn.

But she didn't turn over. She did nothing at all but continue to lie still as a stick facing the wall.

Fine, he thought wearily. He'd tell her tomorrow. He'd had it with her as much as she had with him. They were going back.

His mind made up, he prepared for bed himself, settled down in his own bag and waited for sleep.

He woke at dawn to the sound of her stomping around the cabin.

He groaned and opened his eyes, noticing first that four pans were steaming on the stove. He glanced around, looking for her. He found her standing by the sink, fully dressed, her arms folded beneath that pair of breasts which belonged on a much more amenable female than she'd ever be.

"Good. You're awake." Her voice was colder than the frozen morning mists obscuring the butte that could be seen out the window behind her head.

He sat up and raked his loose hair back from his face. He didn't miss the way she averted her eyes from the sight of his bare torso. He felt anger—and a hot flare of desire—and realized that maybe he wasn't as resigned to giving her up as he'd thought.

She deigned to speak to him again. "I want to take a sponge bath. Get out, and give me twenty minutes before you come back."

Beneath the sleeping bag, his desire increased as he glanced at the steaming pots again and realized she intended to use their contents to bathe. She would strip down, and wet her body with a cloth, then she'd work up a lather, over those beautiful breasts, that flat belly, the soft flare of those hips . . .

He swallowed, then said gruffly, "It's freezing outside. It's barely dawn."

"Wear your coat."

He remembered he'd decided last night that they were leaving. He should tell her that, tell her to forget the bath, she could take it when she got home.

But lust—and her endless orneriness—made him contrary. He wasn't telling her that she'd won, finally broken him down with pure nastiness, while he was sitting buck-naked in his sleeping bag, wondering how he was going to stand up without her knowing just exactly how he felt about her.

She was glaring at him, waiting for him to agree to do her will—or to risk her viper's tongue by refusing. He considered standing up suddenly, as he'd done the other night, shocking her into an uncontrolled response.

But then he knew she'd only act appalled. And he could do without that.

He said, "Fine," and shifted enough in the sleeping bag that she saw he intended to rise.

She turned around and faced the window. He got up and shoved his legs in his pants, then quickly pulled on a thermal shirt and heavy sweater.

"It's safe now," he told her with some sarcasm, and then sat in one of the easy chairs to put on his socks and boots. He winced a little when he sat down. His lust was still not fully under control.

Then he stood up and stalked to the sink. She slid swiftly out of his way. He rinsed his face and brushed his hair and anchored it back in a ponytail. Then he got his coat and wool hat and gloves. He put them on and opened the door, not saying a word.

"Wait." She handed him his watch. "I mean it. Twenty minutes." She went back to the sink and yanked the curtains shut to keep out prying eyes—*his* eyes, he was perfectly aware.

He left, barely restraining himself from slamming the door.

Outside, the morning was cold and misty, as it had been yesterday and the day before. When the mist burned off, the day would be clear and gorgeous—as long as those clouds he could see to the west didn't thicken and move in.

He stomped out into the trees and took care of nature's call. After that, there were a good fourteen min-

utes left before he could return to the warmth of the cabin.
He spent them walking in circles around the clearing,
watching his own breath come out as freezing mist, getting madder and madder as each second passed.

Just who the hell did she think she was, anyway? All
right, maybe it had been a fool's dream, for him to imagine he could win her by hijacking her off into the woods.
But damn it, he hadn't done a thing but treat her with
courtesy and respect this whole time. The one time he'd
almost kissed her, she'd asked him to stop and he had—in
spite of his raging desire to do otherwise.

They'd had a deal: a week of her time for Brendan's rig.
He'd turned over the rig before the week even began as a
gesture of good faith. And now here he was, waiting out
in the freezing cold for her to finish washing that gorgeous body of hers so he could take her back home halfway through the week she'd sworn to give him.

He stopped in mid-pace in the middle of the clearing
and stared at the mist-shrouded mountain across the lake.
When he'd planned this ill-fated trip, in the wee hours of
Sunday morning, he'd pictured them climbing that
butte—Ladyslipper Peak, his father had always called it—
together. It was a challenging hike, but not dangerous,
with a clearly delineated trail around the south side most
of the way to the top.

Sam glanced at his watch. Five minutes to go. She'd be
finishing up rinsing now, dribbling clear warm water over
her shoulders, her neck, the tender valley between her
breasts...

Sam glared up at the mountain again—and decided he
was not going to go meekly back inside and tell her she
was getting what she wanted.

No, by God. They weren't leaving today. They'd leave
when he was damn good and ready.

Yes. Absolutely. He could see now that the mistake he'd made was to meekly hang around the cabin, hoping and praying for a kind word or a soft look from a woman who wouldn't call an ambulance if she found him bleeding in the road.

He'd been here to the lake ten times by himself in as many years. And he'd always, up until now, found his own company plenty to satisfy him.

And it would be plenty now. He'd arranged this week for rest and recreation. And he wasn't leaving without getting what he'd come for, whether the mean little witch inside the cabin joined him or not.

Sam glanced at his watch again. Time was up. He turned from the lake and headed for the cabin, noticing that she'd pulled the curtains open once again.

She was completely dressed, her wet hair in a braid down her back, and making coffee when he entered. He could smell her shampoo in the steamy air. He carried the wood he'd brought in over to the bin by the stove and dropped it in. Then he took off his coat, gloves and hat and put them away.

Next, he went to the refrigerator, took out bacon, an egg and some milk, got the biscuit mix from a shelf and started whipping up a batch of pancakes. She saw what he was doing and fell into step with him, getting down the plates and fixing up the table, putting out the milk and sugar he liked for his coffee, as well as the margarine and syrup for the pancakes.

It was almost spooky, really, the way they worked together. From the first day, when they cleaned the cabin from top to bottom without sharing more than ten words the whole time, it had been like that. They were like two parts of a well-oiled machine when they tackled a task. He'd mentioned it the first day, but she hadn't wanted to hear it. She'd known, of course, that he was thinking of the other things they might do well together.

He was still thinking of those other things. All the time. It was driving him crazy, if the truth were told.

As they sat down to the breakfast table and ate the crisp bacon and fragrant griddle cakes without speaking, he looked longingly out the window at Ladyslipper Peak. Yes, it would be good to get out and take that mountain, a long, hard hike. He would do it today.

Maybe, if she decided to follow along, the view from the summit would soften her hard heart. In any case, the exercise would work off a little of the tension that kept coiling tighter and tighter, like a snake readying to spring, inside him.

They finished the silent meal. Then they got up as one and cleaned the table.

After that, it was near eight. He decided to work for an hour on the carving of the coyote, to give the mountain a chance to warm up a little before he tackled it. He got out his tools and set to work, feeling better than he had in two days.

Though he did his best to pay no attention to her, he couldn't help but notice that she seemed restless. She went out and came in again, settled down with a book, then put it away.

He wondered if she sensed a change in him, if she had a feeling that something between them had shifted, though he'd said not a word about anything at all.

Things *had* changed, he realized. She'd had him on the run, and now he'd decided he wasn't running anymore. She refused to want him. Fine. He was through trying to get her to change her mind.

But she still had her end of their bargain to keep. She was here for the rest of the week, if he wanted it that way.

And, the more he thought about it, the more he knew he did want it that way.

At nine, he put his tools away and found the small day pack he used for hikes. He got out a few of the snacks and drink boxes she'd brought from home and loaded them in the pack. Then he found his canteen and filled it. Though he never glanced her way, he knew she watched his every move.

When the pack was ready, he loaded the handgun—she always conscientiously removed the cartridges every time she put it away—strapped it on and pulled a sweatshirt over his sweater. Then he put on his down vest and pulled on his gloves.

He could feel her eyes on him the whole while, and he knew the only thing that kept her from asking what was up was the knowledge that he was bound by the laws of safety and common sense not to head out without saying where he was going and how long he'd be gone.

He waited, enjoying the upper hand for a change, until he was sliding his arms in the day pack and slipping his canteen on his belt hook, before he said, "I'm hiking up Ladyslipper Peak—the mountain across the lake. There's a trail around the other side that goes to the summit. It's a couple of hours up, and less coming down. I should be back by one or two this afternoon."

She just stared at him, her dark eyes smoldering with all that pent-up resentment—and repudiated desire.

He knew a perverse stab of satisfaction. It was obvious she hadn't the faintest idea what to do about this development. She'd gotten used to him tiptoeing around, waiting for her to make a move so he could react to it. She didn't know how to handle it when he acted of his own accord.

He grabbed his hat and stuck it on his head and turned for the door.

"Wait!" she said at the last minute.

He turned, lifting an eyebrow. "Is there a problem?"

She blinked, her expression bewildered. He had to stifle a smug grin as he watched her furiously casting about for some reason why he should stay here where she could abuse him at her leisure.

"Wh-what if you have an accident or something?"

"We've been through this. I'll fire two shots."

"But I haven't the faintest idea where that trail starts. I don't know the terrain. I would have hiked up that mountain myself if I thought it was safe to go alone."

"It's safe."

"You've done it before?"

"Yes."

"You never mentioned that."

He said nothing in reply. He just gave her a look intended to remind her of everything she'd put him through in the past few days.

She glanced away—rather defensively, he thought. Then she pointed out, "And anyway, if something happened to you, I'd have trouble finding you. That wouldn't be good."

It was an absurdly weak argument, one he demolished without missing a beat. "*If* you hear shots—which you won't—then take the truck back the way we came in, to the last crossroads. Go right. Go right again when you come to the next fork. Go about two miles and you're at paved road. Turn left. From there it's four miles to the ranger's station." He turned around and reached for the door.

He heard her stand up. "Sam . . ."

"What?"

"I . . . I think I'd better go with you."

He felt a hot surge of triumph, a delicious sensation, one he savored fully before turning at last and giving her an unconcerned look. "What for?"

Her face was flushed. She looked confused and adorable and he had to remind himself that just the slightest hint of weakness on his part and she'd be on him unmercifully once again.

"It's . . . well, it's just better if we stick together."

He shrugged. "Nothing is going to happen. And if by some weird chance it did, you know what to do."

"But I—"

"You what?"

For a moment, she didn't speak. He stared at her, at her flushed face, at the wisps of dark hair that had escaped her braid and now kissed her temples, at her stormy dark eyes and her sweet red mouth. He liked staring at her, especially now, when she was at a disadvantage. She looked vulnerable now, which didn't happen often—he could testify in court to that.

"I . . . just think I should go," she said at last.

"No," he said flatly.

Her black brows drew together. That sweet, vulnerable look was fading. She'd be spitting and scratching again in a moment, if he didn't stay ahead of her.

"Unless . . ." He let the word wander off into nowhere.

Her brows smoothed out a little. "Unless what?"

"Unless you just plain *want* to go."

She gaped at him. "Excuse me?"

"You can go if you *want* to go. Do you . . . *want* to go?"

"Well, I—"

"Yes or no? This is not a trick question."

"Well, I . . . yes! Yes, of course." Then she added, unwilling to completely concede to him even on this small issue, "but only because I don't think you should go off alone."

He studied her for a moment, and considered telling her that that wasn't good enough. She either wanted to go or she didn't. But then he decided he'd pushed things far enough.

He looked down at the soft moccasins she was wearing. "Fine. Get your boots on, and get ready. I'll wait outside." With more satisfaction than he'd felt in days, he flung open the cabin door and stepped out into the bright morning.

Delilah, even more at a loss than Sam realized, stared at the closed door for several seconds after he was gone. She knew she should stick her head out the door, right now, and tell him to head on up that mountain without her.

What she'd done, making all those absurdly weak excuses for keeping him here, and then, in the end, virtually begging him to let her come, was a grave lapse. She was supposed to be staying as clear of him as the circumstances would allow, not chasing him willingly up the side of a cliff.

But good grief, she was just so... confused. Not to mention at the end of a very frayed rope when it came to her emotions.

Making Sam's life miserable twenty-four hours a day had not turned out to be an easy task for her. True, she'd had a lot of practice in her life at being mean; a girl didn't grow up in the Jones Gang and live to tell about it unless she learned to get tough when she had to. Yet since she'd grown up, it hadn't been necessary for her to be mean with any consistency. She was out of practice.

Being mean to Sam for two days running had practically worn her out. It took fortitude and stamina to be consistently vicious, she was learning. And it was even harder in this situation, since he'd seemed to get nicer the meaner she became.

It was driving her right out of her mind, to be honest. To be here alone with him, and have to look at him and *feel* his presence every hour of the day—and constantly remember that he was not the man for her, that he'd brought her here as the payoff on a wager, and that she'd only be asking for heartache if she softened toward him one bit.

Sam Fletcher was forty years old. He'd never married, and she doubted he ever would. Not that she wanted to marry a man like him, anyway. No, whatever might happen between them would take place right here, in the next few days, and be over as soon as they went home.

And she didn't want that, a temporary fling. She wasn't the type for a temporary fling.

"So nothing is going to happen," Delilah announced to the empty cabin, and then went to get her heavy socks and boots.

Well, she decided, as she laced up the boots, she *did* want to go with him, and she was going to do what she wanted. She'd go stone cold bonkers, sitting here alone for four hours, staring at the lake and trying to keep from thinking about Sam.

Yes. Going with him was the better option. If nothing else, the heavy exertion would work off a little of the strain that kept building between them, worse every hour.

Delilah stood up and put on a sweater and a sweatshirt and a padded vest, just as Sam had. The layers were efficient for hiking; they could be peeled off and tied at her waist as she grew warmer. She got more food, her canteen and her own hat and gloves and went out to join him where he waited on the log by the lake, taking the key and locking the door behind her.

He stood up when she approached, and saw the extra juice boxes and snack bars she carried. He turned around, without saying a word, so she could add the food to that already in the pack.

"Okay," she said, when the food was packed.

He glanced over his shoulder. "Ready?"

"Yes."

He headed for the trail that she'd taken alone the first day they arrived. She fell in step behind him, glad to be moving, to be going somewhere.

Yes, the hike would be good for her, she was sure. And the lapse of voluntarily going along with something he wanted to do meant nothing. What could possibly happen between them while they were climbing a cliff, for heaven's sake?

But then she glanced up, at the craggy face of the cliff they would be scaling. It looked stark and uncompromising, like the powerful frame of the man in front of her.

A frisson of taboo excitement skittered through her body. She felt reckless and daring, eager for whatever might lie ahead.

And then she froze, her face flaming.

Recklessness. Daring. Such emotions were not for her. Growing up a Jones, she'd seen well enough what happened to people who gave in to their every wild urge.

They got in big trouble. Frequently.

In her mind, the voice of caution advised, *Go back right now. You're playing with fire to go with him. You're breaking your own rules. You're on hazardous ground....*

Delilah shook her head. There was nothing to worry about. She was being plain paranoid. What could possibly happen? It was a hike up a mountain, and nothing more.

She realized she'd stopped moving for a moment, and Sam was getting way ahead of her. She hastened to follow him into the trees.

Chapter Ten

They walked briskly for a half hour, following the trail through the trees east of the lake. But when they came to the place where the path veered to lakeside, Sam went the other way. He strode cross-country for awhile until he reached a different trail. Delilah followed his lead, keeping her eyes open, noticing everything from the occasional deer tracks to the hot pink head of a snow plant poking through the mulchy ground.

It was good, she decided, to be out, moving around, *going* somewhere. It had been the right decision to follow him. She felt better with every step she took. Her fears *had* been groundless after all.

The new trail snaked around to the base of the mountain on the other side. There, it began to ascend on a series of switchbacks that took them ever higher, up the south slope of Ladyslipper Peak. As they climbed, the morning mists faded. An hour after they'd left the cabin, the day had warmed considerably and both of them had tied their sweatshirts and sweaters at their waists.

Delilah, no slouch when it came to hiking, found she had to push herself constantly to keep up with Sam. At one point, they took two steep grades in a row, up which Sam maintained a killing pace. Near the top of the second one, Delilah stopped for a moment to nurse a stitch in her side. By chance, she paused at a gap in the tall stands of evergreens which until then had blocked out a clear view of the sky.

Breathing hard, she rubbed her side. She glanced up— and saw the gray clouds rearing up in the sky to the west. The freshening wind blew in her face—from the same direction as the rising clouds.

Sam, who must have become aware that she had stopped, turned back to check on her. She called, "Wait up!"

He remained unmoving, waiting, as she hustled up the trail to join him. She hurried, not paying as much attention to the trail as she should have. She slipped on some loose shale just as she reached him. She teetered.

He warned, "Watch it," as he reached out and grabbed her.

She fell against him.

"Easy," he muttered, steadying her.

She gasped and gaped up at him, witnessing the swift heat that leapt in his eyes, knowing the answering fire inside herself—a flash fire, racing along every nerve, searing her down to pure desire in an instant.

The whole world surged into sharp focus. She was aware right then of *everything* at once—from the scent of dust and pine that surrounded them, to the call of a hawk in the distance, to the loose strands of her own hair, which the rough wind had whipped against her mouth.

His eyes seared through her. Time spun out. She continued to gaze up at him, so stunned by her own sudden, complete arousal that she couldn't move. The wind sang in the pines to the same wild tune as the blood roaring in her ears.

At last, she remembered herself. She put her hands on his chest. "S-sorry." She pushed, feeling the warmth of him, the strength, the call of his hips against her own....

He let her go. Her body, had it a voice, would have wailed in yearning protest. She looked down at the loose earth that had tripped her, and waited for some degree of composure to return.

When it did, she dared to look at him again. He watched her, through eyes that gave away nothing. She noticed that he had stepped away from her while she collected herself.

She gestured at the incoming clouds and raised her voice so he could hear her against the wind. "Storm coming."

"I know."

"Maybe we should go back."

He shrugged. "It's not cold enough to snow. And a few drops of rain won't kill us."

"It looks like more than a few drops of rain, Sam."

He didn't immediately reply but only stared at her. She saw the look in his eyes, a look turbulent as the wind that whipped all around them. She knew what he was thinking. He didn't want to go back to the cabin, be locked in there with her, until he absolutely had to. She couldn't blame him. She felt the same way.

"I'm going on," he said. "If you want to go back, fine. You know the way now."

She thought about that, as he went on watching her. About returning to the cabin alone, to wait for him.

About sitting there by the fire through the storm, wondering when he would return, trying to read that book she'd been trying to read since Saturday night.

No way, she thought grimly. She looked up at the sky again and decided he was right; it wasn't that cold. If they kept moving, they'd get wet—but nothing much worse.

"I'll go on with you!" she shouted into the wind.

"Why?"

Her gaze did not waver. "I *want* to."

He gave a slight nod. "Fair enough."

He took his canteen from the hook at his waist and drank from it. Then, wiping his mouth with the back of his hand, he held it out to her. She should refuse, she knew it. She had her own canteen. But her hand was reaching out of its own accord. She took the canteen, put her mouth where his had been, and felt the sweet water slide down her dry throat. Then she screwed the lid on and handed it back.

"Let's go," he said.

They went on as the wind swirled around them and the clouds rolled closer still.

The trees thinned visibly as they climbed, and the trail got rougher. There were places where erosion had worn it completely away. There, they clung to whatever rocks or hardy branches were handy and inched their way across. Often Sam, after crossing a rough spot first, would hold out a hand to her.

The first time she almost refused it, but he gave her a look that promised dire consequences should she spurn his aid and get herself in a bind as a result. She could almost believe that he might leave her there, and not help her climb out, should she go sliding down the hillside after scorning his assistance.

She took the hand he offered and felt the heat between them as if it were an electric current, shooting from his palm to hers, right up her arm, through her pounding heart—and down into her most private parts where it pooled and roiled and clamored for release.

More than once, she had that nagging feeling that she should go back. She ignored it.

There was no going back. Not now.

Something had happened. She wasn't sure what, exactly.

All she knew for certain was that now the whole world shimmered with life and beauty and a vibrant intensity. She felt truly free. It was glorious. She never wanted it to end.

The wind howled, as they came out into the open, above the thick close-growing belt of evergreens. Now, the carpet of fir and pine lay all around on the surrounding hills. But they climbed above the trees, in a place of stark, granite beauty, free of snow on this, the south side, because the springtime sun had done its work. Gradually, the only trees that grew were juniper and white pine, their gaunt pale branches twisted and gnarled by the unrelenting force of frequent winds.

Overhead, now, the once-blue sky was obscured by the agitated clouds. Sam and Delilah had been working their way up the granite shelves for perhaps fifteen minutes when the sky lit up, the thunder boomed, and the black sky above opened up with a hard, wet vengeance.

Delilah was crossing a rough spot when the rain began. She glanced up for a moment, and the water beat on her face, whipping and pelting at her with the aid of the torturous wind.

She opened her mouth. The heavy drops were cool and sweet. She smiled, glad with a fierceness that made her breath catch in her throat that she'd come, glad, as the rain rapidly soaked her to the skin, that she was whole and strong and climbing a mountain beneath a turbulent sky.

She looked down again, seeking a foothold to continue. Sam was waiting, arm outstretched.

She put her hand in his. The now-familiar shaft of heat and hunger arrowed up her arm and seared down to the core of her, building the growing need there higher still.

He pulled her across the slick space. She found her footing quickly. He released her and stepped back.

"This is crazy." His low words carried easily; the wind was at his back. "You were right. Let's turn around."

She was silent for a moment, within the rush and swirl of the wind. She felt a sinking feeling—of disappointment bordering on despair.

All her life, she'd been so careful, done nothing reckless, taken no crazy chances. Because she knew what crazy chances got a person: trouble. Her whole family was living proof of that.

But then her lifelong enemy had decided to pursue her. He'd chased. She'd run. As fast and hard as she could. But still he stayed on her tail. He'd forced her to come here—away from her carefully managed life where he'd had no chance of getting through to her—and he'd done his best to break her down.

Well, he hadn't done it. She had held out against him. But the stress had been torture. And now, here they were, on top of a mountain in a pounding gale.

And she felt free and strong and full of energy and heat. She felt gloriously, utterly, completely *alive*.

And she didn't want to go back down, not withou' reaching the top, going over the crest to lakeside, and witnessing the panorama of the lake and the wild land laid out before her while the wind tore her hair and the rain beat down upon her.

"How far is it?" she shouted.

"Not far."

"Let's finish it."

He shook his head. "It's foolish. We'll be drenched."

"We already are." For the first time, of her own accord, with no reason other than to communicate, she touched him. She laid her hand on his arm.

"Lilah..." He stiffened.

"Please, Sam. I want to reach the top."

He met her eyes. And he saw what had happened to her, the wildness in her, that she'd at last let come to the fore. She let him see it, *wanted* him to see it, to share her excitement, catch it like a fever and be willing to go on.

"You're crazy," he breathed.

"Yes. Yes, at last."

"All the way to the top?"

"Yes. You said it wasn't far."

"No. Not far. Not too far..." He touched her face. His rough thumb slid across her lips, back and forth.

"The top," she barely whispered the words, but he caught them, in spite of the wind and the din it made.

"The top," he said back to her.

She released his arm; his warm hand left her face. He turned to the upward trail. They went on.

He'd spoken truly; it wasn't far. Fifteen minutes at most, minutes that burned away to nothing beneath their clambering boots. They cut back to the east, then scrambled up a gully that already ran with water, drenching their boots.

After that, it was bare rock faces, and blasted trees. They struggled up the last of it, on all fours much of the way.

And finally, he hoisted himself over the top, and reached down a hand. She took it, he hauled her up—and into his arms.

She landed against the hard wall of his chest. She looked up. His eyes burned into hers. The world was a wild, wet maelstrom. All rational thought had fled.

He saw what he sought—call it surrender, call it the triumph of her own secret, reckless heart. His arms closed more tightly, stealing her breath and searing her senses. Her breasts grew tender, aching, and full. She boldly thrust them forward, and his big hand came up and cupped one.

He groaned. She sighed. He held her gaze captive, as he thumbed her nipple, teasing it thoroughly through the wet cloth of her nubby thermal shirt.

She said his name. He told her yes.

She reached up, grabbed his big head, and hauled it down so she could taste him, know him, as she had dreamed of knowing him in these last agonizing nights when he lay so close and yet a thousand miles away.

The rain beat down on them. His mouth, hot and hungry, so long evaded, finally sought, closed over hers.

They moaned in sensual glee, as one. His tongue teased her lips, she let it in eagerly, as he rubbed himself against her, and she rubbed back.

The kiss, wild as the storm, went on forever. Delilah, who had never known such delight, gloried in it. He kissed her mouth for a long, drugging eternity. Then he cupped her head in his big hands, and he kissed her cheeks, her nose, her temples, the wet coils of hair that had long ago pulled out of her braid and now lay plastered against her streaming face. He sipped the raindrops from her chin, and kissed her closed eyelids and the soft corners of her mouth.

And Delilah touched him, as he kissed her. She ran her questing hands over his shoulders, found the straps of the pack and slipped it off. It fell to the rock at their feet. Neither of them noticed. She stroked his back through his soaking shirt, loving his hardness, his strength, the bulk of him that seemed such a complement to her slender suppleness.

She was bold—fearlessly sensual. She felt the narrowness of his waist, the tight curve of his buttocks. She cupped his face as he did hers, and matched him, kiss for kiss.

At last, he whispered against her mouth. "Turn. Look."

She stilled, looked in his eyes, her arousal creating a sweet, heavy languor even beneath the fury of the storm.

He smiled down at her, a smile that said everything—what he would show her, the delights they would share.

"Kiss me some more, Sam. Like that. Like you just did."

"You're greedy."

She felt a quick flush of embarrassment.

He chuckled. "It's okay. I like you greedy."

"Oh . . ." She looked down.

"Don't."

She gazed at him once more.

"Better. Much better." He glanced up, at the angry, streaming sky. "We're going to have to head down soon. If this keeps up, we could actually end up in trouble."

She nodded gravely. She remembered that gully they'd climbed, already running with its own overflowing stream.

The dirt sections of the trail would turn to mud, and mud meant the possibility of slides.

"But first . . ." He let his voice trail off.

"What?"

He took her by the shoulders and turned her so she fitted back against his body. "Look."

Delilah blinked away the rain and did as he bid her.

"We're in the slipper," he said in her ear. "Ladyslipper Peak, remember?" She nodded, against his shoulder, liking the feel of his body, behind her, along the length of her, caressing every inch. He explained, "From down by the lake, if you look closely, you can see where we're standing. It looks like a lady's high heeled shoe."

"You'll have to show me."

He chuckled. "Don't worry, I will. If we ever get back down there."

She smiled, and armed away the water from her eyes. Then she gazed down over the glorious panorama spread out below.

On this side, the cliff beneath them tumbled away to nothing in a series of escarpments that eventually widened out at the base to huge boulders that were lapped by the waters of the now-turbulent lake. Across the lake, she could see the clearing, but mistily, through the rain. The cabin was barely visible, and even that was mostly because she knew where to look for it.

The whole scene appeared mysterious and magical, a universe of lake and tall trees—and tucked within it, a tiny fairy glen. The veil created by the rain made the clearing seem incorporeal, as if, should she blink, she might look again to find it gone.

Lightning glared in the sky and the loud crash of thunder came after. "Sweetheart. We have to go."

"I know." She accepted his judgment, and the endearment, without debate. Somewhere on the rocky cliffs of Ladyslipper Peak, the long pitched battle had ended. He had won—or had her wilder self?

For a time at least, in this place, she was his; he was hers.

She bent and took up the pack, helped him slip it on. They turned as one and started down.

Chapter Eleven

The rock faces ran with miniature streams, the dirt turned to slippery mud, and the wind seemed to grow to gale force, screaming like a banshee through the trees.

But somehow, they struggled down the unforgiving granite ridges, into the cover of the trees, and finally down to the base of the mountain, where they followed the trails that at last led to the clearing by the lake.

Nearly two hours after leaving the crest, they fell into the cabin, shivering uncontrollably and covered with water and mud. They pulled off their boots and shrugged out of their drenched outerwear right away, and then worked together to build up the fires, Delilah replenishing the stove and filling the pots with water to boil for bathing, and Sam laying and lighting the fire in the hearth. Soon enough, the cabin was filled with soothing heat.

Delilah, by the stove, looked over at Sam. He knelt by the fireplace on the rag rug, staring into the flames.

Overhead, the rain pounded on the roof, a loud, hollow drone. But Delilah thought of silence, of the waiting stillness between them, beneath the roar of the storm outside and the crackle of the fires in the room.

She stood very still, in her muddy clothes, looking at his back as he bent before the fire. And then she went to him.

He looked up at her, his gaze taking in the whole of her. She knew he could see the pebbling of her nipples beneath her clinging shirt. The thought excited her, and she found, incredibly, that she could let herself feel that excitement, accept it, even revel in it.

The excitement had a taste to it, a sweet taste, like the taste of Sam's mouth on hers....

He said, "You want me, Lilah."

It was the same challenge he'd tossed at her more than once before. Now, strangely, it didn't even occur to her to try to deny its truth.

"Yes."

He reached up, hooked a finger through her belt loop, and slowly pulled her down, so she kneeled, as he did, before the fire. They faced each other.

His hand fell away. "As soon as the sun goes, the temperature will drop."

"I know."

"By morning, there'll be snow."

"Yes, probably."

"If we leave now, we could get out. Otherwise, we'll probably be stuck in here for a few more days."

"Yes."

"Yes, what?"

"Yes. I understand."

"Do you?" He reached out again, as if he couldn't help himself, and he brushed the tightened nipples of her breasts. She tensed, then relaxed, and let the pleasant,

teasing sensation have its way with her body. It felt as if—
the finest thread connected her breasts to her secret feminine heart. His touch tugged the thread. The feminine
heart of her opened, bloomed. . . .

With a small shrug of regret, he let his hand fall away.

"I'll take you back now," he said quietly, "if you want
to go. The bargain we had is met."

She frowned, confused. "Met?"

"The deal. The bargain. I'm . . . satisfied. I'll take you
home now, if you want."

She understood. She allowed herself a secret smile.
"You'll take me home. Now."

"Yes."

"And Brendan can keep his truck."

"That's what I said." He sounded impatient; she suspected he was afraid she would leap eagerly to her feet and
start packing up her gear.

She shook her head slowly, letting her secret smile show.
"You have no mercy."

He didn't move. "You called me a manipulative snake
the other day. And maybe I have been. But not anymore.
If this goes any further, you'll never say you didn't have
a choice."

She took in a shaky breath. "Okay."

He glared at her. "Okay. Okay? What does that
mean?"

"Okay. Yes. I want to stay."

He made a low sound in his throat. And then he
grabbed her and pulled her to him. He cupped her head
in an unyielding hand. Right then, she couldn't have
pulled away if she'd wanted to. His mouth claimed hers,
hard and hot. She answered the kiss in kind. He touched
her breast again, a knowing, maddening touch, and she
moaned in delight.

But then he restrained himself. He pulled back, and turned her, so she lay between his thighs. For a long moment, they stared into the hungry flames of the fire he'd built.

She thought, then, of the little pouches she'd left in the drawer at home. She murmured, "I have nothing... for contraception."

He kissed her temple, smoothed the moist hair there. Then he helped her to sit, slipped out from behind her and padded on stocking feet to his gear. He fumbled in a pocket of one of the packs and returned to her, his hand outstretched. "It's okay. I do."

She looked at the pouches that were like the ones she'd left at home.

He chuckled ruefully. "You can't blame a guy for wanting to be prepared. Just in case his dream comes true..."

"No, Sam. I can't blame a guy for that...." She reached for him, he came down to her, turning her toward the fire again.

She leaned back, so she lay across his lap. He cradled her head and began kissing her all over again, working her braid loose as his lips played with hers, then combing the wet strands with his fingers until they lay in snaky tendrils across his big thighs.

Then, very gently, he worked her clinging, still-moist shirt from the waistband of her jeans. He slid his rough and tender hand under there, and caressed her skin. Delilah sighed, and wriggled a little, eager as she had never imagined she would be to have a man stroke and touch her, and ready her for ecstasy.

He took the wet shirt and pulled it up and over her head. She raised her arms for him, so it would easily slide away. He took a moment to pull his own shirt off and away. Then he looked down at her once more.

He said, "Beautiful..." as he unhooked her bra and tossed it aside. Once she was bare for him, he lowered his mouth and kissed her, taking her breast into his mouth, sucking first gently and then more strongly, until she writhed and moaned for more.

Delilah lay stunned with delight as his hungry mouth began to wander, tasting her, knowing her. He nuzzled beneath the low curve of a breast, a place revealed now since she lay on her back across his thighs. He licked the bottom swell of that breast; his lips trailed up, and he took her nipple in his mouth once more.

Delilah groaned and clutched his head, her fingers threading through his long, wet hair, pulling out the band that held it back, combing through it, feeling it trail in heavy, moist strands over her belly and breasts, teasing the nipple he wasn't sucking on until his hand cupped it and tormented it the more.

Then he raised his head and spanned her waist with his hands. He stood her up, before him. Kneeling in front of her, his light eyes holding hers, his wild mane of hair falling on his bare shoulders so he looked more primitive and feral than ever, he unhooked her belt and unzipped her pants and then slowly, taking her panties as well, he skimmed down her jeans. She stepped out of them. He tossed them aside.

She stood before him in her socks alone. His gaze branded her.

"Sam?"

"Shh..."

He leaned forward a fraction. And he nuzzled her belly.

"Oh!" she gasped in delighted shock.

He kissed her there, then lower, parting her, and touching her most secret place with his hungry lips. She let him do that, *wanted* him to do that. She clutched his shoulders and pressed herself toward him, and he went on kissing the womanly heart of her until she thought she would die of pure pleasure. She flung her head back and cried her ecstasy at the rafters, where the flameshadows danced and the rain beat in hard flurries with each wild gust of wind.

And then, in an instant, he was pulling her down. She lost the dizzying torment of his intimate kiss, only to find herself beneath him. She forced her heavy lids to open.

He looked down at her, his hair touched her breast. She saw his hunger. She saw what he wanted. And she wanted it, too. She reached for his belt, slipped the tip from the loop, the tongue from the hole. She had it undone in seconds. Then she undid his heavy corduroy jeans, pulling the fly apart quickly, shoving the jeans down his hard thighs and pushing his briefs away, too.

He sprang free. She touched him.

"Lilah..." He groaned the word at the ceiling, the tendons in his powerful neck standing out with the strain.

"Yes, Sam. Yes, now..."

He looked down at her again, and grabbed up one of the condoms waiting nearby. He slid it on, with her help.

Then she wrapped her legs around him. He thrust into her.

She let out a long, ecstatic cry.

"Look at me, Lilah." The command was low, weighted with heat.

She looked at him, into his light eyes that seared through her, knowing her, in a way no other human being ever had.

He moved out. She whimpered, a wordless plea for his return. He slowly filled her once more. Then he pulled back again. Her body yearned for his. He gave her what she was longing for.

And all the time, his eyes held hers, so there could never ever be a doubt of what they did with their bodies, here in the center of the storm.

"I've wanted this," he muttered, "dreamed of this..."

"Yes, oh, yes, I know..."

A squall of seeking wind hammered the rain against the little window on the west wall. Lightning crashed and thunder rolled.

Sam took her slowly, watching her build to a shattering fulfillment, holding himself on the brink until she thrust herself against him so hungrily that he knew she was nearing her final spiraling climb to ecstasy.

He levered himself up a little, and held still, so she could find her own rhythm, set her own pace. And when she pressed herself wildly against him, rubbed her soft body all over his, he knew he wouldn't last unless he did something quick.

He rolled, then, so swiftly that she cried out. And then she was on top.

"Oh, my!" She looked down at him, her hair curling in riotous coils all around her face. She looked wild and utterly free, her lips full and red from his kisses, her eyes glazed with her own need. "What is this?"

"Ride me," he instructed.

"Oh, my!" she murmured again. Then she raised herself up, experimentally. "My, my, my..." Slowly, she sank upon him again.

She let her head roll back; her wild hair fell away to expose the column of her neck. She moaned. He felt himself inside of her, sheathed by her—the most incredible creature he'd ever seen, something mythic and too beautiful to tame or possess.

And he knew, down in the deepest part of his being, that no one had ever seen her like this before. And, if he had a damn thing to say about it, no one else ever would.

This was the Lilah he had sought to free. His Lilah. His woman. Now. And from now on...

He thrust his hips upward, to give her more of him, and he gloried in the way she responded, moaning louder, thrusting back. Then she braced her hands on his chest, and she moved against him, faster and faster. Her dark eyes branded him, held him, a willing captive in her erotic spell.

She said, "Oh, Sam, I never thought, I never imagined..." and she couldn't finish. There were no more words.

Her eyes, drugged at last with her own mounting, expanding bliss, drooped shut. Her head fell back. She cried out something feral, something triumphant. Her body rose and fell in wild crescendo, gleaming in the fireglow.

He held her hips to stay with her and found he himself was caught up, rising, going over the edge of the world along with her. They cried out in unison. He thrust the final time into her and felt himself spilling, releasing, a last eternity of pleasure that went on and on, as her softness held him, took everything he had and gave it back to him tenthousandfold.

She fell across him, spent, her magnificent soft breasts crushed against his chest, her breath sliding over his skin, warm and sweet, one hand unconsciously stroking him at first, then lying limp as a fallen flower in the crook of his shoulder and his neck.

He touched her hair, a black tangle all around her head, smoothing it, and then idly caressing it, as he slowly came back to the world.

For a while he merely lay and memorized the feel of her body, limp and satisfied, on his. He heard the rain on the roof and the wind blowing wild outside. And then, lazily, he rolled his head toward the bubbling sound coming from the stove. The pots she'd set out were boiling. The big window, he noticed, was covered over with steam.

He chuckled then. "Sweetheart, we've really fogged up the place."

"Hmm?" She began caressing him again, touching his arm in long, trailing strokes. And then burrowing her fingers in the hair on his chest, making little cooing sounds.

Sam chuckled.

She asked, softly, "What?"

"Nothing. You."

She sat up on him, then. And she was smiling. "What about me, Sam Fletcher?"

"I just never thought I'd see the day, that's all." He grinned back at her, thinking that he'd wanted her to smile for him for how long now? And now she had.

"The day that what?" she prompted. Her full breasts tempted him. He touched one, a feather-light caress. She hitched in a kindled breath.

"This day," he explained. "You and me, together."

She bent and kissed him. "Well, Sam Fletcher. You *have* seen it. And guess what?"

"Yeah?"

"So have I."

"Surprised?"

She tipped her head, considering. "A month ago, I never would have believed it. But lately..."

"What?"

"It started to seem . . ."

"Yeah?"

"Inevitable, I guess." Her expression changed. The firelight licked across her skin, picking up the sheen from the sweat of their lovemaking. Her hair foamed out around her face, a veil of tangled ebony. She looked wild and pagan—and far away from him.

Sam, watching her, found he didn't like that faraway look. He didn't like it at all. "What's wrong?" he demanded. "What is it?"

"Nothing." The look was gone. She smiled down at him once more. She bent her head and kissed him, a sweet, soft brushing of her lips on his.

Then she slid to the side. He sat up for a moment, to get rid of the condom. Once that was taken care of, he went to the bed and came back with the spare blanket. After that, he opened his sleeping bag and laid it out on the rug for them to lie on. He stretched out again. She lay beside him, between him and the fire and he settled the blanket over them. For a while, neither spoke. There was the rain and the fire and the occasional caress, a smile and an answering look.

Finally, across the room, a pot bubbled over, the water hissing and popping as it hit the scorching stove top.

"We can have our baths," she remarked. "The water's boiling."

He reached for her. "The water's not the only thing that's hot. Come here."

Eventually, they got up from the floor and went to bathe, a wholly enjoyable process now that there was no need for either of them to go outside in the storm and wait until the other was through.

They mixed the boiling water with cold, and took turns washing each other, a marvelously sensual experience—not to mention revitalizing.

After that, they both realized they were starving. They prepared dinner, and sat down to eat in a shared mood of quiet congeniality. They cleaned up afterwards, as darkness fell. They turned on the light and Sam set up his improvised woodworking shop and began boasting the head of the mountain lion.

Delilah at last allowed herself to ask the thousand and one questions about his woodworking tools and the whole process of carving that she'd been dying to ask these three days. He answered them all.

And then, later, as they spread his sleeping bag on the bed for a sheet and laid hers over it as a blanket, Sam suddenly went still.

"What is it?" she asked.

"Listen . . ."

"I don't hear anything," she said, and realized it was true. The wind had died down, and the rain seemed to have stopped some time ago. She couldn't have said when exactly.

He prompted, "Yes. Yes, you do. Listen."

She listened—and she heard it. Like a whisper, like a coat made of feathers, drifting slowly down . . .

"Snow."

He smiled and held out his hand.

They went to the big window together. Sam took a towel and wiped away the steam and like eager children they pressed their faces to the glass.

Delilah saw it, falling steady and thick.

Sam turned to her. He spoke with great solemnity. "Miss Jones, we are being snowed in."

She turned to him. "We might never get out."

"Oh, we'll get out. Eventually."

She looked at him from under her lashes. "But what will we do with ourselves . . . until then?"

He reached out and ran a finger down her neck, over the collar of the clean shirt she'd put on after their shared bath, to the soft swell of a breast. "I have an idea or two of how to pass the time."

"You do? Show me . . ."

"I'll be glad to." And he did.

They woke the next morning to a world of white, and found it no hardship to remain in the cabin—except for necessary sojourns into the trees—the entire day, and all of Friday as well.

They ate and slept and made love when they felt like it. Sam worked on his carvings. Delilah whipped through that mystery novel which previously hadn't been able to hold her interest at all.

They avoided, by tacit agreement, talk of what would happen when they returned to North Magdalene. They talked instead of their pasts, of what had shaped them, made them each who they were.

Sam *had* been a preacher's son, the rebel of his family, the black sheep who left home the day he graduated from high school and never went back. His father had been dead for fifteen years, but he still had a mother and a sister somewhere down around San Diego.

Delilah confided what it was like for her, to lose her mother at eleven and be left with a houseful of troublesome males.

She confessed that things had not gotten really bad until her mother died. Before her mother died, the boys smiled a lot. They'd always made trouble, of course—that was bred into the Jones boys from their rapscallion father. But somehow, Bathsheba could always work the troubles out.

That was what Bathsheba Jones had been: a miracle-worker. Doing wonders daily that no one ever knew about—until she was gone. Oggie had always been a borderline case, but somehow Bathsheba made their lives work. And then she died. And nothing was the same. Delilah had tried in vain to take her place. But she'd only botched things up, ending up in screaming battles with her brothers, who weren't about to be told what to do by *anyone,* let alone their bossy sister.

Sam interrupted then. "Your brothers worship you." He chuckled. "Usually from afar, since you won't let them get near you anymore."

"Well, what can they expect? Look what happens when I *do* get near them—I end up wagered to you for a week." She playfully punched his shoulder.

He grabbed her and wrestled her to the rug. Then he kissed her and she kissed him back, and neither of them felt much like talking for a while.

They did the chores together smoothly, as they'd done before, but now they both wore smiles and the words they shared were tender ones. And they each took pleasure in doing little things for the other. She repaired the rag rug that had come partly unbraided. He gave her the coyote and the mountain lion to add to what they'd both started to think of as her "menagerie."

Delilah admired both carvings and stroked them with loving hands. She marveled that less than a week ago she'd told herself she wouldn't keep the wooden creatures he'd left on her windowsills. It seemed impossible to imagine such a thing now. She would never give those beautiful animals up. Never in a million years. . . .

Saturday morning dawned crystal clear. By noon, the temperature was in the high sixties in the sun, and most of the snow from Wednesday's storm had melted away.

Though neither of them spoke of it, their looming departure seemed to hang in the air between them. Tomorrow was Sunday, and they would be heading home.

After lunch, Delilah washed Sam's hair for him, trickling the water gently over his scalp, working up a good lather, and then rinsing it thoroughly and rubbing it dry.

She teased him, as she combed it out. "I don't know, Sam Fletcher . . ."

"*What* don't you know?"

"I don't know if I could ever get too serious about a man with longer hair than mine." She bent over and nuzzled his ear. "I'm a conservative woman."

He caught her arm, and kissed her, a kiss that lingered so long she almost forgot what she'd been saying by the time she went back to work on him with the comb.

His next words reminded her. "There are certain things a man won't do, sweetheart. Even to snare the woman of his dreams."

Delilah's heart leapt at that. To think that he—once her worst enemy—now called her his dream woman. And more amazing, that she delighted in hearing it. She teased him some more. "Right. As if getting a haircut were some major concession."

"For me it is."

"But why?"

"My hair's my freedom. I grew it long when I left home and it's been that way ever since."

"Because?"

"My father used to shave my head."

Her comb paused in midstroke. "Come on. You're exaggerating."

"No." His voice was flat. "He shaved it. With an electric razor, like they do to recruits in boot camp. He thought long hair was the devil's business. Once I pointed out to him that Jesus had long hair. I didn't sit down for a week after that, let me tell you."

"Oh, Sam. I'm sorry...."

"Why? It's not your fault." He said nothing for a moment. Then he seemed to shake himself and added, "Anyway, I left there as soon as I had my eighteenth birthday and a high school diploma."

She didn't want him to stop. "And then what?"

"I went to L.A., got a job as a janitor."

"And?"

"I worked for two years, living in a residence hotel in East Hollywood, taking classes at City College and saving every penny I could."

"What did you study? At college?"

"Shakespeare and jewelry making—with a lot of time out for partying hearty on cheap wine that wouldn't deplete my slowly growing nest egg." He chuckled. "I wasn't a real ambitious guy. I realize now I was suffering from a whopping case of low self-esteem. But back then, we didn't know a lot about self-esteem. Back then, they called guys like me losers—at least that was what my old man had been telling me I was for eighteen years. A bad boy, with Satan in his heart."

Sam's hair now lay smoothly on his broad shoulders. Delilah set down the comb and sat across from him at the table. He smiled at her.

She said, "You were twenty when you showed up in North Magdalene."

"Yeah."

"So. What happened. How did you get there?"

"Well..."

"Honestly, Sam. Don't tease me. I want to know."

"It's nothing exciting."

"Just tell me. Please."

"I never could say no to you when you say please. You say it so seldom...."

"Sam!"

"All right, all right. I bought myself a present for my twentieth birthday—you remember that old van?"

Delilah nodded.

"Well, I bought the van, and I took what was left of the money I'd saved from working, and I got in that van, and I started driving. I drove north. And ten hours later, I came to this little bend-in-the-road town."

"North Magdalene."

"You got it. I parked on the side of the road and I went in the bar, where I met an old geezer named Oggie Jones." He gave her a telling look. "He did ask for my ID, by the way. And when I gave him a phony story, he threw me out. But. As luck would have it, I met a guy on the sidewalk right away, a guy named Jared Jones, the bar owner's son. Poor Jared. He was depressed because his wife had just kicked him out—"

"For the umpteenth time," Delilah couldn't resist pointing out.

"Jared had a bottle," Sam went on without missing a beat. "He *didn't* ask for ID. And he was willing to share."

"How heartwarming."

"Ah, Delilah. You have no idea what it's like when a lonely man at last finds a friend."

"I can imagine.... So you remained in North Magdalene."

He nodded. "Why would I leave? I found my substitute family in your dad and your brothers. And I found my dream."

"And exactly what was your dream?"

"Well, first it was gold. I got a taste of gold fever."

Delilah made a scoffing noise. Except for college and her stint as a student teacher, she'd lived in the gold country all her life. She knew that gold fever was mostly an affliction of greenhorns. Men who hung around the hills a little knew better. Few people got rich anymore mining for gold.

He smiled, and shrugged. "Hell, I was a kid," he said, in explanation of his own innocence then. "And it was damn good to have a dream at last. I bought my dredger—"

"And staked your claim at *my* special place."

"I know." He looked appropriately contrite. "I never gave the tender feelings of a motherless fourteen-year-old a thought. I was obsessed with the idea that I was going to make my fortune. And by the time I realized I wasn't going to find any nuggets the size of my fist, I was already making jewelry and selling it out of the van."

"You found another dream," she said softly.

"That's right. One I could really live with. I opened my store eventually, and I built myself a house. It is a fact that for a few years, I drank a lot. And I got in fights. I made trouble."

He reached across the gouged surface of the rough table and took her hand. He gave it a squeeze. Delilah squeezed back. He continued, "But slowly, as the years passed, as I built my business and started to feel like I belonged where I was, I began to believe my father just might have been wrong. I wasn't a loser, and the devil had no permanent claim on me after all." He paused then. "You hear what I'm saying, Lilah?"

She nodded, wondering why he suddenly seemed so intent.

"I own a store and a house and this ten acres by the lake that my father left to me when he died—along with a note saying I was still his son, in spite of my devil ways."

"Oh, Sam..."

"I'm a man of property, a respected member of my community."

"You are. I know you are."

"I'm not a bad catch, if you know what I mean."

Delilah looked at him, at his handsome face and his long red-gold hair, at his powerful torso and his muscular bare arm that was stretched across the table to her. And she knew, with equal parts joy and despair, exactly what was coming.

"I'm good enough for the schoolmarm."

"Sam..."

His hand tightened on hers, until his grip was almost painful.

She winced. He held tighter.

"So marry me, Lilah. Marry me tonight."

Chapter Twelve

Delilah stared at him, across the table. She hadn't expected this, she hadn't expected *anything*, really. She'd been purposely living for the moment only, not letting herself think what might happen next week—or even tomorrow.

"Well?" he demanded, still crushing her hand.

"Oh, Sam..."

"What?"

"Well, Sam, I..."

He waited, his fervent expression fading.

"Sam, I just think..."

"You think what?" He released her hand, then, and pulled his own back to his side of the table.

She faltered on. "This is so sudden...."

"It isn't sudden to me."

"Well, I mean, we haven't talked about marriage before."

"I know. So let's talk about it now. Marry me. Tonight. We can pack up and head out right away, be in Reno before sunset. We'll get married, spend our wedding night in a good hotel, and then go back to North Magdalene in the afternoon tomorrow just like we planned so you won't have to miss even a day of school."

Delilah bit the inside of her lip, as it came home to her that the wagered week really was coming to an end. She'd be behind her teacher's desk at school just forty-eight hours from now.

Of course, she'd known they were going back tomorrow, but she'd purposely not been thinking about it. Her life back home seemed far away, almost unreal, eclipsed by the immediate reality of the special and secluded world she and Sam had created since the day on the mountain.

She winced as she thought of home, of what it would be like, when they returned to North Magdalene together—that crazy Sam Fletcher and the schoolmarm, Miss Jones. Of Nellie and Linda Lou, and how they loved to burn up the phone lines at even the slightest hint of scandal.

Sam said, "Forget about them. Think about us."

Delilah blinked. "What do you mean?"

"You know what I mean. You're thinking about home. About what people will say. I can see it in your face."

She shook her head, and felt the guilty flush that turned her cheeks hot. "No..."

His gaze was level. "Don't lie to me, Lilah. We don't need lies between us. We've got something better than lies."

Delilah looked down at her hands, ashamed. "All right. Yes. I was thinking of what it will be like, going home."

"Look at me."

She lifted her head and met his eyes.

He said, "You'll find that out when we get there."

She forced a brave smile. "I know."

"Then let it go for now."

"All right."

"Let it go and answer my question. Will you marry me?"

"Oh, Sam..."

"You said that already."

Delilah couldn't sit still. She got up and went to the big window and looked out at the mountain. Most of the snow had melted away in the last few days, but near the crest, glittery fingers of white still filled every gully and crevasse.

She heard Sam rise from the table and approach her. Then his arms came around her. With a sigh, she leaned back in them.

"You never showed me the slipper," she said.

He chuckled, the sound low and good against her back. She felt him relax a little, and was glad. He spoke softly, close to her ear. "See the big round boulder balanced on the ledge about three-quarters of the way to the top?"

She nodded.

"Pretend there's a line straight up from there." He pointed then and she drew a bead on the summit using his finger for a sight. "See it?"

"Yes—yes, I do." She smiled. It was so clear, now she'd found it, the sharp shelf that looked like a pointy toe, the spike in the rock that could have been the high heel, the sloping ridge that formed the instep.

She saw the place where they'd stood in the storm, that high spot that made the cradle where the heel of the lady's foot would rest. It was there that she'd kissed him for the first time, and accepted what would happen when they reached the haven of the cabin once more.

Sam made his demand again. "Marry me."

With him so close, pressed up against her, it was hard to think of anything but him, and what they'd shared, and could go on sharing—for the rest of their lives. Of his hands on her body, his smile across a room, of the way they got in and took care of what needed to be done, side-by-side.

Considered in the light of their commonality, his proposal was more than tempting. But he was pushing her so hard and so abruptly; that bothered her. And there was another thing that disturbed her, too.

He said he wanted to marry her right away—but he hadn't said a thing about love.

But then, to be fair, neither had she.

And, now she was down to it, *did* she love Sam?

He growled in her ear. "Say yes."

"I'm thinking."

"You think too much."

"If you wanted some brainless fool, you wouldn't have gone after me."

"Point taken. Now tell me you'll marry me."

She turned in his arms. "Why?"

That gave him pause. "Hell and damnation, Delilah."

She pushed him away. "Don't swear at me, answer me. Why do you want to marry me?"

He dragged in a breath. "Because we're good together. And I want us to go on being good together, from now on."

"Fine. What else?" She waited, refusing to simply ask the question, Do you love me? and be done with it. She was like any other woman. She wanted words of love, and she wanted them because he chose to say them—not because she'd asked for them.

But he looked totally flummoxed. "What do you mean, what else? What else is there?"

"Oh for heaven's sake, Sam."

"You're mine," he said flatly. "I want the whole damn world to know it."

Delilah felt like screaming. This was getting worse instead of better. "Great. 'You're mine,'" she imitated his possessive words. "You sound like one of my brothers, talking to one of their wives."

"I *am* like your brothers. I've never denied it. I've read a few more books than any of them, maybe, spent a little more time figuring out what I want from life and then going after it. But make no mistake. In the ways that really matter, Jared and Patrick and Brendan and I are all brothers under the skin. We've all got our wild sides. And we've all been looking for the right woman—and scared to death we'd find her."

He came at her again, his jaw set, his eyes lit with a reckless light. She backed up, and felt the sink rim behind her. He put his hands on either side of her, imprisoning her there. "There's nowhere to run, sweetheart. For either of us. I've found the right woman for me—you. And you scare the hell out of me. That's a pure fact. But I won't let you go."

She looked up at him, trying to understand. "*I* scare *you?*"

He nodded. "You bet, sweetheart. I said you were mine. But you didn't let me finish..."

"Y-yes?"

"I'm also yours. At your mercy. You could really hurt me, if you wanted. Because I'm open to you."

"Oh, Sam..." She reached up, touched his lips, felt his breath on her skin. "I would never hurt you. I swear. I... I love you."

The words passed her lips on a sigh. And she had no wish whatsoever to call them back. Because she knew they were true. Of all the sweet, gentle men she might have chosen, it was this wild, troublesome one she would have. She was his, he was hers. She loved him. That was that.

"Then marry me," he said.

She lifted her chin. "All right."

He didn't move for a moment. Then he loosed a triumphant shout that echoed to the rafters. And after that, he pulled her close for one of those kisses that always obliterated rational thought.

She held back. "But not tonight."

He tensed. "When?"

She laid down her terms. "We will be married in the North Magdalene Community Church—and my scamp of a father will give me away."

He looked pained. "Lilah, I have not set foot in a church in twenty-two years."

"It is not God's fault that your father was...misguided. But be that as it may, you are allowed your own beliefs, and you may wrestle with them on your own. However, this is my wedding, too. And I will have it in my church."

"Lilah—"

"I'm not finished. Let me see. I'm sure we can arrange the small ceremony for some time in the next few weeks. And during that time, you can contact your sister and mother and see if they want to attend."

"But I haven't spoken to either of them in years."

"Precisely my point. They're your family. And *my* family too, once we're married. I want to get to know them, if they want to know me at all."

"All right," he said. "Fine."

"What does that mean?"

"It means I agree to your terms. Though it would be a hell of a lot simpler to—"

She touched his mouth again. "Life is not always simple, Sam Fletcher."

His gaze was hot and intense. "It's settled then. You've promised to marry me. You won't find some way to back out once we get home?"

She felt uneasy again. He really did seem to be pushing awfully hard about this. "Do you think I won't keep my word?"

"I think lots of things can happen between now and a church wedding."

"They won't. I've promised. We'll be married."

"Good. Now let me show you what else you can do with those lips, besides giving orders."

"Oh, Sam..."

He grinned. "Oh, Lilah..." The teasing words were husky.

He pulled her close then, and she knew he would not be denied or put off this time. That was okay with her; she didn't want to put him off.

His mouth covered hers with a hot, rash intensity that stole all thought away. Delilah surrendered to his touch, eagerly tangling her clutching fingers in his hair.

He groaned into her mouth, and began tugging her shirt open. After that, he made short work of her bra. He kissed her breasts, one and then the other, standing there before the window, with the afternoon sun slanting in to bathe them in its glow.

And Delilah gloried in it, giving back his hungry touch in kind, feeling his hardness against the cove of her womanhood, rubbing her body against his, driving his passion higher still.

He muttered her name against her heated skin, and then began working at the clasp of her belt. She understood, and helped him, and then set to work on his clothes as well.

Soon enough, they stood before the window naked. He left, and came back with a condom. She slid it on. He lifted her. Her legs clasped his hips and then he was inside her, thrusting, demanding every bit of her.

And she gave herself up willingly, crying his name, as he moved first slowly and deeply, and then faster and faster within her. She held him, as he held her, deep and fast and hard. She cried out his name as she went over the edge and then stayed with him, as he found his release as well.

Sweating, satiated, they remained upright for endless moments, holding onto each other for dear life. And then at last he carried her, staggering a little, to the bed. They fell across the mattress, arms wrapped around each other. He held her close against him. She closed her eyes and buried her head against his neck. He nuzzled her hair and whispered her name.

She could *feel* his love, she told herself, beyond his desire and the commonality they shared. True, he had not actually said the words. But he'd said other words that amounted to the same thing.

She was sure he loved her. Why else would he want to marry her? Of course he loved her. She would allow no doubt in her heart. It was just a matter of time before he told her so.

He moved then, to remove the condom and then flip the blanket over them. She snuggled up against him and let the sweet languor that came after lovemaking draw her down toward the edge of sleep.

She hovered at the rim of consciousness for a timeless while, thinking that soon they would get up, maybe go out for a walk, then come in and make dinner. Then he'd work on his carving for awhile; she might read.

They'd go to bed, make love again, slowly and tenderly. And then go to sleep.

And when they woke up, it would be time to get ready to go home to the real world, where she would start planning her wedding—to wild Sam Fletcher....

Feeling suddenly restless, she rolled over.

"Lilah?" Sam muttered groggily, reaching for her. "You all right?"

"Fine," she told him softly. "Go to sleep."

He snuggled up against her. She held him and lay still. But she found she wasn't sleepy; her sweet lassitude had fled.

They spent the next morning packing up and closing up the cabin, and they were ready to leave at noon. Delilah climbed into the Bronco beside Sam and spared a last, misty glance across the lake at Ladyslipper Peak before they drove away.

"Sorry to leave?" Sam asked from the driver's seat.

"Yes," she confessed. "I guess I am."

"Don't worry. We'll be back."

She smiled. "I'll keep that in mind."

He shifted the truck into gear and turned around, then headed into the trees the way they had come seven days ago.

It was a pleasant, companionable ride home. Delilah looked out the window at the trees and the mountains and gave Sam a warm smile each time he glanced her way. She wondered a little about how her plants had held up, how things had worked out between Brendan and Amy, but she carefully avoided thinking about anything else.

Things would work out. She and Sam would take it all one step at a time.

They stopped in Grass Valley on the way, and bought groceries. Sam suggested they fill either her refrigerator or his. No need to stock two kitchens, since they were together now.

Delilah stopped dead in the aisle. It hadn't occurred to her that they'd be *living* together before the wedding. But apparently, he assumed they would.

He was pushing the cart, and had rolled on to the canned tomatoes before he realized that she was still back with the green beans.

He turned. "Lilah? What's the matter?"

She had a painfully clear image of Nellie, of the way her face would look when she heard the news that Delilah and Sam Fletcher were cohabitating.

It shouldn't matter. Delilah knew it. It was small-minded of her that she *let* it matter. But it did.

"Lilah?" Sam was looking worried.

She hurried to catch up with him. "Sam..." A lady with a toddler in her cart rolled by. Delilah waited until she had passed.

"What? What is it?"

"Sam. I just can't do it. I just can't."

"What?" His eyes bored into her. "*What* can't you do?"

"Live with you before we're married. I know it's old-fashioned. And hypocritical, too. But I'm the school-teacher, and I—"

"You're right," he said. "It is hypocritical."

"Sam, please—"

"But I understand your position."

She gaped at him. "You *do?*"

"You think you have a certain image to uphold."

"Well, I do. I *do* have an image."

"An image you'd have no problem with whatsoever if you'd only marry me right now."

"Oh, Sam..."

"So let's go to Reno."

"Sam..."

"All right, all right. Have it your way. We'll buy food for *both* houses... and that wedding better be coming up pretty damn quick."

She reached up and kissed him, paying no attention to other passing shoppers who eyed them with knowing smiles. "Thank you."

"Come on. Let's get the milk and eggs."

They pulled up in front of her house at around four. Her little hatchback waited on the sidewalk, looking dusty from its week without use.

Her house had been built in the twenties, without a garage. Delilah found herself thinking of how she'd always planned one day to add one. It occurred to her right then that she probably never would. Sam's house was newer, nicer and bigger than hers. They'd be more likely to end up living there. The thought made her feel sad, somehow, that the dreams of her single life no longer amounted to much.

"Lilah?" Sam was smiling at her, leaning an arm on the steering wheel. "Why the glum look?"

She shook her head. "It's nothing. Really."

"You sure?"

"Yes. Really. I'm sure." She opened her door and stepped down from the truck.

The afternoon sun was warm on her back. Here, in North Magdalene, true spring had come. The grass was vibrant green, the trees had most of their leaves. Her

ses, in the small plot in front of the porch, were in full
oom, some of the petals fallen and curling on the grass,
nce she hadn't been here to rake them up.

At the lake, it had been different. There, the winter was
ly just coming to an end. The world had seemed an in-
nate, closed-in place. Just Sam and herself and the
bin, the mountain and the lake and the tall, silent trees
at whispered their windy secrets to each other, secrets no
her ears could hear.

She realized Sam had gotten out on his side and was at
e rear of the truck. He'd opened the back end, and was
atching her.

She caught his look, a waiting kind of look. Though she
w a question in his eyes, he asked nothing this time.

He said, "Let's get your things inside."

"Right. Good idea."

Within minutes, they had all her gear and groceries out
the truck and into the house. Then Sam said he ought
go on into town, check with Marty to see how the store
d fared in his absence, take his things to his house and
aybe pick up the mail.

They were in the kitchen by then, and Delilah was busy
tting the groceries away.

Sam said, "That is one fine-looking chicken," of the
d she was just pulling out of the grocery bag.

She gave him a look. "Translation—you want chicken,
s chicken. You want it tonight, and you're hoping I'll
lunteer to cook it."

"No woman has ever read my mind as well as you do,
eetheart."

She grunted. "Dinner's at six-thirty. Be here or be
ry."

"Yes, ma'am." He grabbed her and kissed her.

"Get my mail, too, would you?" She gave him t[]
combination to her mailbox.

He kissed her nose, hugged her close once more, a[]
then he was gone.

Delilah put the rest of the food away, then unpacked h[]
gear. She spared a moment to add the mountain lion a[]
coyote to the menagerie on the kitchen table, telling he[]
self that later she'd move them, perhaps put a few in ea[]
room, so she could enjoy Sam's beautiful gifts to her []
over her house. After that, she took the now-dry wat[]
trays out from under her plants, which all appeared []
have survived their week without care just fine. Next, s[]
indulged in a hot shower and changed into fresh clothe[]

By then, it was five, and time to get the chicken starte[]
So she washed it off, patted it dry, stuck some vegetab[]
in the cavity along with spices and a little salt, and pu[]
in the oven to roast.

The phone rang just as she was assembling the ing[]
dients for a salad. Delilah froze, with a bunch of radisl[]
in one hand, and a head of redleaf lettuce in the oth[]
The phone went on ringing.

Not many times in her life had she *not* wanted to []
something as much as she didn't want to answer t[]
phone. She knew who it would be: Nellie, or Linda L[]
or someone else wondering where in the world she'd b[]
for a week. Or worse, *knowing* where she'd been, a[]
dying to hear all about it.

The phone rang again. And again. And Delilah kn[]
that, while she could refuse to answer this time, []
couldn't go on not answering forever.

She was going to marry Sam. The truth would co[]
out. Might as well be open and aboveboard from the st[]

Delilah set down the lettuce and radishes and went[]
the phone in the living room.

"Hello?"

"Delilah? You're home. At last." The breathless voice belonged to—who else?—Nellie.

"Yes, I'm home."

"Are you all right? Did he . . . hurt you in any way?"

"Who, Nellie?"

"Why, that wild man, Sam Fletcher."

"So you know I was with Sam."

Nellie drew in a sharp breath. "Sam? You call him *Sam* now?"

Delilah sighed. "Nellie? Are you my friend?"

"Well, of *course* I'm your friend. . . ."

"Then will you stop making shocked little noises and tell me what is going on?"

Nellie was silent for a moment. Then she complained, "You could have said something, you know. You could have *confided* in me. What are friends for, after all?" Nellie paused, but not long enough for Delilah to actually answer her. "And why should I tell you what's happened since you left, you haven't told me a single thing about *anything*. And I was worried sick about you, too. Linda Lou and I didn't know what to do when you didn't show up for church and then didn't answer your phone for two days. I finally had to see Sheriff Pangborn—and you know how *he* is."

After a quick gulp of air, Nellie imitated the Sheriff's laid-back manner. "'Now, Miss Anderson, don't you go havin' a coronary on me there. I'm sure Miss Jones just forgot to mention she was going out of town for awhile, that's all. She'll turn up.' Can you believe that? 'Turn up,' he said, like you were something missing from a kitchen drawer or something. I vow, I have no idea who keeps electing that man. But I stood firm. And finally he agreed to check with those brothers of yours and your father and see if they knew anything."

Nellie paused, but only for breath. "And he did. And it turned out that little Amy knew exactly where you were, though she asked the sheriff not to tell *me*, only to say you were okay, because *you* had asked that she say nothing unless she had to. I was never so hurt in my life."

"Nellie..."

But Nellie was not through. "And then, of course, it ended up being spread all over town anyway. I think the sheriff told his wife, Leona, and Leona just couldn't resist whispering it to Marcella Crane, and, well, you know how these things are. Now everyone knows, about the card game and the wager of that truck of Brendan's, and how Sam Fletcher said he'd take a date with you instead. But then that rotten rascal wasn't satisfied with only a date, oh no, he had to sweep you away to some... wilderness area, I think everyone said and—"

Nellie went on talking, but Delilah missed what came next, because someone knocked on the front door. Delilah knew a massive feeling of relief. No matter who it was, it couldn't be worse than this.

"Nellie..."

"—and everyone over at that bar of your father's has gone—"

"Nellie."

"—insane over this. You won't believe—"

"Nellie!"

She must have finally gotten through. Nellie hitched in a breath. "Yes? What? What is it?"

"There's someone at the door. I'll have to call you back."

"But—"

"Talk to you soon."

Nellie's voice babbled on as Delilah quietly cut off the connection.

The knock came again, more insistent this time. The blinds were drawn across the big window by the door, so Delilah, standing in the middle of the living room, had no idea who it could be. It was too early for Sam to be back. And besides, the door was unlocked. She had little doubt that Sam wouldn't hesitate to walk right in.

It was probably Linda Lou, she thought grimly, come to express her outrage at Delilah's actions right to her face. Oh well, she decided, straightening her shoulders and smoothing back her hair, she had never kidded herself that this was going to be easy.

The knock came again. "I'm coming!" she called. She strode across the room and pulled open the door.

Her second brother, Patrick, stood on the other side. He looked like he'd just lost a best friend.

"Sis, I've got to talk to you."

Chapter Thirteen

Delilah peered at her brother suspiciously. A week ago, in the middle of the night, she'd opened this door to find Brendan standing where Patrick stood now. Brendan, too, had said he *had* to talk. And later she'd promised herself she wouldn't get involved in her brothers' problems ever again.

But Patrick really did look miserable.

She asked in a wary tone, "What is this about?"

He looked around. "C'mon, sis. Have a heart. Not on the front porch. Let me in."

Delilah, still undecided, did nothing for a moment.

"Please, sis . . ."

"Oh, all right." She stepped back and he entered.

Then he just stood there, looking glum. Finally he wondered, "Got a beer?"

"I might, somewhere. Come on." She led the way into the kitchen, gestured at the table for him to sit, and then found a bottle of light beer in the back of the refrigerator. "Do you want a glass?"

He shook his head. "That's fine." He took the beer from her and had himself a long swallow. Then he set it down. "Thanks."

"It's okay. Now what's going on?"

He was staring at the carved figures, which still waited on the table. "Sam made those for you?" In spite of the rising inflection at the end, it was a statement requiring verification, not a question.

Delilah realized that, whatever rumors were flying around town, Patrick had heard at least a few of them. She began to suspect that this visit had something to do with Sam. The thought increased her uneasiness.

"Yes," she said cautiously of the carvings, "they're from Sam."

Patrick took another drink, then shook his head. "Hot damn. Everything changes, and that's a fact." He stretched his booted feet out in front of him and stared at the beat-up toes. Then he looked up at Delilah, his blue eyes—their mother's eyes—full of bewildered sadness. "A man can't count on anything to stay the same. Things I always would have sworn were impossible are actually happening. Things like you running off with Sam Fletcher, and Chloe dating some stranger...."

Delilah felt her uneasiness fade a little when he mentioned Chloe. Maybe this visit had nothing to do with her and Sam after all. Maybe Patrick had just decided he needed to talk about Chloe Swan and had chosen Delilah for a confidante. It didn't make a lot of sense; Patrick had never confided in her in their lives. But it was possible.

She volunteered, "Sam told me he saw Chloe at The Hole in the Wall with a man he'd never seen before."

Patrick nodded and took another drink of beer. "That was a week ago. She's been out with him twice since."

Delilah hid a knowing smile. "You're keeping an eye on her, are you?"

"Of course not. Chloe and I are...friends, everyone knows that. It's nothing more. It's never been anything more. I just, well, I just hope she knows what she's doing with that guy, that's all." Patrick began peeling the label off the beer bottle.

"You came here to talk about Chloe, then?"

"No. Not exactly. Chloe's just...on my mind, that's all. Like all the things lately that can't be counted on to stay like they were. Like my ex-wife moving to Arkansas and taking our two girls along with her."

That bit of news shocked Delilah. "She isn't."

"She is."

"But Patrick, I'm sure that has to be illegal, for her to take your children out of the state without your consent."

"So what am I going to do? Sue her from two thousand miles away? And is that going to be good for the girls, anyway? And besides," he confessed, "Marybeth said if I wasn't careful, she'd just ship those girls right back to me. And I could raise them on my own."

Delilah thought about that. Patrick's daughters were eight and ten. She couldn't in a million years see Patrick raising them alone. She decided to give no more free advice on this subject. She said, "I'm sorry, Patrick," and meant it.

"Hell," he replied. "It's all just part of what I was talking about. Nothing can be counted on anymore to stay the same."

Delilah sighed, knowing what he meant. She felt cast adrift herself, after that abortive phone conversation with

Nellie. She realized more and more all the time that, with Sam in her life, things would not be as they had been. She felt sympathy with her brother; she could see he was suffering from the way things were changing, too.

"Yes," she agreed softly, "things do change."

Patrick spoke to the beer bottle. "Like my sister, going off for a week with a man she's hated since the first day she met him."

Delilah heard the disapproval in his voice and did not like it. "Did you come here to lecture me, is that it? A heck of a lot of room you've got for lecturing *me*, Patrick Jones. You've hardly led a blameless life."

Patrick looked up sharply. "Look. This is no lecture. I just want to know..." He paused. His face went beet red. "I mean, he *forced* you to go, didn't he? What choice did you have? It was either that, or Brendan and Amy lost everything."

Delilah suddenly decided she should get going on the salad. She turned to the sink, and started washing her hands.

"Delilah?" her brother demanded. "You gonna give me an answer or not?"

She squirted out the liquid soap and began furiously lathering, as if she could wash Patrick's question away with a good scrub.

"Delilah?"

She knew she should just agree with him. What he'd said was only what she'd told herself; that she'd had no choice, for Brendan's family's sake.

But in her head she kept hearing Sam's voice. *If this goes any further, you'll never say you didn't have a choice....*

She pinned her brother with a piercing look, "He didn't drag me off. I agreed to go. I *had* a choice."

"Well. Fine. But you never would have gone if it hadn't been for the bind Brendan was in."

"That's true."

Patrick nodded, broke the hold of her gaze and stared at his beer bottle some more. "Are you glad you went, now it's over?"

Delilah ripped off a paper towel and dried her hands. "What are you getting at here, Patrick?"

"Well, sis, I don't rightly know how to say this..."

"I can see that."

"People are talking, about you two."

"So I've heard."

"And, over at The Hole in the Wall..."

"What?"

"Well, there have been bets placed."

Delilah's throat went dry. She tried clearing it, and when that didn't work, she stuck a glass under the tap and took a quick drink. When she felt she could speak, she said, "Bets? About me and Sam?"

Patrick looked out the window, at her liquidambar tree, with such avid concentration she would almost have thought he'd never seen a tree before. "Yeah. About you and Sam."

"Wh-What kind of bets?"

Patrick kept ogling the tree. "I put my money on you. I figured, if there was one thing that would never change in this world, it would be the way you hate Sam Fletcher."

"How many bets, Patrick?" Delilah's voice had acquired an edge. "And on what?"

Patrick glanced at her, winced, and then swiftly looked away again. "Two bets."

She waited.

He shot her another pained look, then began, "One on whether Sam would..." Patrick faltered and then forced himself to go on. "... get you in the sack, if you know what I mean."

Delilah stared out at the liquidambar tree herself for a while, until she thought she could speak without shrieking in mortified fury. Then she said in measured tones, "And the other?"

"Whether or not he's talked you into marrying him." Patrick sat up a little, probably feeling better now the bad news was out. "I put my money on you, like I said. I bet that you'd hold out. On both counts."

Delilah felt sick to her stomach. She'd known people would talk, but this was worse than her wildest nightmares. They'd actually been *betting* on the outcome of her wagered week with Sam.

And beyond her dismay, she was confused. The bets didn't add up, or at least not the second one. She could understand the wager on whether or not she and Sam had slept together. It was the kind of thing over which the yahoos at the bar would love to lay their money down. But the other bet, the bet on whether she'd said she'd marry him... who could have known that Sam was after marriage? She certainly hadn't, not until he'd asked her. And even then, she'd been surprised.

"I don't understand," she said carefully. "Who came up with the idea that Sam wanted to marry me?"

"Dad."

"Father?"

Patrick shot her a condescending glance. "Aw, c'mon, sis. You know how Dad hates it that you've never got yourself a man."

"So?"

"So he and Sam had a long talk about a month ago, one night after closing. He convinced Sam to go after you and get himself married to you. He's bet a thousand dollars that Sam proposed, and got you to say yes."

Delilah stared at her brother, thinking the best thing to do right now would be to tell him to leave. She was just asking for hurt to continue with this. But somehow, she couldn't stop. She demanded, "And just how is Father supposed to have convinced Sam Fletcher to go after me?"

Patrick granted her a pitying look. "You don't know, then? That bastard didn't tell you?"

"If I knew," she pointed out with great reasonableness, "would I be asking you?"

Now Patrick looked guilty. "No, no. Of course you wouldn't. Aw, sis. I'm sorry."

"You have as yet failed to answer my question, Patrick."

"Sis . . ."

"Answer. Now."

"Well." Patrick also appeared suddenly to have a dry throat. He coughed. Then he muttered, "It was a damn bribe, that's what."

"Father bribed Sam to marry me?" Her own voice sounded hollow, far away.

"You got it."

"With what?"

"The Mercantile."

"Father said Sam could have The Mercantile if he'd—"

"—Marry you. Right. Can you believe it? The Mercantile. *My* inheritance. *I* couldn't believe it. But when I asked our dear old Dad what the hell he was doing breaking his word to me, he winked and said 'Don't worry about that, boy, I always take care of my own. You'll get yours. You just sit tight.'" Patrick lowered his voice to a growl. "The lying old coot. I don't buy his promises for a New York minute. And that's why I'm here. Because I want you to know that I'm not putting up with this. I may have to stand by and watch Chloe wreck her life with some out-of-town stranger. I may decide it wouldn't benefit anyone to sue Marybeth about the girls. But you can be damn sure I'll sue my father if he thinks he can take back what he's promised me all my life just to buy a man for you!"

At last, Patrick fell silent. Delilah stood at the sink, gaping at him, realizing it was time to tell him that she'd heard enough. He could leave now. But her fickle voice had deserted her again.

"Sis?" Patrick was at last looking at her—staring at her, actually. "Sis, you all right?"

She managed to murmur, "I'm fine." She wasn't, of course. But no way would she admit that to Patrick.

"Aw, sis. You really do love that wild man, don't you?" The question was rhetorical and anyway, Delilah wouldn't for the life of her have answered it right then. Patrick continued, "Haven't you figured out that a guy like that is no good?" He gave a wry chuckle. "Especially after growing up with three brothers just like him?" Delilah turned away. Her brother said, "Aw, sis. I really messed up here, didn't I? You poor kid. I'm sorry...."

She didn't want that. She didn't want anybody feeling sorry for her. She drew on all her reserves and said, "Thank you for the information, Patrick. You can be sure I'll make use of it. And now you may go."

"But, sis..." Patrick had started to look sheepish. "Look. I guess I went a little far there with that remark about Dad buying you a man and I—"

"Stop it, Patrick. That's enough."

"Oh, hell."

"Would you please go?"

"But—"

She took a few steps in his direction, to let him know she meant business. "Just go, Patrick." She had her arms tightly folded under her breasts and she gestured with her chin in the direction of the door. "Now."

"Okay, okay..." He stood up and backed out of the kitchen toward the living room. "Sheesh," he said as he reached the front door. "Lately, I can't open my mouth without sticking my size ten in it..."

"Goodbye, Patrick."

At last, he opened the door and went through it, closing it soundlessly behind him.

When he was finally gone, Delilah hadn't the faintest idea what to do with herself, so she just stood there, between the counter and the kitchen table, staring into space and trying, though her heart balked at the prospect, to come to grips with the information her brother had just provided.

The thought she kept having, the really hurtful thought, was that if what Patrick claimed was true, then all the strange contradictions in Sam's behavior would finally make sense. From the abrupt and relentless way he had pursued her, to his insistence that she marry him in Reno—before they came home and she had a chance to learn that it was more than a lifetime of love he was after from her.

In fact, she could see now, love had had nothing at all to do with any of it. Sam had never said he loved her. And at last she was beginning to understand the real reason for that.

But then, with a rush of emotional pain that felt as real as a blow to the stomach, she thought of his kisses, of his tenderness, and his light eyes looking into hers, as he said,

We don't need lies between us. . . . You could really hurt me, because I'm open to you. . . .

All that, all they'd shared, had been true, she was sure of it. Okay, perhaps her experience with loving a man had been limited. But her instincts about what was truth and what was a lie couldn't be that bad.

Or could they?

For twenty years she'd had sense enough to keep clear of Sam Fletcher. She hadn't trusted him an inch. Over the last month, she'd changed her mind about him, since he'd kept after her constantly until she finally broke down.

But which perception of him was the true one? The one she'd held for twenty years, or the one he'd *forced* on her in the last few weeks?

Another arrow of hurt pierced her right to the heart, doubling her over. She dropped to the chair Patrick had vacated. She had to wait, till he came back, she knew it. She had to wait and be fair and ask him if what Patrick said was true.

She reached out and picked up the exquisite wooden doe he'd left on her windowsill. She stroked its smooth flanks.

No, she decided. He couldn't have taken a bribe from her father to marry her. Sam would never, ever do something like that.

Or would he?

Chapter Fourteen

Something was bothering Marty.

Sam sensed it the minute Marty joined him at the store, which had been closed to the public for the holiday. But Marty didn't say what was bothering him until forty-five minutes later, when the two of them were sitting side by side on folding chairs going over the receipts.

After several injured glances, Marty finally came out with it. "Mr. Fletcher, how come you didn't tell me you were going off with Miss Jones?"

Sam eyed his clerk uneasily. "Who says I did?"

"Come on, Mr. Fletcher. It's all anybody in town has talked about since the middle of the week."

Sam shook his head. He supposed he'd expected as much. "What are you complaining about, then? You found out soon enough."

"Well." Marty really sounded hurt. "It would have been nice to have been told by you. It would have been nice to know you trusted me."

"Look, Marty. It was between Miss Jones and me. I didn't think it was any of your concern."

"Well, you were wrong. It did concern me."

"How?"

"Have you talked to Jared Jones yet?"

"No." Sam closed the ledger; it was in fine shape anyway. "Jared's in town?"

"He was, as of yesterday morning."

"And?"

"He came looking for you."

Sam smiled, thinking of his old friend. "Jared and I go way back."

Marty shook his head. "Mr. Fletcher, you're not getting my drift here. Jared Jones wasn't behaving like he wanted to talk over old times. In fact, he grabbed me by my shirt and lifted me off the floor and said if I knew where the hell you'd headed out to with his sister, I'd better say now, or I'd never be a father in this lifetime."

Sam was quiet, digesting this. Then he asked, "Did you tell him?"

"Hell no. I *like* this job."

"Still got your manhood?"

"So far, yes, sir, I do."

"Thanks, Marty," Sam said, wincing at the thought of what might have happened if Jared Jones had appeared at the cabin in a rage. He realized he probably should have expected this. Of the three Jones boys, Jared had always seen himself as the protector of his sister's virtue. Just because Sam and Jared had always been close friends, didn't mean Jared would think Sam good enough to get near Delilah.

"What will you do now?" Marty asked.

Sam considered the question and couldn't immediately
come up with anything too satisfying. In the old days Sam
and Jared, side-by-side, had taken on ten fools in a bar in
Redding over some minor insult that Sam couldn't even
remember now. When the dust cleared, Sam and Jared
had been the ones still standing. Sam wasn't sure who'd
end up upright if the two of them went at each other. He
fervently hoped he wasn't about to find out.

Marty coughed nervously. "Er, Mr Fletcher?"

Sam remembered he'd been asked a question. "Look.
Don't worry, Marty. Everything will be all right."

Marty didn't consider that any kind of an answer. "But
what will you *do?*" he demanded again.

"If I can get him calmed down, I'll talk to him. The
problem will be that Jared's not a very good listener when
he's mad." This was the understatement of the year, Sam
admitted to himself. He decided not to dwell on that,
though. He finished on an upbeat note. "But as soon as
Jared sees what's really going on, he'll settle down."

Marty just couldn't help but ask, "And what *is* really
going on, Mr. Fletcher?"

"Nothing. Everything is fine."

"Er, could you be a little more specific, Mr. Fletcher?"

"Hell, Marty."

"C'mon. For the guy who risked future generations of
Santinos just to keep your whereabouts a secret..."

"Hell."

"Yeah?"

"We're getting married."

Marty's brown eyes grew wide. "No kidding? You and
Miss Jones." He settled back in his folding chair. "Well,
ain't that a kick in the pants.... When's the wedding?"

"In a few weeks, over at the Community Church."

"Well, what do you know."

Sam allowed himself a smile. "Yeah. It's a crazy world, isn't it?"

Marty grinned right back, and then moved a little closer. "Mr. Fletcher?"

"Yeah, what?"

Marty lowered his voice, his eyes on Sam's hair. "You want to really thrill Miss Jones, you know what to do."

Sam gave the boy a forbearing look. "What is it with you, Marty? You think just because your father's the barber you can't rest until every guy in town's got a buzz cut?"

"Look how far you got with her once you got rid of that beard."

"She likes my hair," Sam muttered, remembering the feel of her tender hands, massaging his scalp when she gave him that shampoo, and of the way she combed through it with her fingers when they made love. At the same time he tried to forget how she'd teased him about cutting it, saying she'd never take him seriously while he had hair longer than hers.

Marty wore a sagacious expression. "Yeah, but if you're gonna end up having to beat up her brother, it's better if you got an ace up your sleeve. Some way to show her how much you really care. You just think about it, okay?"

"All right, all right." Sam pushed the ledger aside. "We're finished here." He grabbed the checkbook and wrote Marty out a check. "Thanks." He tore it off and handed it over. "A little bonus. For a job well done."

Marty's eyes grew big again as he looked at the amount. "Like I said, I like this job. And I think I better get on home. Mom's got dinner on." He got up. "See you tomorrow, then."

Sam waved him out the door.

After that, he locked up and went across the street for the mail, thinking that maybe he ought to go looking for Jared to tell the poor fool what was going on. But then, he had no doubt Jared would find him soon enough.

He opened his mailbox and had to virtually pry the stuffed-in circulars and bills out. Next time he and Lilah left town, he'd have Melanie Swan hold his mail—or have Marty take care of it.

Once he'd liberated his mail from the box, he spent several minutes sorting the junk and tossing it out. Then, setting everything else on the little counter that was provided in one of the corners, he went to Delilah's box. He had it open and was trying to pry her mail out, when Linda Lou Beardsly came in.

She saw what Sam was doing and gasped, "Stop that this instant, Sam Fletcher!"

Sam turned. Linda Lou was a tall, big-boned woman, with a long face. Sam couldn't help thinking that she looked, right then, like an outraged mule.

Sam decided to try for lightness. "Got a problem, Mrs. Beardsly?"

"I certainly do, Mr. Fletcher. That is Delilah Jones's box you've just broken open."

"I know that," he replied, the soul of calm rationality. "And I haven't broken it open. She asked me to pick up her mail."

Linda Lou heaved a massive breath. "I find that difficult to believe."

Lord, Sam thought, she was a steel safe of a woman. It was said she was good with children, and that all the little kids she taught until they got old enough to graduate to Delilah's class adored her. But right then, Sam couldn't help thinking it was no mystery why her husband, Owen, spent so much time in The Hole in the Wall's back room.

"Believe it," Sam suggested, his voice dripping patience. "It's true. How else would I get the combination, unless she gave it to me?"

"I could think of ways. I know how you are."

Sam sighed. He knew he should probably advise Linda Lou to check with Delilah and find out the truth. But Lilah had been on edge when he left her, he'd seen that well enough. She'd been nervous about their relationship, and about how people in town would take it. There was no telling what damage an outraged call from Linda Lou would do to her equilibrium right now. Old Nellie Anderson had probably given her a call already, if he knew Nellie at all.

Linda Lou was still sticking out her chest and pinching her thin lips together. "You have already done enough, I'll have you know. It's disgusting, that's what. A man like you abducting a sweet, good person like Delilah. But then everyone's always known how much you've always hated her, that you were out to destroy her life if you ever got the chance."

"Look. Mrs. Beardsly..."

Mrs. Beardsly wasn't finished. "It is unforgivable what you've done to her—"

"Mrs. Beardsly, she's fine. She's home right now, cooking a chicken for our dinner."

"Cooking a chicken for your dinner! What kind of fool do you take me for, Sam Fletcher? Delilah Jones would never willingly cook a chicken for you."

Sam realized he was getting nowhere. "Mrs. Beardsly, this is really none of your business."

"None of my business!" She couldn't seem to stop repeating what he said. "I'll have you know that Delilah Jones is my dear, dear, friend. And we all know that she never would have gone away with you of her own free will, that she only went to save one of her no-good brothers from ruin."

"Everybody seems to know just about everything around here," Sam managed to interject.

"This is North Magdalene. It's everyone's *business* to know. Where was I? Oh, yes.... But now her ordeal is over. She's paid her brother's debt to you. And I want you to leave her alone."

Sam eyed the old battle-ax, wondering what to do now. He was beginning to think that she'd go after him with tooth and claw if he actually dared to reach in Delilah's mail box and extract the contents.

Sam felt weary suddenly. He thought of Jared, threatening his clerk to find out where he and Lilah had gone. And now this confrontation with Linda Lou. No wonder Lilah was anxious about what people would think.

And beyond weariness, he experienced disappointment. Since he'd risen above his father's tainted image of him, he'd let himself imagine that most people were basically open-minded. He'd begun to believe that not only could people change, but that other people could learn to accept those changes—or at least that they'd take the time to ask what was going on before assuming the worst. Right now, though, looking at Linda Lou Beardsly's outraged, mulish face, he was beginning to doubt his own hard-won beliefs.

Linda Lou jabbered on. "But *this* is the pinnacle, the summit, the crowning glory of contemptibility. For you to steal her mail.... I tell you, I am *speechless*—"

"Good," Sam said. "Then shut up."

"I beg your par—"

"Shut up!"

Linda Lou sputtered for a moment, and then actually held her tongue.

Sam said, "Thank you."

He paused before he went on, giving her a threatening stare that kept her quiet—probably in fear for what that evil Sam Fletcher might possibly do to a poor woman alone in the deserted post office on Easter Sunday afternoon. He considered telling her that he and Lilah were getting married. But he doubted there was even the smallest chance she'd believe him. The news would have to come from Lilah.

And the mail would have to wait. He and Lilah could come here after dinner and pick it up together. He really did believe that if he tried to take it now, Linda Lou would either physically attack him, or run out the door screaming "Thief!"

"Look, I'll leave the mail." He turned quickly, shut the little door and spun the lock. "See?"

Linda Lou folded her arms. "Hmph."

"Delilah will come over for it herself later."

"You had better believe she will, Sam Fletcher."

He edged around Linda Lou and collected his own mail, wondering grimly how he would explain this confrontation to Delilah without her getting all upset.

He was worried, he realized, worried for the first time since she'd agreed to marry him about how all this was going to work out.

Sam burst out of the dim post office like a prisoner busting out of jail—fast, with a lot of relief at the sight of the clear, early-evening sky. He started walking fast, too, wanting to hurry back to Lilah, even though it was still an hour before he was due at her house. He wanted to touch her and kiss her and be reassured that, even if most everyone else in town was up in arms about wild Sam Fletcher running off with the schoolmarm, what the two of them shared remained the same.

Unfortunately, he had to pass The Hole in the Wall to get to Pine Street, which led to her street. And he was on foot, since he'd left his truck at home; it was a beautiful spring afternoon and he'd thought the walk would be agreeable. He hadn't stopped to consider that being on foot would leave him vulnerable to greetings—and questions—from anyone he happened to pass on the street.

As he went by the bar, Rocky Collins was just coming out through the double doors.

Rocky, who looked as if he'd been celebrating Easter Sunday by knocking back some serious shots of his favorite tequila, crowed at the sight of him, "Whoa, Lordy! What have we here! It's the man of the hour, or I'm a ring-tailed raccoon."

Sam didn't much care for the greeting—and had no desire to hang around and find out exactly what it meant. He said, "Back off, Rocky," and kept on walking.

But Rocky had never had sense enough to come in out of the rain, let alone not bother a man who didn't want to be bothered. "Hey, c'mon Sam!" he called. "I want to ask you somethin'!"

Sam heard Rocky's lurching footsteps, dogging his own. With a muttered oath, he turned. "What do you want? Make it fast."

Even Rocky, not famous for his brains, finally understood that it probably wouldn't be such a good idea to trifle with Sam right then. And Sam was one of the few men in town that Rocky, who always seemed to end up in a fight, never chose to mess with. Still, Rocky wanted more than anything to be the first of the guys in the bar to know the answers to the burning questions of the day.

So he smiled his friendliest smile and asked real politely, "Well, what I'd really like to know, Sam, that is, if you don't mind my askin'—"

"Get to it, Rocky."

"What we're all wonderin' is—"

"Yeah?"

"How'd it go with the schoolmarm?"

Sam looked at Rocky for a long time, long enough that Rocky was already backing away when he answered, "None of your damn business."

"Well, sure, yeah, I knew that. . . ."

"Then why'd you ask?"

"I dunno. Plum stupid, I suppose."

"Get lost, Rocky."

"Yeah. Right. I am gone." Rocky turned and hurried off up the street, as fast as his unsteady legs would carry him.

Sam watched him go, and wondered if everyone in town had gone crazy since he and Delilah headed off for Hidden Paradise Lake. He'd left Lilah at her house less than two hours ago. In that short time, everyone he'd run into had had something to say about the two of them. If this was the kind of reaction he was getting from people, what must she have heard in the time since he'd walked out of her house?

He realized he was nervous. Nervous as a kid about going back to her. And scared. He had pushed her, he knew it, forced a commitment from her before she was really ready to give it.

Because he'd been afraid of precisely this: that they'd get home and everyone would start in on them, and she wouldn't be able to take it. She'd tell him she just wasn't cut out to be the wife of wild Sam Fletcher. She'd break it off with him.

But she was a woman whose word a man could trust. A promise that she'd marry him would be a binding thing to her. He'd been certain it would be enough to keep her with him, until the talk died down, until she was as sure as he was that what they had at the lake could be theirs for a lifetime—if they'd only reach out together and claim it.

But now...now, damn it, he just didn't know. He'd expected there to be talk. But not what this was beginning to look like. Hell, he'd hazard a guess that everyone in town was in on this.

And he wondered if a mere promise, and a hesitantly granted one at that, was going to hold up against the wagging tongues and the sly, knowing winks, against Jared's misguided protectiveness and Linda Lou Beardsly's upright outrage.

He didn't know.

God—if there was a God—help him. He just didn't know.

He wanted to run to her.

But he also needed to be sure she would still know, when she saw him, that she'd made the right choice with him.

He wanted to give her something, a talisman, a proof of his regard.

So he turned and went back to his store. He dropped off his mail there and picked out a ring, a diamond solitaire that he thought might please her. He put the velvet case in his pocket and let himself out again, and then he stood by the door for a time, knowing that jewelry just wasn't enough.

Not for her, not for Lilah, who was fire and laughter, beauty and strength. There had to be something *more* he could give her, so that she'd know without another doubt that her promise had been wise.

And then he knew what he would do.

He took the few steps to the store next to his, Santino's BB&V, and he pounded on the door.

He kept on pounding until Julio appeared, with a napkin stuck in his collar and a half-full glass of red wine in his hand. "What's this?" Julio demanded. "A man can't enjoy his Easter dinner in peace around here?"

Maria, his wife, peered over his shoulder. "Come in, come in, Sam. Join us upstairs for our Easter feast."

"No, thanks. I, well, Delilah's cooking dinner for me."

Both Maria and Julio grinned at each other the way married couples do when something they've discussed is confirmed. Then Maria asked, "Well then, what is it? What can we do for you?"

Sam shrugged. "Well, I was hoping for a haircut. But I didn't stop to think that Easter Sunday at dinnertime is probably not the right time to visit the barber."

Maria and Julio looked at each other again. And then both of them laughed, sounds of pure delight. "I'll send Marty down with another glass of wine for you," Maria said to her husband. "And one for you, too, Sam."

Sam gave them one more chance to back out. "You're sure you don't mind...?" He hoped they wouldn't take it. He wanted that haircut.

He needn't have worried. Julio was so tickled at the idea of giving a good cut to one of North Magdalene's staunchest longhairs, that he couldn't have cared less right then if his food was stone cold when he finally returned to it.

"Let's go, Sam." Julio turned and led Sam to the back room.

Sam sat in the chair and Julio set to work. They were interrupted once, when Marty brought them the wine and gave Sam a high sign that signified his enthusiastic approval. After that, Julio went about his work with calm concentration. When he was done, and the long, shining swatches of hair lay all around Sam's chair, he turned Sam to the big mirror.

Sam grunted. It wasn't as bad as he'd thought. From the front, it didn't look much different than when he'd pulled it back in a ponytail.

Julio gave him the hand mirror so he could see the back.

Sam laughed.

"Something wrong?" Julio, who took pride in his work, looked apprehensive.

"Hell, no," Sam replied. "I was just thinking that, after twenty years of fighting it, I now look respectable both coming . . . and going."

"I think it looks fine," said Julio.

"I do, too. And thanks."

Julio removed the big apron and brushed off Sam's nape. "That's it then," he announced.

Sam thanked him again and paid him enough to make up for interrupting his dinner. Then he went out the front door and headed for Lilah's with the ring making a reassuring bulge in his pocket and his head feeling lighter than it had in a long, long time.

He was still early, but not by too much. And he was still nervous about how she might have handled whatever had come up since they parted.

But he felt much better now that he had concrete ways to show her how he felt.

And he was relieved, too, that he made it past the post office and the bar without being accosted by any scandalmongering citizens. He turned onto Pine and walked briskly to the corner of Rambling Lane, where he turned again. He was mounting Delilah's front step in no time.

The door was unlocked. He went on in. The house was warm and cozy. He realized how much he liked her house. And it smelled of savory roast chicken. Sam's stomach growled. He was suddenly starving.

He caught a glimpse of her, in the kitchen by the sink. He stood for a moment, just inside the door, thinking how good it was, to be here, where she was, in the warmth of her house, with the smells of the food she'd cooked for him fragrant on the air. He noticed that she'd pulled all the carvings he'd made for her away from the window, to the near side of the table; he could see them from where he stood now.

He smiled. It looked as if she'd sat down with them, and just looked at them for awhile. The thought touched him.

However, the chicken, most likely, was ready by now. It smelled ready. And the table wasn't set. That was something he could do while she put the finishing touches on the meal.

He moved forward, into the heart of the room and beyond, through the doorless arch to the kitchen. She was standing in front of the sink, with her back to him. She appeared to be just staring out the window.

He glanced toward the stove. The chicken, still in its roasting pan, sat on top. It looked done.

But nothing else was. Greens for the salad lay in their plastic bags on the counter. Raw broccoli and potatoes waited there, too. All of this, he perceived in an instant.

And he also knew it was all strange. Wrong. Not good.

Still, he tried not to know. He went up behind her and put his arms around her. She stiffened.

"Hey. It's only me." He nuzzled her neck.

She didn't move, didn't sigh, didn't relax in the slightest. She could have been a mannequin, one made of flesh and blood, but lifeless all the same.

"Lilah?" He took her by the shoulders, turned her, stiff but not really resisting, until she faced him. "What's the matter? What's wrong?"

She moved then, to get away from him. She went and she sat at the table, in front of the wooden menagerie.

"Lilah? Talk to me."

She picked up the raccoon, the rough willow piece he'd carved for her that first night, when he'd come here hoping and praying she might agree to go out on a date with him. She looked at it, and then she turned to him, still holding the wooden creature in her hand.

"I've been wondering, Sam." Her eyes were flat, like unpolished black stones. "I've been wondering—do you love me? Do you love me at all?"

He felt fear. Was she all right? He pleaded tenderly, "Lilah, what's wrong? Talk to me, sweetheart."

She chuckled. The chuckle was ice-cold. "Oh, come on, Sam. Just answer the question. Just answer it straight. I asked you if you loved me. It doesn't take a college education to answer that. All I want is a yes or a no."

"Yes," he said flatly, feeling irritation rise and trying to remember that they couldn't both go off the deep end or disaster would follow. "Now what the hell is going on? Has Nellie Anderson been jabbering at you? Or did Linda Lou give you a call?"

She totally ignored his question. She set the raccoon on the table.

"Lilah, talk to me . . ."

She shrugged. "Somehow that *yes* was not totally convincing." Her voice was light, hollow at the core.

"Lilah, will you please, for godsake, look at me?"

She didn't, but she did volunteer, "Patrick was here."

"And?"

"And he said the bets are flying fast and furious over at The Hole in the Wall."

"Bets about what?"

"About us. One, whether you'll get me to go to bed with you."

Sam swore softly.

"That's not all. The other's whether you'll get me to say I'll marry you."

"Lilah—"

She waved a hand over her shoulder at where he stood by the sink. She still conscientiously refused to look at him. "I thought that was strange," she continued. "That they'd bet on whether *you* got *me* to agree to get married. That's not the kind of bet men make, as a general rule. Men always think of women as the ones who want to make it legal—though I can tell you that there are a lot of women out there who'd like nothing better than to just be left alone by men."

"Lilah." Sam was really trying to hold on to his patience now. "What is this? Get to the point."

"I thought it was strange, that's all, that they'd bet *you'd* get *me* to marry you. But then Patrick explained the rest to me, and it all made perfect sense. He said that you'd discussed me with Father a month ago, and that Father had told you he'd give you The Mercantile if you'd take me for a wife." She cast him a quick look over her shoulder, as if checking to make sure he'd heard that she was on to him at last.

"Lilah."

She waved him silent again, a jerky, pained movement. "I told myself I would wait, and talk to you, and find out if it was true, before I started thinking too much about all the...contradictions in everything you've done. But then, I couldn't stop my mind from thinking, and I couldn't help but remember that day I went collecting donations for the bell tower. My father told me that day that he was tired of waiting for me to get married, that he'd found a man for me and I should expect that man to come calling soon." She laughed, a choked sound that was really more like a barely contained sob. "Of course, I thought that was so totally ridiculous, I didn't give it a second thought. But then, when I went into your store, you asked me if I'd been talking to my father. Remember?"

"Yes."

"And then, it was after that, that you started...looking at me strangely every time I saw you. And then soon enough, you showed up here to ask for a date. I asked you then if my father put you up to it. And you denied it. But you lied."

"Lilah—"

"Wait. Just wait. Let me finish. I'll be finished soon enough." She sucked in a breath, and then her words picked up speed, until they tumbled over each other, accusation following accusation, "You wanted that building, and you were willing to go after me to get it. You never said you loved me. Because you *don't* love me. You told me how you and I didn't need lies between us, we had something better than lies. But that was a lie, it was all, all lies. All the time, all of this, nothing but a great, big whopping lie!" She pounded the table with a tight fist. The wooden animals jumped, wobbled, and then righted themselves.

After that, she was quiet. Standing very still behind her, Sam waited, listening to her breathing as she controlled herself, made it even and slow.

The silence was never ending. At last, she couldn't stand it anymore. She twisted in the chair and looked at him—or at least aimed a frozen glare at where he was standing. But she wasn't really looking at him, she wasn't looking at him at all.

"Well?" she demanded, all injury and outrage.

"Well, what?"

"Do you have a single thing to say for yourself?"

He shrugged. "Why should I? It appears to me you've said it all."

For an instant, the real Lilah peered at him through the mask of affronted pride. She said in a small voice, "Say...it's not true..." She stopped, and the rage and belligerence took over once more. "Say *something!*" she demanded then.

"All right." He folded his arms across his chest, mostly because he'd caught himself in the act of stroking the back of his neck. He didn't want to do that now. She'd been too caught up in her own wounded rage to notice that his ponytail was gone. And now, he wanted to get out of here without her finding out. He didn't want her to see the ridiculous grand gesture he'd made for her. Not now, when he knew at last how little she believed in him.

He had to come to grips with reality here. It was never going to work between them. He'd been living a fool's dream to think that a woman who'd hated him enthusiastically for two decades was ever going to become his best friend and his wife.

He'd always known he'd lose her when they returned to North Magdalene. And he had been right.

She was biting her lip in frustration at his extended silence. He took pity on her and spoke. "Why should I argue with you? You've already made up your mind about everything."

She said through clenched teeth, in a parody of reasonableness, "*Did* my father offer you that building if you'd marry me?"

He shrugged. "Yes." He knew he should just let her go ahead and think what she wanted, but some idiot part of him still hoped she might understand. "But—"

"But what?"

"But that isn't why I went after you."

"It isn't?"

"No, it isn't."

"Oh, really?" She looked at him, narrow-eyed, not giving him an inch.

Sam's anger kindled and grew hot. Not only had she already judged him, she wanted him to try to defend himself after the fact. Well, to hell with that.

He inquired with leashed fury, "You want to call it off, is that it?"

She said nothing, she just glared at him, her eyes brimming, her chin high and haughty.

He went on. "Well, fine. You call it off. But don't try to tell me any lies, all right? Let's have it out on the table like it really is."

"Don't call me a liar," she sneered. "Don't you dare call me a liar. We both know who tells the lies around here!" She gripped the back of the chair, as if she were restraining herself from leaping up and jumping on him the way she'd done at the river all those years and years ago.

He looked right at her as he said, slowly and softly, "I call you a liar because you are one, Lilah. And what's more, I think somewhere inside you, you know that you're lying." She gasped. He went on before she could gather herself for more denials. "Deep in your heart, you know what you're doing. And it's not the fact that you never got fancy words of love from me that bothers you now. And it's not your father promising me The Mercantile if I'll marry you, either. What's really bothering you is who you are and who I am. Or at least who you've told yourself for twenty years I am—without ever bothering to make sure."

Her face wore a stricken look. He hardened himself against it and continued, "I thought maybe, after this week, that you *did* see the real me now. But you don't. Or you won't. Any more than you see yourself as you really are—"

Right then, she managed to mutter, "No... that's not true...."

He overrode her weak objections without effort. "It is true. You have an…idea of yourself, of the person you've made of yourself in spite of your rowdy relatives. You came back here after college when you could have gone anywhere, started from scratch. But you had something to prove to this town, didn't you? You came home and you taught at the school and you never got near a man and you purposely made friends with the most upright, narrow-minded citizens you could find. You *created* yourself from scratch. A Jones who wasn't a Jones, who led a quiet, uneventful life, a dedicated teacher who went to church every Sunday and spent Saturday night watering her plants. You made yourself up. And the person you made up would *never* go for a man like me."

"No, I—"

"I'm not finished." He gave her a look that silenced her completely. Then he went on, "You swore you'd never fall for me. But you *did* fall for me. And you loved it. From that day on the mountain until you got home. But now you've probably had a few choice words with Nellie or Linda Lou. You've heard about the bets on us over at the bar. You see how it's going to be, the way people will talk about the schoolmarm hooking up with that wild Sam Fletcher. And you're embarrassed. You want to go back to who you *think* you are. And you want *me* to be the rat you always *knew* I was."

"No—"

"Yes." He dropped his folded arms to his sides and took the two steps that placed him right behind her chair. She remained twisted from the waist, facing him. He looked down into those dark eyes, the eyes he'd dared to dream he might look into every day for the rest of their lives. "Well, fine," he said flatly. "Tell yourself lies. Have it your way."

She looked up at him, speechless, stunned, and he saw the slow realization come over her fine, strong face. He saw the precise moment when she understood that every word he'd just uttered was true. She had lied, the worst kind of lie... she had lied to herself.

She whispered, "Oh, Sam..." She reached out for him.

He stepped back. It was too late. And not enough. He couldn't trust her now. Hell, he'd never be able to leave her alone without wondering what he'd be accused of when he got home.

She'd always doubt him. He saw that now. A whisper in her ear might sway her against him. He wouldn't spend his life convincing his woman that she could trust him.

He raised his arm, so full of hurt and rage—and thwarted longing—that he wanted to strike out.

"No, Sam!" She grabbed for him.

He shook her off—and he swiped the carved figures off the table. The wooden animals went flying, some arrested by her chair, others sailing halfway to the stove, before they clattered to the floor. Then, when the last wooden figure had landed and fallen still, they stared at each other, over a chasm of inches that might as well have been ten thousand miles.

He said, very quietly, "Goodbye."

And then he walked past her, through the living room, and out the front door.

Chapter Fifteen

Delilah couldn't bear to watch him leave. She closed her eyes as he swept past her, and didn't open them again until she heard the closing of the door. The tears, unchecked now, ran down her cheeks and onto the hands that lay limp in her lap.

Sam was gone. And the unbearable fact, the horrible truth, was that she herself had sent him away.

At her feet, the little raccoon lay, staring brightly up. She slid off the chair and took him in her hands, setting him carefully back on the table. Then she crawled around the room, collecting each of the wooden treasures, her heart breaking anew when she saw the crack in the doe's slender foreleg, the chip in the beak of the owl.

She tried, as she assessed the damage, not to think at all, to close off her mind for awhile, until she could stop crying and look at what had happened from a more balanced frame of reference.

But her mind would not shut off. Everything, *everything* Sam had said to her was brutally, horribly true. Her carefully constructed image of herself had had no room in it for Sam; she had been subconsciously waiting for any excuse to send him on his way. The issue of The Mercantile had been just what she'd been waiting for.

Delilah sat in the chair again, still holding the wounded doe. Slowly, she ran a finger over the cracked leg. She could feel the sharpness of the break. A fresh onslaught of tears ensued.

And then the doorbell rang.

Delilah looked up, and swiped away the tears with the back of her hand. But then she only sobbed again.

"Oh, to heck with it," she muttered. The last time she'd answered the door, she'd had to deal with Patrick.

Who could say what would be next? She just wasn't up to it, not today. Whoever it was could just keep ringing until they tired of it. And then they could go away.

There was a silence. Then another ring.

Delilah waited to be left in peace.

But then, the door slowly swung inward. "Delilah?" It was Nellie's voice.

Oh, no! Delilah wished she could just shrink down to nothing and disappear into thin air. Nellie was the last person she wanted to see right then. She considered sliding off the chair and running out the back door.

But she didn't act quickly enough. Nellie was already peering cautiously around the edge of the door. She spotted Delilah and her little eyes widened. "Oh!" Nellie said, surprised for a moment. Then she saw the tears and the abject misery on Delilah's face. Nellie sighed and her own eyes filled with sympathetic tears, "Oh, honey. What has he done to you?" Nellie pushed the door all the way open.

And that was when Delilah saw that Linda Lou was with her.

Delilah opened her mouth to tell them to go away, she wanted to be alone. But the two of them swept in like a pair of oversized mother hens, clucking in sympathy and ready to take charge.

They fluttered across the living room and right into the kitchen, where they swept her up and engulfed her against their bosoms and clucked in her ear not to worry, not to worry at all, nothing was that awful that it couldn't be made right.

"You just come on in the living room, honey. Yes, you sit here on the couch...."

"Better, much better. Here's a tissue...."

"That's right. You just cry...."

"You just let yourself go...."

"I'll put on some hot water, a nice cup of tea...."

"Yes, tea. Nellie will make us a nice cup of tea...."

Nellie got up then, and went back into the kitchen. Linda Lou stayed with Delilah, patting her hand, smoothing her hair and clucking all the while.

"There, there," Linda Lou said, "you've had a traumatic experience, but it's all right, you'll be fine in the end, just you wait, you'll see... I swear, that man ought to be shot, and that's the Lord's truth."

Delilah, who'd been rather enjoying all the clucking and stroking from her female friends, made herself pull away from Linda Lou. She'd already betrayed Sam in her heart. No matter if he could never trust her, she would not betray him with others ever again. "No," she managed on a sob. "You don't understand...."

"There, there. I certainly do. I understand well enough. That Sam Fletcher is crazy—"

"No, no. Oh, Linda Lou, you just don't understand."

"Of course I do. I understand. We all understand. And everyone in town admires you, Delilah, they truly do, for sacrificing yourself for your brother, for going off with that horrible man for an entire week just to—''

"Stop," Delilah said. "Just stop right there." She blew her nose and then sat up tall. "You're my dear friend, Linda Lou, and I think the world of you. But I won't have you saying things against Sam."

Linda Lou blinked. And then she started clucking again. "You are a truly noble soul, I must say. After everything he's done, to refuse to disparage him—''

"Oh, come on, Linda Lou," Delilah objected, and paused to blow her nose again. "Listen to yourself. What you're saying makes no sense at all. Have I ever refused to disparage Sam Fletcher before?''

Linda Lou thought about that. "Well, no. I can't say as you have."

"Of course I haven't. In fact, I've always been the one most willing to explain in detail what a low-down, mean, rotten rat he is."

"Well, yes," Linda Lou allowed, "I suppose, now you point it out, that that is true."

"You'd better believe it's true."

"And you were right," Linda Lou announced staunchly.

"No. I was wrong."

Linda Lou blinked again. "Wrong?" The word was disbelief personified.

Delilah nodded. "Yes, wrong."

Linda Lou did not take this information well. Her browless eyes were all scrunched up, her mouth pursed tight. But then her long face softened, and she looked pitying again. She started patting Delilah's hand once more. "Now, now, dear. It's going to be all right. You just need a little rest, that's all. You can take some time off from school and have a long talk with Pastor Johnson. . . ."

Delilah batted the soothing hand away. "Stop it, Linda Lou."

Linda Lou remained undaunted. "You've been under a lot of strain, dear. Just try to—"

"There is nothing wrong with me."

"—relax. The hysterics will pass, and you'll feel much better very soon."

"I am not having hysterics."

Linda Lou shook her head. "Fine, fine, dear. Whatever you say."

The patronizing tone was too much. Delilah stood up. "Look at me, Linda Lou. Look at me real well. Do I look crazy to you?"

A terribly pained expression crossed Linda Lou's face. "Now, dear..."

"I do? I look crazy, is that what you're thinking?"

Linda Lou blinked again and looked away.

This was too much. Delilah shouted. "Nellie!"

"Yes, honey?"

"Nellie, get in here!"

"But the tea—"

"Forget the tea. In here. Now!"

Nellie flitted in. "What in the world is the matter?"

"Sit down," Delilah commanded. "There. Next to Linda Lou."

Nellie looked at Linda Lou. "Is she all right?"

Linda Lou went on looking pained, but wisely refrained from answering.

"Nellie." Delilah's tone gave clear warning. "Sit."

"All right, I'm sitting." She dropped down next to Linda Lou.

"Now," Delilah said. Two pairs of eyes watched her, wide and wary. "You two are my very dear friends, and it is my hope that you will both remain that way. But it has recently come to my attention, through personal and intimate experience—" Delilah paused, irritated no end as she watched her friends share a shudder and a significant look "—that I have been cruel and nasty and completely off-base about a certain man we all know. And you both know who I mean. I mean Sam Fletcher."

"Oh, no, you haven't been," Linda Lou protested.

"Not for a minute," Nellie declared.

"Yes." Delilah held firm. "It's true. I've misjudged him for years. But not anymore. And I've made other gross errors in behavior as well. I've been . . . dishonest, with myself and with everyone I care about. I've pretended for years to be less than my whole self. Because really, deep down, I'm a lot like Sam is. I've got wildness in me, just like he does, a wildness I've denied for years."

"No," Nellie breathed, as Linda Lou murmured simultaneously, "It's not so."

"It is so." Delilah looked right at Nellie. "Nellie, he asked me out the night you called two weeks ago."

Nellie gasped. "I knew it. I knew something was going on even then—"

"You were right. And I wanted to go out with him then—"

"No!"

"Yes. But I was too foolish and full of myself to admit it. He was forced to resort to desperate means to get my attention."

"The wager," Linda Lou breathed.

"Exactly. And now he *has* my attention."

Nellie rose up and then sat down again. "Delilah, what are you saying?"

"He asked me to marry him."

"He didn't." Linda Lou spoke with awe.

"He did. I said yes."

Nellie sputtered, "You never—"

"I did."

"Oh, my heavens!" Linda Lou put a hand to her heaving breast.

"But then, I didn't really believe in him, not deep down, and I've hurt him very deeply, I'm afraid. I'm afraid, to be honest, that he's never going to forgive me, no matter what I do...."

Nellie longed for the details. "But what *happened?*"

"It's too involved to explain right now."

Both women sighed in mutual disappointment.

"But the point is," Delilah went on. "I love him."

Nellie and Linda Lou gasped in unison at that.

"It's true. I love Sam Fletcher. And you can call me crazy, you can shake your heads in pity and say I should visit Pastor Johnson. You can do and say whatever you please. It doesn't matter. Because Sam Fletcher is the man for me. He's *always* been the man for me, whether he ever lets me near him again or not. And anyone who says *anything* against him will not be someone with whom I choose to associate on a regular basis. Is that understood?"

Both Nellie and Linda Lou stared at her with their mouths hanging open.

"Is that understood?" she repeated once more.

"But, honey—" Nellie began.

"But, dear—" said Linda Lou.

And then both of them fell silent at the sound of heavy, hurried footsteps on the porch. They stared past Delilah. Delilah turned just as her baby brother appeared in the open front door.

"Brendan," Delilah muttered. "What now?"

"Sis..." Brendan gulped in air. His hair was windblown, and his face was flushed. He looked like he'd just run a hard mile. "I have to talk to you!"

"Come in," she told him. "Don't just stand there. And for heaven's sake, close that door."

Brendan stepped over the threshold and shut the door as he'd been told. He nodded at the wide-eyed pair on the couch. "Ladies..."

"Good evening."

"Hello, Brendan."

"All right," Delilah cut through the pleasantries. "What's happened now?"

"It's Jared..." He eyed the women on the couch. "Sis, could we talk alone?"

"What for? Whatever it is, they'll find out soon enough anyway. This is North Magdalene. We have to face facts." Delilah approached her brother and looked at him closely. "What's this?"

"What's it look like? A black eye." He winced. "Hey. Hands off."

"You and Jared got into it?"

Brendan nodded. "He got on me for my part in you going off with Sam. And sis, he's—"

Delilah shook her head. "Jared's always been trouble looking for somewhere to happen."

"That's what I'm trying to tell you—"

"So tell me. I'm listening."

"That's what you say, and then you interrupt."

"Brendan, get to the point."

"Okay, okay. It's like this...Jared's been looking all over for Sam, swearing he's going to beat the bejesus out of him, for taking you off against your will, even though Dad has been trying to get him to see that Sam really only wants to put a ring on your finger—"

"So?"

"So Jared finally found him. Just now. Over at The Hole in the Wall. And Sam, instead of being reasonable, is acting crazy as Jared, like he was even *looking* for a fight himself, you know what I mean?"

Delilah's heart sank. She knew exactly why Sam was in such a troublemaking mood. "They're beating each other up," she said grimly.

"Are they ever!" Brendan replied. "And since you went off with Sam for my sake, when I saw the trouble happening, I thought just in case you *did* care for Sam, I should tell you—"

But Delilah was already moving. She flew into the kitchen and grabbed her keys from the peg there, then rushed back to the living room, shot around her dumbstruck brother and flung open the door.

As she went by, Brendan asked, "But what are you gonna do, sis?"

"I'll figure that out when the time comes." She rushed out into the twilight and slid behind the wheel of her car.

She no sooner had the door shut than Brendan was dropping into the passenger seat and Nellie and Linda Lou were piling in the back.

"What are you two doing?" Delilah demanded over her shoulder, as she pumped the pedal and turned the key.

"Well, if you love him, dear—" Linda Lou said.

Nellie finished. "We *are* your friends, after all."

"Things could get pretty rough," Delilah warned.

"We can take it," Nellie vowed. Her eyes were shining—just like Linda Lou's. It occurred to Delilah that this was probably more excitement than either of them normally saw in a month of Sundays.

And then there was no more time to think of Nellie and Linda Lou. The engine sputtered to life. Delilah switched on the lights and shoved it into gear. The tires squealed as she swung around. She peeled rubber down the street and almost ran into Roger McCleb who was crossing the street at the intersection of Pine and Main. Luckily, she missed Roger and made it onto Main.

She found a free space across the street from the bar, and slammed into it, missing the car in the space in front by mere inches. She was out of the car and striding across the street for the bar within seconds.

She paid no attention to whether her brother and two friends were following. Her concentration was on the double doors, on the sounds of cursing and crashing from beyond them. She thought for a moment that maybe she ought to call Sheriff Pangborn, but then she realized the odds were ten to one someone already had. He'd be there eventually—when the fighting got loud enough.

Her toe touched the sidewalk in front of the doors—and the doors burst open. From inside, unmuffled now, came the sound of a splintering table, the crashing of a chair. A loud *splat* followed by a man's groan.

Two locked bodies rolled out, tussled briefly at her feet, and then struggled upright and forged back in again. The doors swung shut.

"Sis," Brendan warned as he came up behind her. "This is entirely out of hand. It's no place for a woman."

"Shut up," Delilah told him. "And come on."

She put her shoulder against the door, and encountered some resistance as someone fell against it on the other side. She shoved again, harder. The door swung in. She went through.

She faced pure chaos. Swiftly, she tried to assess the situation—no mean feat, as she kept having to duck flung beer mugs and flying furniture. Still, she managed to scan the room—and spotted Jared and Sam going at it like a couple of pit bulls in the center of the fray. Both of them, at this point, looked bloody, dogged and determined, the way men get when they're evenly matched and neither of them has the good sense to give it up.

She saw her father, then, beyond them, trapped across the room from the bar where he'd probably been when the trouble broke out, trying to convince them the fight wasn't necessary, and then, when that didn't work, ordering them to take it outside.

That's what he was still shouting now. "You hooligans! You get your butts out the door! You're wreckin' my place! Get it out, get it outside now!" He kept yelling orders, with only an occasional pause to punch any fool who got close enough to make him nervous. Then he'd start in shouting again.

The situation assessed, Delilah wasted no time. She dropped to her knees and scurried to the bar. She ducked behind it just as a pool cue soared tip-first into the big mirror on the wall over the register. The mirror cracked, the way ice does on a frozen pond, in sharp splintering fingers. But miraculously, it stayed stuck to the wall while the pool cue clattered to the register counter, knocking over bottles, which shattered and spilled their contents all over the counter and down to the floor.

Delilah crept along behind the bar, trying to avoid the puddles of peppermint schnapps and orange liqueur, looking up at the underside of the bar and the counters, watching for what her father had always kept somewhere back here, since she was a child.

She found it, at last, right next to the seltzer fountain. Her father's .38 special, strapped under the bar in a tacked-up beltless holster, where he could easily yank it out whenever things got out of hand—as long as he had sense enough to stay behind the bar.

Still crouched where no flying objects could reach her, she drew the gun. She broke it open. The gun was fully loaded, just as she'd expected.

Over her head, a chair came sailing, hitting the mirror squarely and sending the splintered pieces flying.

Now, she thought resolutely, was as good a time as any.

So she rose up, quick as a cat, and leapt onto the bar. Below and all around her, the fighting continued unabated. Over by the door, she spotted Linda Lou, sticking out her foot to trip a brawler who dared to get too close. When he got up and came at her, Nellie brained him with a beer bottle. Across the room, Owen Beardsly spotted his wife. "Linda Lou!" he shouted, "My God, Linda Lou!"

"Oh, settle down, Owen!" Linda Lou advised and gave another man a shove who came flying out of the fray and got too close to her for comfort.

In the center of the floor, Sam, swaying on his feet, aimed a punch at Jared. It connected, Jared went down, and doggedly rose up once more.

"Gentlemen!" Delilah shouted, "Gentlemen! Please!"

She might as well have tried to stop a stampede with a feather duster. No one even paused to look her way.

Resigned, she aimed the gun at the big light fixture that hung over the center of the room. She fired off four shots, until each of the bulbs in the fixture was no more than splinters and dust.

Somewhere around the destruction of the third light bulb, the battling patrons ceased trading blows and dived for cover—all except for Jared and Sam, who simply stopped fighting and stared at her, their mouths hanging open.

When all four light bulbs were no more, she announced, "That's enough, gentlemen!" She was gratified to discover she had everyone's attention. "Wrap it up. This fight has reached its conclusion."

"Delilah!" said her father, scratching his head. "Delilah, you shot out the lights!"

She gave him an infinitely patient glance. "Someone had to do something."

"Well, I know that gal. But I swear I never thought I'd see the day..."

"Don't worry, I'll replace them." Slowly, around the battered barroom, the men were picking themselves up and checking themselves for damages. Delilah, too terrified that Sam might reject her to look at him, aimed a glare at her oldest brother. "And just what in the world do you think you're doing, Jared Jones?"

Jared, never known for his sweet disposition, swiped the blood out of his eyes and glared right back at her. "Sticking up for you, sis. What the hell do you think?"

A murmur of agreement went up from the crowd.

"Yeah, right on, Jared..."

"A man's gotta do what a man's gotta do...."

"Stick up for your sister, whatever it takes!"

Linda Lou cut them short. "Hush up, you roughnecks! Let Delilah talk."

The man she'd tripped turned on her. "Hey, you're the old bitch who hit me with that beer bottle...."

Near the curtain to the back room, Owen Beardsly spoke up. "You watch how you talk to my wife, mister!"

"Yes, you watch it, young man," Nellie piped up. "And she didn't hit you with that bottle anyway, that was me. Want to make something of it?"

The man muttered another insult and took a step toward Nellie.

Owen was already elbowing his way across the room. "You leave her alone. You want to fight with someone, you fight with me!"

"Don't trouble yourself, Owen!" Nellie called. "We can handle this moron!"

"Moron!" The man was furious now. "Who you callin' a moron, you old—"

It was obvious to Delilah that another brawl was in the offing. So she aimed the gun at the ceiling and fired it again. Plaster flew and rained down. All fell silent once more.

"I have one more shot, Gentlemen," Delilah announced. "Don't make me use it."

A sea of subdued male faces stared up at her expectantly. But Delilah was aware of only one pair of eyes. She could feel those eyes watching her; she just didn't have the nerve to look into them yet.

She focused on her brother once more. "I appreciate your efforts on my behalf, Jared, but next time see me first."

Jared totally ignored her real point and took issue with the sincerity of her thankfulness for all he'd done. "Yeah, well, you don't seem too damn grateful. In fact, you don't seem grateful at all."

Oggie cut in. "And why should she be grateful, you idiot? You're beating up her fiancé!"

Jared glowered at his father. "He never said so. I asked him straight out, 'You gonna marry my sister?' and he never said yes. You heard it. You were here. He said what he and sis were gonna do was nobody's business but theirs. And when a man won't answer if he's gonna do the right thing by a woman straight out, then as far as I'm concerned, it's a done deal. He's got what he wanted, and he's out the door."

Oggie turned to Sam. "Tell him, Sam. Tell him right now. Tell him you and my little girl are walking down the aisle side by side. Shut this blockhead up, and make me the happiest old man on earth."

The time had come, Delilah knew it. She had to face Sam now. She forced herself to look at him, at his bloody face and his ice blue eyes. He was looking right at her, as she'd known he would be, staring right through her, right down into her heart.

She said to her father, to Jared, to everyone in the bar, to the town, to the whole wide world, and most of all to Sam, "Yes, we're getting married. We love each other more than anyone else can know. We've had our... difficulties, but we'll come through them, side by side." She kept looking at Sam, willing him to know, to understand, to give her one more chance to show him she was a woman he could trust forevermore. He looked back but said nothing. Her heart sank. She asked, "Aren't we, Sam?" And a pleading note crept in.

"Answer her," Oggie hissed.

"Shut up, Oggie," Sam said softly. And he started moving forward. The crowd melted out of his way, leaving a clear path to Delilah where she stood up on the bar. Sam came on, closer and closer.

And then he was there, at her feet. She stared down at him—and at last she saw what had heretofore escaped her notice.

"Sam! Oh, Sam...." Her voice said everything. It was the voice of a woman long-gone in love. "Sam Fletcher, you went and cut your hair!"

So deeply moved was she, that she forgot momentarily that she was still holding a gun. It fell from her suddenly limp fingers. Several quick-thinking patrons hit the floor once more. But luck was with them. Brendan, who'd moved behind the bar when Delilah leapt up on it, caught the gun before it could go off and actually hurt someone.

A collective sigh of relief went up from the awestruck crowd.

And it was as the sigh faded that Delilah Jones leapt from the bar and into Sam Fletcher's waiting arms. He caught her without effort. His lips came down on hers.

Neither of them noticed the cheers and catcalls. They were lovers, loving, and the rest of the world meant less than nothing at all for a time.

Eventually, though, they came up for air. And that was when Sam said, "I love you, Delilah Jones."

And Delilah, hearing those precious words at last, felt her heart rise up, light as a sunbeam, carrying her with it, into an infinity of bliss. She said, "And I love you, Sam Fletcher. Till death do us part."

"So what does this mean?" Jared was still demanding. "He still hasn't said he'll marry her."

"He's marrying me," Delilah told her brother, never taking her eyes from the man who held her in his arms. There was a cut over his left eye. She gently wiped the blood away, clucking, "Oh, Sam...."

Oggie cleared his throat, "Uh, Sam, I gotta ask you. About The Mercantile..."

Delilah looked at Sam with appeal in her eyes.

"Keep it," Sam Fletcher growled, smoothing Delilah's hair. "I got everything I wanted out of you, Oggie Jones."

Oggie winked at Patrick, who stood over near Owen Beardsly, by the curtain to the back room.

Delilah said, "I have everything I ever wanted, too. Now Sam, may we please go home?"

"Which home?"

"It doesn't matter. Your house or mine. Home is either one of them, as long as you're there."

With a deep, joyful laugh, Sam Fletcher hoisted his woman high in his arms. He turned for the double doors.

"He gave up The Mercantile and that fine truck of Brendan's just to get him the schoolmarm," Rocky Collins declared in total bafflement, as Sam pushed through the double doors.

"Was she worth it?" some smart aleck nearby inquired.

"You better believe it, bud," Sam tossed the words over his shoulder as he kicked open the door.

Delilah sighed and laid her head against his heart as the man she loved carried her out of The Hole in the Wall and into a magnificent starry spring night.

* * * * *

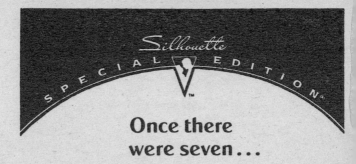

Once there
were seven...

Seven beautiful brothers and sisters who played together,
and weathered adversity too cruel for their tender ages.
Eventually orphaned, they were then separated.

Now they're trying to find each other.

Don't miss Gina Ferris's heartwarming

FAMILY FOUND

Full of Grace   February
Hardworking Man   April
Fair and Wise   June

Available at your favorite retail outlet from Silhouette
Special Edition

Silhouette
SPECIAL EDITION

Continuing in March
be on the lookout for

MAVERICKS

LISA JACKSON'S
MAVERICK MEN

They're wild...they're woolly...and they're as rugged as the great outdoors. They've never needed a woman before, but they're about to meet their matches....

HE'S A BAD BOY (#787)—January
HE'S JUST A COWBOY (#799)—March
HE'S THE RICH BOY (#811)—May

All men who just won't be tamed!
From Silhouette Special Edition.

Silhouette
SPECIAL EDITION ™

It takes a very special man to win

That
SPECIAL
Woman!

She's friend, wife, mother—she's you! And beside each Special Woman stands a wonderfully *special* man. It's a celebration of our heroines—and the men who become part of their lives.

Look for these exciting titles from Silhouette Special Edition:

January **BUILDING DREAMS** by Ginna Gray

February **HASTY WEDDING** by Debbie Macomber

March **THE AWAKENING** by Patricia Coughlin

April **FALLING FOR RACHEL** by Nora Roberts

Dont miss THAT SPECIAL WOMAN! each month—from your special authors.

AND

For the most special woman of all—you, our loyal reader—we have a wonderful gift: a beautiful journal to record all of your special moments. See this month's THAT SPECIAL WOMAN! title for details.

TSW1